ALSO BY KIMBER

Notebook Mysteries Series

Divided Lives (aka K.R. Mullins)

1897 A MARK SUTHERLAND ADVENTURE

1897

KIMBERLY MULLINS

1897 A Mark Sutherland Adventure

Copyright © JKJ books, LLC 2023

First edition: October 2023

Mailing address for JKJ books, LLC; 17350 State Highway 249, STE 220 #3515 Houston, Texas 77064

Library of Congress Control Number: 2023915432

ISBN (paperback) 979-8-9886080-4-2

ISBN (hardback) 979-8-9886080-5-9

ISBN (ebook) 979-8-9886080-3-5

This is a work of fiction. It is based on historical events within the US and Canada during the time period of the 1897.

Edited by Kaitlyn Katsoupis, Strictly Textual

Cover Art by More Visual, Ltd

My books have themes—Mystery, adventure and teams. We are nothing without the people around us. Joshua, Jonathan and Claudia- this is for you.

PROLOGUE

February 1898, Yukon, Canada

Mark shivered as he huddled beside the large rock. He pulled the bag closer to him and watched the snow pile up. He'd been grateful when that snow covered his trail, but now he silently cursed it, knowing it could lead to his imminent death.

"Did you find him?" one of the men yelled over the howling wind.

"He has to be around here," came another voice.

"If he is, he's half frozen. Let's go back to camp."

"I want to find him."

"He can't go anywhere. We'll find him and take the gold from him even if we have to pry it out of his cold, dead hands."

The voices trailed off and Mark was left alone. He burrowed further down and tried to remember the last time he'd been warm. *Texas and Oklahoma,* he thought. *Now, that was heat; so dry I felt like I was breathing in dust.*

The more he thought about that time, the warmer he got. The last conversation he'd had there drifted through his head,

Gus was saying, "The Yukon sounds interesting and it might be where I go next. I'll see."

I wonder if he is on his way and if I'll live to see him?

CHAPTER 1

*L*ate April, 1897, Chicago, Illinois, USA

The editor of the newspaper, Don Galloway, looked down at the paper in his hand and out into the area where his reporters sat. He scanned the room and his gaze settled on a young man hunched over his typewriter.

"Mark!" he called out.

The young man looked up and brushed his dark brown hair off his forehead. "Just a minute, I need to finish this story," he said in a distracted voice and started to type.

The editor nodded and called back, "Come see me after you get that done." The paper would need to be turned in by the evening. He knew Mark would have his story in on time.

Galloway went back into his office and pulled other story ideas he needed to assign.

Bang! The door to his office hit the wall. The editor looked up abruptly at Mark.

Mark grabbed it and closed it quietly behind him. "Sorry about that," he said.

Galloway didn't comment. Instead, he asked, "Did you get your story in on time?"

"Just now," Mark confirmed as he ran his hand through his thick hair.

"Sit down," Galloway directed.

Mark sat in the chair opposite the editor's desk.

He picked up the paper lying in front of him. "I have a story idea for you. You haven't been out on the road for a while and I thought you might want it."

"Definitely!" Mark sat forward eagerly. He didn't like to stay in one place for too long. The goal was for him to see as much of the world as he could. "Did you figure out a way to get me to the Yukon?" He had been campaigning to go as soon as gold was discovered the year before.

Galloway looked over his glasses at Mark. "Not yet."

"Yet. So, there's a chance?"

"I'm not ready to share that information," he said dismissively.

"Oh. What's the story you want to brief me on?"

Galloway handed the paper to him.

Mark read it through twice before he looked up in disbelief. "Outer space?"

"You like adventure, don't you?" the editor asked, sitting back in his chair. He waited to see what Mark's response to this story would be.

"Yes, yes I do." Mark had been working in Chicago the last few weeks and was itching to get back out on the road. But was this something he wanted to investigate? He shook his head. "Don, was someone drinking and telling stories? You don't really believe this?"

"Well," Galloway quantified, "what we know or what's been reported is that a 'flying object' was seen and it appears to have hit a local judge's property."

"What's the judge's name?" asked Mark, taking notes.

"Judge J. S. Proctor. Witnesses reported a cigar shaped craft with bright lights passing low. The object hit the judge's windmill and it broke apart. People heard an explosion and a fire was reported that could be seen for miles."

"Where did this happen?" Mark asked, hoping it was at least somewhere interesting.

"Texas."

"That's a big state. Can you narrow it down?" the reporter asked, still unsure if this was the story for him.

"Aurora, Texas."

Mark frowned. "I don't think I know that town."

"It's somewhat northwest of Dallas. The town is small."

Mark thought about that and thought this might turn into something interesting. And he hadn't been to Texas in a while. He made up his mind. "I can do it. When should I leave?"

The editor smiled; the story should stir people's curiosity and sell papers. "You should go soon. This type of story will be in all of the newspapers. Good human interest stuff."

"I'll get my tickets and head out tomorrow."

"Report back as soon as you conduct the interviews."

Mark went back to his desk and pulled out a map of the US. Much of it was now composed of individual states. Reviewing the route, he was thankful that the trip would be primarily by train. Traveling from Chicago to Dallas would require multiple transfers. The final part would be some type of alternate transportation from Dallas to Aurora. He gathered some gear into his shoulder bag and pulled on his suit jacket. He didn't include a knotted tie in his daily wear. Mark swung his bag on his shoulder and put his hat in place. He walked over to the editor's door and knocked lightly. When Galloway looked up, he said, "I'm headed out. I'll let you know what I find there."

"Mark, there have been other sightings that match the one you're investigating. Take it seriously. Also, keep your eyes open for any other events we can have articles written on." Mark's on-the-road articles usually generated interest.

"I will," he said and waved absently as he exited the office.

Mark whistled as he descended the stairs to the ground floor of the newspaper office. Even though he wasn't excited about the story, he was happy to be on the road again. His first stop would be the train station to get his tickets, and then he would head home by walking and catching the trolley.

By the time all of his errands were completed, it was late in the afternoon and the sun was starting to set. He was headed home to the boarding house where he and his family had lived since he was twelve. George and Elizabeth Sutherland had moved to Chicago to give Mark a safer environment to grow up in. The owners of the boarding house had saved them from a kidnapping and had continued to be their close friends.

He looked up at the four-story building with a large stoop in front. *Home*, he thought. It was somewhere he would always treasure.

He went in and made his way upstairs, waving at the people in the sitting room. Packing was foremost on his mind, and he wanted to get organized before the dinner bell rang. He entered his room and went over to the closet to pull out his carpet bag. The trip, for the piece he'd been assigned, would be a little over a week. His packing would have to include clothes for any detours he might encounter before he returned home. He dropped the bag on the bed and went to the dresser to get his shirts and socks.

The door opened abruptly and Mark didn't turn toward it. Instead, he continued to pack. The individual entered at a run, jumped on the bed, and bounced Mark's bag to the floor.

"Hey, Enzo," Mark said, looking over at the other man before bending down to pick up his bag and placing it back on the bed.

Enzo stretched out, making himself comfortable.

"Hey," he said.

"Move over," ordered Mark.

Enzo moved. He sat up, braced himself on his elbows, and watched Mark continue to pack. "Where to now?" The two were about the same age—in their twenties—and had grown up together. Enzo had moved into the boarding house when he turned eighteen.

"A little town in Texas," Mark said shortly, not wanting to share more information about the trip. He still wasn't sure how he felt about it.

Enzo saw the hesitation and immediately questioned, "What're you going to cover?"

"It's nothing," his friend said dismissively, hoping Enzo wouldn't press him.

Enzo saw Mark's face reddening and knew there was something more. "Tell or I'll torture you," he threatened lightly.

Mark looked at him and his build; he was more muscular than Mark and had wrestled him to the ground before. He gave in. "Okay, fine. There was a flying object that crashed and the thought is it might be from outer space."

"Wow," Enzo said and sat back. Now, he wanted to go with his friend. "When do you plan to come back?" He had some time between his engineering projects.

"It could be a while. It'll take time to get there and back."

"Oh, well, that won't work. It does sound interesting." He laid back on the bed and shot up a second later. "But you'll be back by May?"

Mark frowned. "What's the reason you want me back on a specific date?"

"Well, you might miss the wedding," he said, smiling brightly.

"You haven't proposed to Ruth yet!" Mark exclaimed. He stopped his packing and walked to his desk chair to sit down. He began jotting down some notes for the trip.

"I will at some point and I'll want you to stand up for me."

Mark shook his head. He knew Enzo always had a plan. "If it happens, I wouldn't miss it. You need to give me plenty of notice to get back home."

"How come? Isn't it just the one story?"

"Yes, but you never know, other things might pop up."

"Like in Boston," Enzo said knowingly. Two years ago, he had been assigned a project to work as a structural engineer on the Boston subway. Mark had gone to cover the news of how the city planned to take the business street and place it underground. The story had changed in April, when workers discovered human remains under Boylston Street.

"That story was too good to miss, and then the bodies!" Mark remembered.

"Yeah, you ended up staying almost as long as I did."

"I got two articles out of that trip. My editor was happy with that one."

"Plus, it was fun to be away and hang out together," Enzo reminded him.

"Won't you be headed back to Boston soon?"

"Yeah, they want to start this thing up in September. So, if I'm not married, I guess I'll go back."

"I think you're going to Boston," Mark muttered.

"What was that?" asked Enzo, though he had heard what his friend said.

"Nothing, not a thing."

Enzo let that go and changed the topic. "So, Texas—with travel time?"

"At least a week of travel, then the time there and maybe another week back. If I don't find another story."

Enzo looked down, his smile gone. Mark noticed. "Hey, I'll be back," he assured him.

"I know. It would be nice if you worked around here."

That isn't who I am, Mark thought. "Enzo, you know I get antsy if I'm not on the road, looking for the next adventure." So many things were changing; he wanted to see them all. Reporting was the one job that combined his two talents: writing and adventuring. "Take me to the station tomorrow morning?"

"Yeah, I guess so," his friend said in a low voice.

"Hey. Cheer up. I am here now."

At that moment, the dinner bell rang.

"Come on. It's dinner time. That should cheer you up," Mark said.

Enzo already looked happier. "I hope there's pie."

They went down the stairs together and into the dining room. Everyone was seated at the table. The first person Mark saw as he entered the dining room was his mom. He went to her immediately and kissed her cheek. He nodded to his dad. "Dad ," he said. His dad nodded back to him.

Enzo claimed his seat next to Ruth. Mark noticed she pulled away from him as he scooted closer to her. She also didn't return his smile. *Odd*, thought Mark and put it out of his head. Dinner was delicious as always and the conversation loud.

Everyone else filed in as Mrs. Spencer and her assistant Hazel finished putting food on the table. The food was passed around and conversation flowed between the people. Around the table were his mom and dad, Enzo, Enzo's brother Marco and sister-in-law Mara. Other boarders included two engineers from Prussia, Karl and Wilhelm.

Mark mentioned his trip the next morning. "Do you need me to take you to the train station?" his dad, George asked.

Mark took a quick drink of water before saying, "No, Enzo's going to take me."

Enzo paused as he reached for a tray of meat and grinned. "I'll make sure he gets there."

"Can you tell us about where you're going next?" asked Mara.

Enzo laughed loudly. Ruth squirmed next to him as he teased his friend. "Yeah, tell them about it."

Mark's face infused with color and he glared at Enzo.

His father noticed and said, "Now I have to hear about this trip."

Mark finally commented. "It's a human interest story, not a big deal. Someone saw something and I'm going to interview him."

"What did he see?" prodded Marco.

Mark mumbled, "Something that flew through the air."

His dad heard and frowned. "Was it a balloon?" he asked.

"I don't think so," Mark said noncommittally.

His mother looked thoughtful. "I've heard of flying machines."

"That's right," said his dad. "Wasn't the first flight in an airship made by Ernst Jägels?"

"Ja, that is right. Unfortunately, it crashed and the flying machine was beyond repair," commented Wilhelm.

Mark looked interested and said, "Just a minute." He went to the sideboard and got his notebook. "Can you tell me where this was?"

"Prussia," volunteered Wilhelm.

Mark's dad turned to the other man. "You know the details?"

"I do. It's a type of airship in which there's an envelope of lifting gas that's supported by an internal framework," Wilhelm explained.

"Are they over here yet?" Mark asked, taking fast notes.

"Nein, not yet," Wilhelm said. Karl nodded in agreement.

"Oh," Mark said, disappointed. "I don't think my editor would approve a trip to Prussia."

"Do you think someone has a similar type of flying machine over here?" Mark's dad asked.

"You should tell them," teased Enzo.

Mark ignored him and said, "We're not sure what was seen, but theories exist that it was not of the Earth."

Elizabeth, Mark's mom frowned. "If not from the Earth, where else would it be from?"

"Outer space," said Enzo.

The entire table went silent and looked at Mark.

"Surely not," said his mom, her voice going high.

"Yes, that's the human interest part; you saw how you all couldn't wait to hear more about the topic? I'm going to investigate and see if it was man-made or not."

Mr. Galloway was right, this could get some readership. He made some notes on the questions he was receiving.

"How would you know? Was it just a sighting? Or did they actually find something?" asked Enzo.

"They found something. It appears that whatever it was crashed, so there should be a debris field to review."

"Do you believe it could be from space?" Ruth asked in a low voice.

"I have my doubts," he said.

The conversation continued about life on other planets. Was it possible?

"Mark," commented his dad, "keep an open mind and don't make fun of the people you interview. They will want to be taken seriously."

"I agree," said Mark. "This shouldn't be a funny piece. The interviews should be handled in a professional manner. There were also additional sightings that support the event may have actually happened."

He thought about this as he went upstairs to his room; they'd given him a new direction for the story, one that excited him. His bags were on his bed and he took the opportunity to finish packing. When he finished, the bags were moved to sit beside his desk. Before bed, he went downstairs and stepped outside to enjoy the silence and smoke a cigar. He wanted to gather his thoughts for his upcoming trip.

The smoke floated in the air as he exhaled. The night was warm and it allowed him to relax. He took a final pull on his cigar and put it out with his shoe. He turned and started to head back in when a soft voice stopped him. "Mark, could I speak with you?"

He looked over and saw Ruth standing in the shadows. With a wide smile, he teased, "Where's Enzo gotten to?"

"That's what I wanted to talk to you about."

He felt uncomfortable with the direction of the conversation.

"Ruth," he started, "Enzo—"

"Mark," she interrupted, "I want to go with you when you leave."

"With me? Ruth..." he started hesitantly, trying to let her down gently. "Ruth, I like you, but not like that." He was afraid this was a romantic overture.

"Mark," she said firmly, "I don't like that you way either. I just want to get away from here, from making decisions."

"What decisions?" he asked tentatively. He didn't want to accidentally mention Enzo's proposal.

She frowned. "I know Enzo's going to propose at some point and I'm just not ready to make a decision like that."

"Do you think running away is the answer?"

"I think distance would be a good thing," she insisted. "We live here together; we see each other every day. Is it love or just convenience?" Ruth had moved to the city when her parents died. She and Enzo had been inseparable ever since she arrived.

"I just thought," she said miserably, "I could go on this assignment with you, as your assistant or something."

"It wouldn't be a good idea for us to travel together. I won't have Enzo hurt that way."

"I understand. Then I'll have to go on my own," she said defiantly.

"Isn't there an easier way?" he asked. "Someone you could go stay with?"

"There's no one," she said miserably.

"What about Clair? She has a number of locations where she could arrange employment for you and get you away from here." Clair Spencer ran a charity that was wide ranging and helped women move forward.

"I don't know her that well."

"I do. I'll organize a note to send to her but," he cautioned, "I won't help you until you've talked to Enzo. There'll be no running off or disappearances. I won't see him hurt like that."

She moved to a chair and collapsed. She started to cry. "I just need some time and space. Can't you see that?"

What he saw was a very young girl who wasn't ready for marriage. "Talk to Enzo and then I'll help. But it has to be tonight. I'm leaving in the morning."

"Yes, your trip." She thought about the packed bag in her room. Then she thought about Enzo, really thought about him. She looked up and said in a clear voice, "I'll go to him now."

Mark nodded and watched her leave. He'd wait to write the note; Enzo might want to discuss it with him. He looked at the squashed cigar with regret. He had hoped to feel more relaxed before going to bed. He shrugged philosophically and headed back into the house. On his way to the stairs, he noticed the doors to the study were closed and raised voices could be heard. *I guess she found Enzo.* He hastened his steps to allow them their privacy.

Once he was in his room, he walked to his desk and put together the letter for Ruth. Whatever the outcome of the meeting, he wanted to have it ready.

There was a tapping on his door. *Enzo already,* he thought, not looking forward to the conversation. He folded his letter to Clair and called, "Come in." He was relieved when the door opened and his dad walked in.

"All packed?" George asked.

"Yes, early train in the morning."

"Be safe and let us know when you'll be on the way home."

"I will."

"Goodnight."

"Night, Dad." Mark watched his father leave and got ready for bed. As he climbed into the bed, he heard a knock. He got up quickly and pulled on his pants. Another soft knock sounded as he opened the door.

It was Ruth and Enzo. Ruth's eyes were red and swollen and Enzo's hair stood on end from repeatedly running his fingers through it. Both seemed out of sorts. Enzo spoke for them. "Can we talk to you?"

"Of course, downstairs?" He was in his nightshirt and wanted to change.

"Yes," Enzo said.

As the duo headed downstairs, Mark changed quickly and pulled the door shut behind him and followed them to the sitting room. The house was quiet; everyone had gone to their rooms. The stairway and foyer were dark, the only lights illuminated from the sitting room. Mark took a deep breath and entered the room. Ruth and Enzo were sitting together. That seemed to be a positive sign. He sat and waited for them to start.

Enzo nodded at Ruth. "Mark, could you send Clair the note about the job?" she asked in a rush.

"Are you sure?" He looked first at Ruth, then at Enzo.

"I am," she said firmly.

Enzo spoke up. "I'll support her and, if this is what she wants, then yes, please send the letter."

"I have the note here," he said and patted his pocket. "I'll have Hazel take it over tomorrow morning."

"Thank you," Ruth said. She squeezed Enzo's hand and kissed him on the cheek. "I'm going up to bed now."

They watched her go. Once they no longer could hear her on the steps, Mark turned to Enzo. "Are you okay?" he asked.

His friend sighed and leaned back. "Yeah. I think the space will be a positive thing. We've lived in each other's pockets since we met. She just wants to be sure of our feelings for each other."

They had nothing more to say, so they stood and walked up the stairs together.

"See you in the morning," Mark said when they reached his floor.

"Yeah, in the morning," Enzo muttered.

CHAPTER 2

$\mathcal{M}$orning came quickly and a knock on his door reminded Mark to finish getting ready. "Come in," he called out.

Enzo stuck his head in. "Ready to go?"

"I am." Mark placed his extra notebooks and envelopes in his bag. Preparation was key when he was on the road. The bag closed with a snap and the latch was secured. He grabbed his jacket and hat. Enzo took his bags, and they moved downstairs. The bags were left by the door, and the two headed to the kitchen. It was early, but Mrs. Spencer and her helper Hazel were working on breakfast. The bacon was sizzling on the stove.

"Mind if we grab something here?" Mark asked Mrs. Spencer.

She looked over at the pair. "Your father left instructions for an early breakfast. Sit down. We have your plates ready. Eggs, toast, bacon, and pastries."

"Thank you," both men said gratefully.

She watched them dig in, satisfied with the clearing of their plates.

Mark stood and took his and Enzo's plates to the sink. Hazel took them from him. "Could I ask you a favor?" he asked her.

"Of course." Hazel had been at the boarding house for about five years and did occasional errands for the boarders.

"Can you see that Clair gets this letter?" He pulled it out of his pocket and handed it to her.

"I will," she promised and placed it in her pocket.

Enzo and Mark started to head out, but Mrs. Spencer called out to them. "Don't forget your lunch." Mark went back and took the can. "This should keep you for a day or two," she said.

He opened it and saw the amount of food she'd packed. "That'll work. I shouldn't need to buy anything for a few days. I'll miss your cooking," he said and kissed her on the cheek.

She waved him on his way. "You go on now! Don't miss that train."

"We won't," promised Enzo. "I have the wagon outside."

They exited the house, climbed up on the buckboard, and started to the train station. Once there, Enzo turned to him. "Have a grand adventure!"

"I will, and I'll let you know how to reach me."

"I may not be here."

Mark frowned and something came to him. "Will you go to Boston for the final build?"

"Yes, it's just the distraction I need."

"I'm sorry I got involved."

"No, you helped when she asked. I'm thankful for that."

They heard a voice call out, "All aboard."

"That means me," Mark said, and he jumped down and ran toward the train and his next adventure.

Enzo turned the wagon around and headed back home, his head hanging a bit lower.

CHAPTER 3

*T*exas
The trip to Texas was long but uneventful. Mark carried books to read to help him fill the time; his bag was weighed down more by them than clothes. He took over the seat next to him. The paper had paid for the travel, so he was in second class. There would be no beds, but there was more room than in third class. Once he was settled, he thought about Enzo and Ruth and hoped distance could bring them back together. Time would tell.

There were multiple stops and train switches before they stopped in Dallas. Mark descended the steps into the station and walked over to a station worker. "Good morning, do you know where I might get transportation to Aurora?"

The man waved over to a local wagon delivery location.

"Thanks!" he said and hurried over to the small building with a stable attached. The man working there called out, "Yes, can I help you?"

"I was hoping to catch a ride to Aurora."

The man looked through his deliveries for the day. "You're in luck, we have one headed there this morning."

"Can I wait here or should I come back later?"

"Stay around. My drivers are getting their wagons loaded now."

"I'll stay."

Mark had planned on breakfast, but if they were leaving, he didn't want to miss the opportunity. It didn't take long, and the boxes were loaded on the wagon near the office. Two horses were hooked up and the clerk called to him, "If you want to go, you need to go now."

Mark took him at his word and ran to the wagon.

"Jump in back," the driver instructed.

Mark tilted his cloth hat and threw his two bags in the back, jumping in behind them.

"How long until we get there?" he asked.

"A few hours. We should be there around lunch time."

Mark nodded and settled back against the boxes, rubbing his growling stomach. They were silent as the scenery went by. The rocking of the wagon lulled him to sleep. He woke abruptly when the driver called back, "We're here." Mark opened his eyes and saw the small, dusty town of Aurora for the first time. *That jacket I brought won't be of much use here,* he thought and pulled at his collar, trying to get some air. April in Texas felt hot after the cooler temperatures of Chicago.

The driver pulled to a stop. "The hotel is over there," he said and gestured to a building to their left.

That held little interest for Mark. What he needed was food. "Can you tell me where I can get something to eat?" he asked.

The driver motioned down the street. "Just head that way, up to main street. There's a café there. It'll provide you some good food."

"Thanks for that!" Mark said as he jumped off the wagon with his bag.

The driver watched Mark walk away. He shook his head. Since that object had been sighted, there had been more and more people wanting transportation into town. It had been dying slowly with new generations moving away. It might keep the town alive, but at what cost?

Mark continued on and hoped the man's suggestion was correct. The cafe he recommended was just where the driver said it would be. The door opened easily, and he entered and looked around. What he saw was clean and smelled wonderful. He continued to stand in the doorway, looking at the full tables and food being served. *Popular, the food must be good,* thought Mark.

One of the waitresses spotted him and waved him to an empty seat at the counter. He held up his bag, and she pointed to the closet. With the bag stored he walked to the counter, sat, and opened the menu quickly. The food on the trains had been filling but just standard fare.

"Mind if I join you?" a man's voice inquired.

Mark turned toward the man who stood next him. He had dark hair and brown skin; he was short in stature, but appeared solidly built. "Sure, have a seat. I'd like some company," Mark said.

The man sat and took the menu as Mark looked around for the waitress. He wanted to put his order in.

The man appeared to have made his decision quickly also and laid his menu down on the counter. "My name is Gus Lopez."

Mark reached out his hand, who took it in a firm shake. "Nice to meet you. I'm Mark Sutherland."

"What brings you to Aurora?"

Instead of answering, Mark asked, "Are you from here?"

"No. And by the looks of you, I'd say you aren't either."

Mark looked down at his city clothes and hat to admit the man was right. Most people in the room wore rough clothes you'd expect in a rural community. Even being wrinkled, dusty, and dirty from travel, he didn't fit in here with his dress pants, shirt, vest, and jacket.

Gus, on the other hand, *did* seem to fit. His clothes were rough, not polished. He also didn't look like someone afraid of hard work. When they shook hands, Mark had felt the scraping of old calluses.

"No, I'm traveling. I report on news and write articles for the *Chicago Tribune*. What about you?" Mark asked.

Gus sat back on the stool. "I also travel for work."

"What kind?" Mark asked curiously.

"I mostly find work here or there, whatever's interesting. I like to use my hands," Gus said.

Mark looked down at them again. That explained their condition. "And when it becomes uninteresting?"

"Then I move on to the next thing," Gus said simply.

Mark nodded; he understood the urge to keep moving. Whenever he felt the walls closing in, he went on to the next project.

At that moment, the waitress approached them and asked, "What can I get you?" She wore a long skirt, a button up shirt, and an apron. There were no frills to her appearance and no small talk. Not wanting to hold her up in such a busy place, they answered promptly. They placed their orders and, when she left, Gus started the conversation again.

"What story are you here for?"

Mark looked around before he answered. He said in a low voice, "There was a report of a flying machine in the area. It may have crashed."

Gus frowned. "Flying machine? Who saw it?"

"A local man, Judge Proctor, reported it."

Gus looked on with interest. "I'd love to accompany you when you talk to him."

Mark thought for a long moment and shrugged. *What harm*

could it do? "I don't see why not," he said. "I do want to stress that we take it seriously and don't make fun of him."

"I won't," he promised. "I'll just observe."

Mark nodded, happy for the company.

Their food was delivered, and they settled in to eat. Gus talked as he ate; he kept an ongoing stream of conversation. All of his stories were about his jobs, most on the railroads or general construction. "The country's growing, and I move to where I'm needed."

They finished their lunch and, when Mark headed out, Gus followed.

On the way, there was no shortage of conversation. Gus rushed in to fill any void created. He continued to talk about the parts of the country he'd traveled to and where he hoped to go. What he didn't talk about was family or where he was from.

Mark tried to dig further. "Where are you from originally?"

"Nowhere really," replied Gus, then continued on with his meandering of the same topics as before.

Mark listened and wondered if Gus had gone to college. He appeared to be well read but there was no mention of higher education. He was contemplating the upcoming interview and didn't offer much to the ongoing dialog. Gus seemed happy to talk for the both of them.

They got closer to the ranch; it was just outside of town. The heat was beating down on them and they hurried up the wide wood steps onto the shade of the porch. The house needed a coat of paint, but appeared to be in good shape.

Mark knocked on the door and Gus hung back, going silent. It was like a constant buzzing sound had stopped and it disorientated Mark for a moment. He shook his head and waited for someone to come to the door.

A woman answered. She smiled wide, wiping her hands on her apron. "What can I do for you?"

"Hi, I'm Mark Sutherland, and this is Gus Lopez."

"It's nice to meet you," she said. "I'm the judge's housekeeper. Is there something I can do for you?"

"We wanted to speak to him about something that happened on his property," said Mark.

The housekeeper's face went blank, and she stated coldly, "If you've come to make fun of him. . ."

Mark interrupted. "No, ma'am. We heard he had an interesting story to tell. I'm with the *Chicago Tribune*; I write human interest stories."

She looked doubtful at that. "I'm still not sure if he'll talk to you."

"Could you tell us where we can locate him? If he says no, then we'll leave."

She gave him a long look and finally nodded. "He's out walking the property and should be around soon for something to eat. You can wait on the porch." She pointed to a couple of chairs. Mark and Gus moved to them and sat down. She relented and asked, "Would you like some lemonade?"

They both nodded; it'd been a long walk from town. She went back into the house.

Gus looked at Mark. "Do you know any more details about what happened here?"

"The initial report said the object flew across the property and hit a windmill about 6am on April 17. The rest will have to come from the judge," said Mark.

Gus started to talk as they waited. The screen door slammed into the wall and the housekeeper came out with their lemonade. "There he is now," she said, pointing out to the road.

An older man walked toward them. He was distinguished, his clothes fine and his manner refined. As he climbed the steps he said in greeting, "Who do we have here?"

"They're here about the flying thing," the housekeeper replied before Mark could answer. She turned and took the lemonade back into the house without giving them their glasses.

Judge Proctor put his hand to his face and scrubbed it before answering. "Yes, well, that happened. What would you like to know?"

"Tell us what you saw that morning," Mark prompted.

"I didn't see anything," he admitted. "But I did hear an explosion and saw smoke."

"What did you do then?"

"I headed out to the area where the smoke could be seen, about a mile that way," he said, pointing north.

"What did you see when you got there?"

"My windmill was gone and the debris from the machine was scattered all around."

"Can we see the windmill?" Mark asked.

"There's nothing to see," Proctor explained.

"What about the debris, can we see that?" *Is there any evidence?* he wondered.

"No, I gathered it up and buried it."

Mark frowned. "Was something or someone found inside of the craft?"

"Yes."

"Can we see the body?"

"No. We had a traveling pastor, William Russell Taylor, say prayers and the body was buried in the local cemetery."

"Can we see that?"

"No. We don't want people to be in the area, for fear they'll try to dig it up."

No evidence, thought Mark. "What would you say about the body when you found it?"

"Not of this world. Like nothing I'd seen."

"Could you describe the body to me?"

"No more than I've told you."

Mark stared at the judge and finally said, "I guess that's about it." *What a waste of time.* He looked to Gus, then back to the judge and said, "Thank you."

"When will this be in the paper?" Proctor asked.

"Soon," Mark said as he closed his notebook.

"Good, good," the judge said. "Will you head back today?"

Again, Mark said, "Soon." He looked at Gus and asked, "Ready?"

"Yes," Gus said. They walked away from the house. "You didn't believe him, did you?"

"Not a word. They should've had some evidence to show."

"How will you write it?"

"I'll write what I was assigned: a human interest story. A 'craft' was seen and crashed."

"Why would they do it?"

"Make up this story? You see the town appears to be dying. How much would an influx of people help?" His mind on this article, Mark went quiet on their walk back. Gus started discussing previous places he'd worked.

They made their way back to main street and Gus said, "You know, we never did get to drink that lemonade."

"That's right." Mark looked around and asked, "Cafe?"

"Yes."

They headed over and were able to get a table this time.

Mark pulled out his notes and started reading through them. Gus tapped his arm. "Yes?"

"I think someone's trying to get your attention."

Mark looked over at the window and saw a young girl of about fifteen waving to him. Looking over at Gus, he said, "Wait here."

Gus said, "I'll order for us."

Mark headed out the door and the girl said, "I have information for you."

"What can you tell me?" he asked.

She looked around. "Over here. My dad runs the store." They went behind the mercantile; it backed onto an empty field. They wouldn't be seen there. When they stopped, she turned to him. "I'm Eliza Cain, and my parents saw the flying machine."

"Did you see it?"

"No, but my parents told me about it."

"Can I talk to them?"

"No," she said loudly. She lowered her voice. "A lot of the town's laughing at us and the story. It started to affect Dad's business and he said not to discuss it."

Witnesses, that's promising. "What did they tell you?"

"They were stocking the store at the time and they saw something through their front windows. They went out and followed it on foot."

"Was it going slowly?"

"No, I don't think so. They were able to follow the smoke," Eliza explained.

"It was already burning?"

"Yes, and they were close when it exploded on the judge's property."

More confirmation of the details from the judge, thought Mark.

"Other people saw it also," she said.

"Can you tell me their names?"

"Charlie Stephens saw it, but his dad wouldn't let him investigate. He's eight."

Mark looked down at the notes he'd taken. "This is good information. I appreciate you taking the chance to talk to me. Can I use your name in the article?"

Eliza chewed her lip. "This would be in Chicago?" She'd heard he worked for a paper there.

"Yes."

"That might be okay. We don't get a lot of papers from there."

"One last thing."

She nodded for him to continue.

"Can you map out the location of the crash and the cemetery?"

"Can I borrow your notebook?"

He gave it to her and she drew the location of the landing and handed it back to him. "Thank you," he said, studying it.

They parted ways, going out separately.

Mark returned to the café and found Gus sitting with several empty glasses. He was making his way through a piece of chocolate cake. "How long was I gone?" he asked wonderingly, looking at the glasses and the cake.

"Long enough," Gus said and waved at the waitress. She brought over a lemonade for Mark and a piece of cake.

"Thanks," Mark said. He ate quickly and drank down his drink. Taking a deep breath, he let it out before saying, "I needed that."

"What did she have to say?" Gus asked in a low voice.

"She changed my mind," he said thoughtfully.

"You now believe something from outer space landed here?" Disbelief was clear in the man's tone.

"No, not that. But I think something did happen. It seems like more than one person saw this event take place. I do wish we had pictures of the craft or machine that crashed." As he pulled out his paper to take notes, he thought of Jake. He was a photographer for the Chicago Police Department. But, as much as he wished it, Mark knew Jake would be out of his comfort zone here. He liked routine and his travels were anything but routine.

Rather than let the silence linger, Gus started talking about the weather. Mark couldn't pay attention; he concentrated on the article. It came together quickly. Everyone he talked to seemed sincere, and he planned to include that in the final article. Mark mulled over his outline, trying to see if he should say where the object or body had been buried. He decided not to; instead, he'd include a statement that said he hoped future people could figure out what had crashed in Aurora, Texas, in 1897.

"You know, I would like to see the site and confirm the marks on the ground and the missing windmill," said Mark, looking down at his story.

"Do you know where they are located?"

"Yes, the girl gave me directions."

"Want to head over now?"

"Yes," Mark said. They paid their check and walked out. "This way," he said after looking over the map.

A man sat in a rocker outside of the café and watched them closely. He heard everything they said and commented, "The grave isn't where you think it is."

Mark and Gus looked over at him. "Excuse me, do you have information on where the actual burial is located?" Mark asked.

"If you want to find it, go to the cemetery. There'll be a huge old oak tree, just south of the entrance. You should see a beehive in the tree. Look around the tree for carvings. That'll tell you where the body's buried."

"Sir, did you see them put the body in the ground?"

The man rocked back and forth before replying. "I can't say I did, but that is where it is."

"Thank you."

The man nodded and continued to rock.

Mark and Gus started their walk. It took them a few miles outside of town. "Eliza's parents followed the craft this far?" asked Gus.

"Looks like," commented Mark. According to the map, they'd arrived at the location of the crash. Is *there any evidence?* They walked on the property; they weren't in view of the house. Gus jogged ahead, examining the land.

"Hey, over here. There appears to be a burned path," he called.

Mark joined him and looked at the burned trail. "It could be man made."

"It could. Let's follow it."

Mark followed Gus and it led to four white posts sticking out of the ground. The burn marks were visible. "The windmill?" Gus asked.

"Or what's left of it. It also looks like freshly dug ground under it." Mark sighed. "As much as I want to, we can't dig into the judge's yard."

"Then what next?"

"The cemetery."

Gus shrugged and followed. *This is getting interesting.* "What if we're seen?"

"Not sure," Mark said.

The cemetery was a few miles from their current position, but the idea that there was the possibility of a person from somewhere other than Earth being buried there had them hurrying. They entered per the man's directions and headed to the tree. It was gnarled and very old. Mark and Gus separated to find the carving. Mark stopped and traced the crevasse. "Gus, here it is." Gus came around quickly to see what Mark had found. It was as described, shaped like the description of the flying machine.

"Look where you're standing," Gus said.

Mark looked down; it was freshly dug soil. He jumped quickly back. "This is it!" He dropped down and started to dig.

Gus stopped him. "Mark, I don't think we should be digging up anyone, whether from around here or not."

"But we need proof!" Mark pulled desperately at the ground with his fingers.

"For who? I think we can both agree that something happened here and someone died."

Mark stopped digging reluctantly and slowly sat back on his

heels. "I guess we'll leave it up to future investigators to find out if he is a man or something else."

"I think that's for the best. What now? Will you include the locations of the wreckage and the body?" Gus asked.

Mark said stood and dusted off his hand on his pants, "Yes, this changed my mind, I'll include that it's on the judge's land. That's a fact."

"And the cemetery?"

"I'll include the location of the cemetery and the fact a funeral was conducted." *I'd like to come back one day and find out what, or who, is buried here, he* thought. "Let's head back to town. I need to sit and write my article; my notes are pretty complete."

They walked back to town and Gus asked, "Have you gotten a room yet?"

"No," Mark admitted, "I'd hoped to be out of here before that."

Gus nodded. "We can go over to the hotel where I'm staying and use the lobby. I think there's some desks or tables there."

"Sounds good. I'll need to get my bag from the café."

They headed that way for Mark's bag and then walked to the motel. Once there, Gus found Mark a place to work. In about an hour, he had his article written and proofed. He folded it and put it into an envelope. He waved to Gus, who was sitting on the couch reading the paper. "Post office?" asked Mark.

Gus nodded. He folded his paper and they headed out. Once the letter was dropped off, they exited and stood on the sidewalk.

"Where to now?" asked Gus.

"Home, I guess," Mark said, looking around to see if there was transportation out of town.

"How about coming with me?" asked Gus unexpectedly.

"Where are you going next?" After listening to his travel stories the last two days, he knew he must have another destination in mind.

Instead of answering, Gus asked, "Know anything about oil?"

"Oil? Sure, it's that stuff they're using for heat now? Comes from the ground?"

"Yep, I'm headed to an oilfield in the Indian territory of Oklahoma. I hear they're looking for men to work the field. Interested?"

"Always." Mark would send the story idea to Galloway, but if not approved, he'd go anyway. It was an experience he couldn't pass up. "I'll need to send a telegram to my editor, then we can go."

They headed there first, and Mark sent the telegram and told Galloway he'd contact him again from Oklahoma.

Mark looked at Gus. "How do we do this?"

"We get a ride to Dallas, then trains to Oklahoma."

Mark spotted the Wells Fargo Wagon. "Hey, let's see if he can take us."

They both jogged over to the driver and Mark called up, "Hey, can you take two people?"

"I can," he said. "Climb in." They followed his direction and started their first leg of the trip.

The wagon bumped and the dust kicked up behind them. Gus filled the silence with an ongoing stream of conversation. The topic now was Indian territory.

"Who owns the land where the oil is?" Mark asked.

"It's Tribal land—Choctaw, Cherokee, Seminole, Creek and Chickasaw. Two of the tribal ladies married George Keller and William Johnstone. The tribe trusted them, and they built a business, sure there was oil. They formed the Cudahy Oil Company."

"Do you think they'll find oil?"

Gus shrugged. "Maybe, maybe not. I'm looking forward to finding out."

CHAPTER 4

*L*ate April, 1897, Oklahoma

After a long train ride, they finally arrived in Bartlesville, Oklahoma.

It wasn't much to see. Another dusty small town. What was different from Texas was the people. Mark looked in interest at them. Choctaw, Cherokee, Seminole, Creek, and Chickasaw, just as Gus had said.

Main street had a long row of brick buildings at various heights. Each featured many windows with shops featured at the bottom of each. Roads weren't paved and dry dirt was kicked up as horses pulled wagons through the town. "Not much to look at," Mark commented.

"Not now, but if an oil boom happens, this place will change quickly," Gus said.

Mark nodded. "Money would lead to change. Where do we go now?"

"Cudahy Oil must have an office in town. We should be able to find it quickly."

"You looking for the oil hiring office?" a young man asked as they walked by him.

"We are," said Gus.

"It's just down there and to the right. You'll know it by the men lined up in front of it."

"Thanks!" Mark said.

They followed his directions and spotted a line of approximately ten men. They looked at the sign: HIRING OFFICE.

They got in line and waited patiently as each man was processed. Their turn came up and the man at the desk waved. As they moved forward, a voice called out, "Gus!" They looked toward it and saw an older man, red cheeks and a large belly straining a white shirt. "Gus, I didn't know you were in the area!"

"Yeah, good to see you, Joe," Gus drawled. "I was in Texas and thought I might come up here and work for you."

"Wonderful," Joe said, taking Gus' hand, pumping it up and down. "We need oil men. When can you start?"

Mark looked at his friend in astonishment. After all of the talking he did, he didn't mention he had experience in the industry.

Gus looked over at Mark. "Oh, and my young friend here, he could use a job."

The man looked him over and asked, "Will you vouch for him?"

"I will," Gus confirmed.

"Then I'll take the chance." He stuck out his hand to Mark. "Joe Wilson."

Mark took the offered hand. "I appreciate you taking a chance on me."

"If Gus recommends you, I'm good. I need you both out at the oil field. Barney!" he called over his shoulder. "Take these men down to the field. Set them up with a place to stay."

Barney stood and walked to the door and turned the sign to closed. The men waiting protested. "I'll be back; we'll open again in another hour. Follow me," Barney said to Gus and

Mark as he pulled the door closed. They moved out back to a horse and wagon. He walked over to the driver's seat. Once he'd pulled himself up, he looked back and motioned to them. "Hop in."

They climbed in and Joe got the wagon moving with a click at the horse. Mark looked at Gus and asked, "We aren't staying in town?"

Gus laughed loudly. "No, this type of work goes 24 hours until oil's found. What little sleep we'll get will be in tents."

"Tents?" asked Mark. He hadn't thought of that.

"Yes."

Well, I wanted adventure; this is part of it, thought Mark. They went past the town and he couldn't see anything in the distance. He looked over at Gus and saw that he'd taken the opportunity to close his eyes.

Mark stayed awake, observing the area around them. The trip was long and hot. *Is there anything green in Oklahoma?* Mark asked himself.

They arrived at the oil field. *As far as adventures go, this one's had a slow start. No baths in my immediate future,* thought Mark.

They finally pulled to a stop. Gus woke and yawned, stretching out his arms. "Here already?"

"This is it," said Barney, pointing to their left. "Go over to the sign-in area. They'll give you your work assignment and tents."

Gus looked around at the tents and some half-completed oil derricks in the distance. He gestured to the one that was completed and said to Mark, "That's where we'll be working."

They walked to the tent area where other men were checking in and joined the line. It moved quickly and the man working at the table looked at them. "You and you," he pointed to Gus and Mark, "sign in here." As they signed their names to the check-in sheet, he continued, "You both share a tent." It wasn't a question. "Over there." He pointed and continued.

"There are outhouses dug around the perimeter. We'll be providing food in the lunch tent for breakfast, lunch, and dinner. Payday will be Fridays. We'll review your assignments each morning." Mark and Gus nodded. "Grab your bags and get settled in." When they hesitated, he said, "Move on." They heard the next person in line being given the same information.

Mark and Gus walked over with their bags and entered their assigned tent. It was so small, they could barely stand. There were cots with blankets. Mark sighed in relief; he hadn't wanted to sleep on the ground. "Not a lot of extras here," he commented.

"No. This type of work is focused when we're on the job. There won't be time for much else."

"The foreman said our first day would be in the morning," commented Mark. "Can you show me what we'll be doing?" He dropped his bag down on his cot. He wanted to start an article on the first day at an oil camp.

"Yeah. As long as we don't get in anyone's way, it should be okay," Gus replied.

They walked toward the completed wood derrick. It was actively running.

"How does this thing work?" asked Mark as he walked around the tall structure.

Gus studied it. "You ever hear of Thomas Derrick? The hangman who lived in the Elizabethan Era?"

"No, I don't think so."

"This thing," his friend said, patting the structure, "started off as modified gallows. You've seen them on your travels?"

"Gallows? Yeah, unfortunately." They were still being used as lethal punishment in parts of the United States and Territories.

"This uses a similar supporting framework in its design and that's why it carries his name now."

Mark walked around it and looked at its height.

"These wood structures are built over the suspected oil wells, and all the machinery is installed on the site itself. Once constructed, it plays an important role throughout the entire task of oil extraction, right from drilling, pumping, to storing. It's based on weights and balances."

"What's that at the top?" Mark asked as he leaned in.

"That's a mobile boom with a cable, pulley, and crane arrangement, which is capable of hauling heavy equipment from one place to another."

"All of this for oil. Why is it so important?" Mark asked wondrously.

"The future. It'll be something we use in machines. Great turbines and other types of moving machines."

"How does it work exactly?"

"A large heavy rod or pole is used to dig the Earth's surface to reach the oil reserve beneath it. The pump has repeatedly beaten the Earth's surface until the layers of rock and soil give way. That hole you see came from that process. It already has some extraction pipe in it. It'll be our job to make sure that pump works and doesn't overheat. Once that happens, crude oil and natural gas can be pumped out of the inserted pipes in the freshly dug holes."

"Where have you done this work?"

"I've participated in sinking wells in Texas and Oklahoma. The first derrick is the test one to see if the field has oil."

"There's still a chance we won't find oil?"

"Yeah, some areas are dry and will be a bust."

"What about here?" Mark asked.

"I think there's a good chance this field is valuable."

They headed back to their tent and the call came for everyone to meet in the dinner tent. The tent had long wood tables full of men eager to start work the next day. Joe spotted them and carried over his coffee to their table. He sat.

"Gus, I want you to take over the operation of the current well. I'll move the men to other rigs. We need those to be ready to go when this one comes in." He looked over at Mark. "You stay with him and follow directions. I'll see you at the rig in the morning."

CHAPTER 5

*A*fter breakfast the next morning, they walked over to their rig. Joe was already there waiting for them. When they started the inspection, Gus asked, "How deep have you gone?"

"We're 200 feet. That's why I want you on this rig."

"And you going deeper?"

"I have faith that we're close. Take over as the rigger. I want you here if we find oil. We need someone experienced when it comes in."

"Are you expecting a gusher?" Gus asked.

Mark looked on but stayed silent.

"Better than that, we're planning a nitro drop in a few weeks."

"You feel that sure?"

"I do, and we'll need to react quickly. You take over here and keep the drilling going." He looked at his watch. "Get to work. Your crew should be on their way soon. I'll check on you later."

They watched him walk off. "Gusher? Nitro?" asked Mark.

"If the nitro is used and oil is there, then it'll be spilling out until we can get the piping under control."

Mark thought about the articles he'd write about the buildup.

The men walked up and looked to Gus for direction. He set them all to their jobs and had Mark shadow different men during the day. Joe had kept them together and stopped by several times on the first day to check in. He watched Mark's work and nodded to Gus. Mark would stay.

The days were shifts of 12 hours and were long and hot. The first few weeks, Mark just collapsed on his cot after finishing work and had to be roused by Gus to go to dinner. He was always glad when he got there, as the food was filling and flavorful. The owners understood groups like this ran on their stomachs.

The drilling had gotten well over 300 feet and they still had found nothing. Mark thought about that as they sat outside their tent looking at the night sky. He found that Gus would often sit silent in the evening and Mark would try to shake him out of his ennui.

"I'm from New York," Mark said one night as he and Gus sat outside their tent drinking beer.

That stirred his friend from his contemplation of the sky. He looked over and commented, "I thought you mentioned Chicago."

"Now, I'm from Chicago, but I was born in New York."

"How did you end up in Chicago?"

"That's a story." Mark saw that Gus had sat forward, interested.

"Well, go on," he prompted.

"My mom, dad, and I lived in New York. I wasn't interested in school and started to hang out with a local gang. They started teaching me how to pick pockets."

Gus' eyes widened. "How long did you do this?"

Mark laughed abruptly. "Not long," he admitted. "I was

caught rather quickly by a lady detective. She had me by my collar before I could take anything from her."

"A lady detective?" Gus asked, fascinated.

"Oh yeah. And she had definite ideas on how to change my future."

"How did she do that?"

"Books. We started to trade books through the mail. As long as I stayed in school, I received books."

"Like the ones you're always carrying?" Mark had a book with him when not sleeping or at work.

"Exactly."

"Where did she live?"

"Chicago."

"Where you live now? Did she have something to do with that?"

"Yes," Mark admitted. "That gang decided they needed to make an example out of me so that the other boys wouldn't quit. We ended up being kidnapped and held under the Brooklyn Bridge."

"Kidnapped? Who helped you? The lady detective?"

"A member of her team brought help in the form of an off-duty policeman and some Pinkerton detectives. They got in and managed to get us out safely. After that, my parents thought it best to leave New York."

"How was the lady detective involved in your move?"

"They own the boarding house we moved into. We stayed very close to them."

Gus laughed and asked, "Did you continue to stay in trouble in Chicago?"

"No, I was too busy with school and things happening around us."

"Having to do with the female detective?"

"Sometimes," Mark said, thinking of how he and his parents had helped in several kidnap cases.

"Now, you're running toward your own adventures?"

"Always." He looked from the sky and over at Gus. The man had loosened up; he was on his second beer of the evening. Mark chose that moment to ask his first question. He was curious about Gus' family and where he was from. *Why was he on the road with no apparent plan other than to keep moving?* It reminded him of Ruth. "You seem to be running away from something.' When he didn't hear anything, he prompted, "Gus?"

"Yeah," his friend drawled, leaning back again in his chair, and looked at the sky.

"Are you married?"

The silence stretched out between them and Gus kept his face directed up. This taciturn man was different from the one Mark had traveled here with. He could talk your ear off about the heat, his other jobs from Mexico, Arizona, Texas, and here. But this question seemed to have switched off his ability to talk.

Gus finally looked over and shook his head. "No." He didn't comment further.

"What about family? Where are you from originally?"

Gus still didn't answer.

Have I asked too much? Mark thought to himself. Just when he started to apologize, Gus started talking. Mark went silent, giving him the space.

"I was away at school."

Mark wanted to ask what kind of school, but he stayed quiet.

"My family… we had property in Texas."

Past tense, thought Mark.

"My wife and son…"

Son?

"My wife and son," Gus continued, "were staying with my parents. They were ranchers. We'd moved from Mexico twenty years before and settled there. I left for school and I went home after graduation. I arrived in Corsicana, got off the train, and expected to be met by my dad. Instead, it was the local sheriff."

Gus felt himself being pulled back into time as he told the tale to Mark.

~

A tall man walked over. The sun hit the man's badge and briefly blinded Gus. He held up his hand to block the glare.

"I'm Sheriff Isaiah Ball. Are you Gustavo Lopez?" he asked.

"I am," Gus replied, looking around for his father. He'd promised to pick him up.

"Sir," the sheriff tried again to get his attention, "sir, there's been an event."

Gus frowned and finally looked the sheriff in the eye. "An event?"

"Yes. Your family got caught up in a fight over land and water rights."

"I don't understand. What's this about water? Is my father okay?"

Ball sighed and tried again. "Why don't we move over to the bench?"

"No, just tell me."

The sheriff put his hands on Gus' shoulders. "Sir, they burned your family's home when he chose sides in the fight about who has access to the water."

Gus felt his world shift on its axis, and he said with no inflection, "My wife? My son?"

"Gone. Your mother and father also. It was the middle of the night when it happened. They barred the doors to prevent their escape."

"Where are they?"

"What's left of them is with the undertaker."

Gus shook his head. "No, the people who did this to them."

The sheriff knew what Gus was considering. "We have them. They'll pay for what they did."

"Can you take me to my ranch?" Gus asked.

"Yes, I have some horses here to take you."

Gus nodded and followed him. They each took a horse and rode to the ranch in total silence. They pulled into the property marker and rode the miles to the house. The smell of smoke washed over them as they rode. Gus let the extra energy overtake him and he pushed the horse into a faster gallop. Sheriff Ball didn't say anything but increased his pace to follow. They reached the burned-out house at the same time.

Gus slid off the horse and ran toward what was left. There wasn't a door there anymore, but that's where he entered. "Nothing," he said out loud. "There's nothing left."

"No. They didn't want anyone as witnesses."

Gus turned toward the sheriff. "How do you know you got the right people?"

The sheriff rubbed his neck and said, "It was a family member who turned them all in."

"How do you know you can trust them?"

Ball looked him square in the eye. "Because it was my wife, Martha, who turned them in."

Gus slumped down on the ground; tears formed but stayed frozen in his eyes. There was no one left.

"Come with me," Ball said, pulling Gus to his feet. He walked Gus to his horse and shoved him on. Gus let the horse guide them back to town.

The sheriff stopped the horses in front of a small house. He climbed down and went to Gus and pulled him down. They walked together to the door. It opened as they approached it and Martha Ball stepped out.

"This is Gus," the sheriff said simply.

Martha did not hesitate she went to Gus and hugged him tightly.

ourt
    Gus sat alone on the benches in the courtroom. *The trial is over. How is it over?* He looked toward the two Wilson men who had murdered his family. They were laughing and hugging one another. *How?* Martha Ball was a witness, but their lawyer discredited her and said she did it out of spite. The Wilson's pointed at him, laughing, and continued out of the doors, calling for a celebration.

Their lawyer stayed behind and walked over to him. "Mr. Lopez, I have an offer for you. We'd like to buy your property."

Gus didn't spare him a glance and walked away. He went straight to the sheriff's office. When he entered, he saw Sheriff Ball and Martha hugging.

She was inconsolable; she'd done what she could. Her testimony should have locked the murderers up permanently. Instead, the court was convinced she'd made it up.

Ball didn't say anything. He'd convinced her they would hear her out and know it was the truth. He'd been wrong. He saw Gus over her shoulder and whispered to her. She turned her tear drenched eyes to him.

Martha ran over and hugged Gus. He stood for a moment, then hugged her back and let the tears flow. "I'm so sorry," she said over and over.

When they finally seemed to run out of tears, she stepped back. Ball brought a glass of water for them both.

Gus reached into his pock and took out a piece of paper. "I want you and Martha to have this. I can't stay here," he said. They both looked bewildered but took the paper offered.

"Sit," Martha said and they sat. They read the paper he'd given them.

"Gus, we can't take your land!" Ball insisted.

Martha said, "No, we can, Isaiah. We'll take care of it for you, Gus, and when you return, you'll come back to us."

"You're sure?" Ball murmured.

"Yes. We need to take care of it for him," said Martha.

"Okay." He knew he couldn't stay on as sheriff after the injustice that had happened.

"What'll you do? Can we convince you to stay here with us and rebuild?" Martha asked Gus hopefully.

"No, I can't stay here," he repeated.

They understood the pain he'd feel, trying to live by the men who killed his family. They'd still be neighbors.

"Do you really want us to take it and live there, work it?" Ball asked.

"Yes, I want to know that the land's safe and not in the Wilson's hands."

"Even though Martha's related to them?"

"She proved who she is with in court. She's a brave lady."

"Yes," Ball said, "she is."

They went with him to the station. "You'll let us know where you are?" Martha asked.

Gus hesitated and Ball said, "I might need to know where you are for the business."

"I'll send an address."

Since that time, he hadn't stayed in any location for too long.

~

"I am so sorry," Mark said. "I shouldn't have pressed."

"No, that's okay. I haven't talked about it since that time."

"Will you go back? Ever?"

Gus looked up at the sky again, silent.

Mark stared at him but didn't say anything else. He turned his eyes to the sky.

Their next day was the only day off they'd get for the week. Mark got up and walked toward his cot. He glanced back and saw Gus still sitting there, not moving, lost in his memories. He shook his head and went to sleep.

CHAPTER 7

$\mathcal{T}$he next morning, Mark woke up and looked immediately to Gus' cot. It didn't look slept in. He shot up, worried that he'd stirred memories Gus may not be ready to contemplate. He dressed quickly, pulling on his suspenders over his unbuttoned shirt, and left the tent. The day had already started and the men were at their jobs.

Mark and Gus were part of the shifts that had the day off. The other men were hanging around their tents. He waved at some in greeting and looked around; he didn't see Gus anywhere. Going back into his tent, he buttoned up his shirt and combed his hair. He exited and tried the first man he saw. "Seen Gus?"

"Nope, not this morning," the reclining man answered.

Where could he have gotten to?

"You might try Joe's tent," suggested the man. "I thought I saw him over there earlier."

Mark nodded and headed that way. When he got to the large tent, the opening was pulled back and he could see Gus inside. Mark sighed in relief. Gus looked like he normally did. He was also talking animatedly. Joe spotted Mark and called, "Come in, come in."

Mark went; he looked quickly toward Gus.

"Good morning," Gus said with an easy smile.

"Hey," said Mark.

Joe started. "I know it's your day off, but I was hoping I could send you both to town for the mail and a few other things."

"Sure," said Mark. Gus nodded.

"You have the list?" Joe asked Gus.

He held up a paper and waved it. "I have it here."

"See me when you get back."

"Breakfast first?" asked Mark.

Gus responded, "I'll walk you over." They headed to the tent. At the entry, he said, "When you get done, meet me outside. I'll bring the wagon over."

"Okay." Mark watched him leave, his brows furrowed.

"You going to eat?" the cook called. "I need to start prep for lunch."

"Yes, please," Mark said eagerly and hurried over. There was slim picking at this hour. The cook gave him a plate with slightly rubbery eggs, bacon, and a couple of biscuits.

"You get what you get at this hour," the cook warned him.

"I understand. It'll be fine."

He quickly sat and gobbled down the food. It wasn't the tastiest meal, but it was filling. He took his plate back over to the cook. "Thank you for holding some for me."

"Yeah, yeah," the cook said and continued to cut onions, his mind occupied with meal prep. He yelled to his helpers, "Potatoes, get those peeled!"

"Yes, sir!" the two helpers called back.

Mark headed out. He didn't have to go far, as he saw Gus waiting just outside the tent.

"Ready to go?" Gus asked.

"Yeah." Mark hopped up and sat next to friend on the seat.

Gus clicked his tongue, and the horse started forward. They rode past the work site and onto the long dirt road to town. The quiet was uncomfortable for Mark and he asked hesitantly, "Did I ask too much last night?" He couldn't let it go. *Why can't I just leave the man in peace?*

Gus stared ahead and said, "No, you just got me thinking. Only a few people know that story."

"Why me?"

"You asked," he said simply, "and I was ready to share."

"Does that mean you might be ready to go back home?"

"I'm not sure," Gus admitted. "I don't think I'm ready for that quite yet."

Mark let that lie and settled back to watch the scenery. Gus reached into his pocket and handed Mark the list. He opened it and found mostly supplies for the cook, mail delivery, and feed for the horses. Folding it back, he held it until they got to town.

It was busier than expected, with people on the sidewalks and the road. "More people than last time," commented Mark. "These don't look like locals."

Gus looked in the same direction, noting the pants and suit jackets and fancy hats.

"Any idea why they're in town?"

"Yeah, I think we're getting close to the drop."

"Drop?"

"Yeah, Ed mentioned to us on our first day that the plan was to stop drilling, put a pan of nitroglycerin in, and then drop the Go-Devil —a heavy dart that will dislodge the nitroglycerine and cause an explosion."

"Nitro," Mark said. "Isn't that dangerous?"

"It can be if not handled properly."

"Who'll he get to do it?"

Gus looked over and said laconically, "Me."

"You!" Mark said, shocked.

"Yeah, Ed and I have worked together before, and I've handled it many times. I can do it safely."

"Is that why he was so happy to see you?"

Gus grinned. "Yeah, the guy he hired backed out. Something about a nervous wife."

"What'll you do?"

"My main job will be to get the nitro moved from its container into the pan and lower that into the well."

"I can help with that."

Gus frowned. "You'll have to take instructions; there won't be time for conversation. We'll practice over and over before the actual event."

"I can handle that." He saw the post office in the distance. "There first?" he asked.

"Yeah. There should be a large amount for us to pick up."

Mark pulled out several bulky envelopes he needed to drop off.

"Are those articles?"

"Yeah, day to day stuff on how to work on an oil rig and general life around the camp."

"Think readers will be interested in that?"

"Yeah, and I can't wait to write about the nitro."

"It'll be something to see."

"How soon do you think?" Mark asked, thinking about the article and timing. He'd want to get it in the mail as soon as possible.

"Soon," he commented.

"How can you tell?"

"The monitoring time has increased and we aren't going any deeper. Joe said the samples from the drill show that something's beneath the shell."

"They haven't told the men?"

"No, no announcements. At least not yet."

"Hmm," Mark said.

He expected them to stop at the post office but Gus continued on. "Hey!" Mark exclaimed. "Where're we going?"

"Changed my mind. I think it might be best to get the supplies first," Gus said. "I don't want the mail to get lost. It's too valuable to the men."

"Oh, right," Mark replied. He'd talked to the men at the rig and they hadn't been home in months. Working as a wildcatter could be a strain on the families.

"Once the field is set up and running, will the men be able to bring their families here?" asked Mark.

"It depends on what's going to be done with the oil."

"What do you mean? Won't they sell it?"

"Yeah, but transportation's the issue. Look around. It would be by barrel to the surrounding areas."

"But what about bigger cities?"

"How would you get it to them?"

"Rail? No," Mark answered his own question. "There isn't one here. What about pipeline?"

"None in the area."

"What'll they do?"

"My guess is they'll have to cap it and wait."

Mark made a mental note to put that in his final article.

They got to the mercantile and both men jumped down. Gus tied the horses to the post in front of the store and they entered. There was a line and Gus and Mark looked around as orders were filled. The line moved forward, and it was their turn. The man there asked, "What can I get for you?"

Gus said, "I'm here for the Cudahy Oil Company to pick up the supplies." He handed the man the list.

The man pulled his glasses out of his pocket, put them on, and looked it over. "We have everything you need. I assume you'll be charging this to Cudahy?"

"Yes."

The man called out, "Boys!" Two boys ran out of the back;

they looked about twelve and fourteen. "Help this man with these things." He looked at Mark and directed him with, "You can follow them and load the items on the wagon." Mark nodded and accompanied them to the back, helping them haul the heavy bags of flour, sugar, and other items to their wagon.

While that was happening, Gus and the store clerk were gathering the other items from the shelves. Once completed, he signed for the bill and met Mark at the now full wagon.

"Post office next?" Mark asked.

"Yes."

They moved the wagon a few buildings down and pulled over. "Go in and tell them who you're picking up for. They should have them ready," Gus said.

Mark knew someone should stay with the wagon. He headed in and went to the desk.

"Yes?" asked the clerk.

"I need to pick up the mail for the Cudahy Oil Company," said Mark.

"We have the bags ready for you."

"Bags?"

"Yes, the men tend to get a lot of letters and packages," the clerk said over his shoulder as he went to the back room.

Mark wondered about the packages as he waited. The man returned with one bag over his shoulder and one carried with his other hand. He ran over quickly to help out. He took the bags, one in each hand.

"Got it?"

"I do, thank you. Oh. I almost forgot." He set the bags down and reached into his pocket. "I need to mail these."

The clerk took the envelopes and told him the fees to send. Once their transaction was completed, Mark took the bags and headed out to the wagon.

Gus jumped down to help when he saw him. "Two bags!"

"Yeah, he said one is full of packages."

Gus grinned. "That's probably food."

"Food? Who would send food?"

"Wives send sweets, cakes, and pies."

"Nice! Will they share?" Mark asked, looking at the bag.

"Some will."

Mark considered writing to Cousin's Bakery back home and asking if they would send some sweets to him. He didn't want to hold them up, though, and helped Gus place the bags in a secure location. They moved to the front of the wagon. Once settled on the seat, they pulled out and headed back to the oil field.

Their arrival must have been expected; the men surrounded the wagon as they pulled into the site.

"Can you distribute the mail?" asked Gus.

"Sure."

"I'll start taking the supplies to the food tent." He jumped down and gabbed the bags to move to the tent.

Mark was happy to pass out the mail; he hoped he had a few letters as well. The articles he'd been sending in should have been printed by now. He opened the bag and started to call out names. The men yelled, "Here!" Gus' letters started piling up. He put them to the side, along with the letters addressed to himself.

As the men started to walk off, he called out, "I have another bag. This one is packages!" A cheer went up. Evidently, the men knew what tended to be in the packages. As he handed out each one, he noticed they didn't open their items in the bigger group.

The crowd broke up and the men headed back to their tents. The mail not distributed would be held for the men at the rigs. He moved the bags over to a corner in Joe's tent. He started to leave when Joe called, "Wait, did you get anything for Gus?"

"Yeah." He took them out and waved them. "These will make him happy."

"I don't think so. You can give those to me," Joe stated as he walked over and held out his hand.

Mark frowned and didn't hand them over. "Why would you take Gus' mail?" He started to back away.

Joe sighed. "It's nothing nefarious. Gus just doesn't want his mail. On his instructions, I've been collecting it for years."

Mark thought of the story Gus had told him. "Is this related to his family and what happened to them?"

Joe looked surprised and said in a low voice, "Yes. He doesn't normally share that story. May I have the mail, please?"

Mark had a moment of hesitation but handed the letters over.

Joe took them and said, "He won't want to know that these came."

"Understood," said Mark and turned to head back to his tent. The men he passed looked preoccupied and were reading their letters.

Mark got to his tent and pulled out the ones he had received. One was from his mother, two were from his editor, and one from his friend Emma Evans. There were also several rolled-up newspapers that were marked with his name on them.

That one will be interesting, he thought, looking at the letter from Emma. *Mom first.* He sat down on his cot and opened it. The letter was newsy, lots of information about her classes and what they were studying. His parents were gifted teachers. Everyone was healthy and they missed him. In the last part of the letter, she mentioned Ruth and Enzo. Clair had taken Ruth and given her a job at one of the women's shelters near New York City. Clair had many such shelters set up throughout the states to help women and children in troubling circumstances. Elizabeth also indicated that Enzo was working in Boston and they'd heard he was healthy but little else. They were worried about him. Mark made a note of Enzo's address and would write to him that night.

Next were the ones from the editor. The articles published from the flying machine seen in Texas had generated a lot of interest for the small town. He had word that people had been going there to see where the flying machine landed.

Galloway indicated that the oil field articles had also done well and he wanted more. *Good thing I already sent those to him,* thought Mark with a smile. *Attached is your check. Let me know if you aren't able to cash it and I'll make sure that your family gets it for you.* He unfolded the check and looked at it. There was a bank in town, but with the distance from Chicago, he wasn't sure if he'd be able to get the money. It was okay; the oil company was paying him in cash and he had enough money, especially since he wasn't paying for food or board.

He folded the check up and put it into his wallet. He'd go to the bank on his next day off. The papers were next; his articles appeared on the first two pages. He read through each one and was happy to see that little had been changed in them.

Mark went back to the letter from the editor and saw nothing about his next assignment. He'd hoped that some word had come back about his trip to the Yukon. *I guess it's a long shot.* It would be an expensive trip and he wasn't sure the paper could afford to send him.

On to Emma's letter. She mentioned her current case and the books she was reading and a little about her family.

Once he finished, he folded his letters and put them into his journal for later. He left the newspaper out in case Gus wanted to read them. *Why didn't Gus want his mail?* He mentioned he moved around a lot. *Does he do that to stay ahead of the mail?* He'd said his family had been taken from him almost ten years ago and he hadn't been back since.

Mark leaned down, opened his bag, and pulled out the journals he'd carried around since he was a kid. Emma had gotten him his first ones. The journals were about the California gold rush in 1849. He'd always been fascinated by the stories that came out of that time. Men moved their entire lives to a territory and created a state out of almost nothing. Many got rich; many didn't. But most stayed in the new state. He tried not to romanticize it, which was why he liked the journals. They gave realistic accounts of the hardships faced. The Yukon was his chance to live this dream. There were obvious differences between California and the Yukon, but both panned for gold and operated sluices.

It was a dream right now. He had friends he could ask for the money, but that didn't feel right. He had his savings; his parents hadn't let him pay for his room at the boarding house. They wanted him to save, so he had. He'd started to research the ticket prices and transportation to Dawson, the city from which the gold rush would be from. The main issue was the supply list. It was an extensive list that was required for entry into the Yukon.

He lay back on his cot, studying the journal. The section that caught his eye was claim jumpers. It was a big issue in the California mines and could be dangerous.

Gus came in. "Dinner bell will be ringing soon."

He laid down the journal and sat up. "Great."

Gus saw the newspapers and asked, "Would you mind?"

"No, go ahead. I left them out for you."

"Thanks!"

"No problem." They both read in silence.

"Those were good articles," Gus said. "I like the way you wrote up the flying machine one in Texas. You took them seriously."

"Yeah, I like that slant. The people we talked to were sincere. Something happened there; we just don't know what exactly it was."

"Yeah." Gus finished the paper and went on to the next one. Mark's oil articles were included in this one.

He read it thoroughly. "They turned out pretty good."

"With your help on the terms it did. Thanks for that."

"No, it's your writing. The two articles you took in today…"

"Yes?"

"How many more do you think you will write?"

"At least one more. The Go-Devil and nitro will make an amazing story."

"Yeah, Joe caught up with me. Looks like we're a few days out."

"Why the delay? You mentioned that we're probably ready now."

"Yeah, but there'll be guests."

"Those arriving in town? Is that safe?"

"Yeah." Gus chuckled suddenly. "I'm not sure people are aware of how dirty this is going to get."

"The gusher you mean?"

"Yeah, once it hits, we'll do all we can to get the oil into the pipes."

"Will the pump move the oil?"

"The pressure from the oil coming up should provide enough without the pump."

Mark hadn't experienced this before. "I wish I had a camera!"

"Oh, they'll have someone here taking pictures."

"Do you think I could get a copy?"

"Talk with Joe. I bet he can help you with that."

"I will," Mark said. He'd notified Joe before he sent in his first article. He had let him review the contents and he had approved it immediately.

Gus said, "Why not take the paper over to him and ask him about the pictures?"

"I will." Mark took the paper and walked over to Joe's tent.

"Sir?" he asked when he saw Joe at his desk.

He looked over at Mark. "Come in."

"Sir, I have the paper with the published article if you'd like to see it."

"I would." Mark handed it over and Joe read it quickly. "Yes, that's what I expected. These are good."

Mark stood silently and Joe asked, "Is there something else?"

"Yes, I wondered if I could get copies of the pictures of the rig, if a gusher comes in. Gus mentioned you'll probably have a photographer here."

Joe sat back and his chair squeaked. "I don't see why not. The more people that know we struck oil, the more customers we can get. I like that idea. We'll get that organized for you."

"You're that sure there's oil there?" Mark asked.

"Son, I'm banking everything I have on it."

"Good luck."

"We won't need it," he said positively.

Mark headed back out to his tent and, once there, the dinner bell rang. Gus exited and asked, "Everything go okay?"

"Yeah, Joe said he'd get me a copy of the pictures."

"Great."

They headed to the tent for dinner.

CHAPTER 8

few days later
A   "Pipe!" Gus called. Mark and two helpers moved the pipe into place and watched as the rig lifted and dropped, pushing the pipe into the ground and removing sections as it pulled back. The new pipe was fitted and moved into the ground by Gus and a helper. Gus worked as the driller, operating the cable and pulleys. Others worked as motor men, floor workers, tool pushers, and general workers. Mark's job was general focus, ensuring the rig remained clean.

Mark wiped the sweat and dirt off of his face and looked over at Gus. "He wants us to keep digging to the center of the Earth, I think. We're at one thousand three hundred feet." They watched the pump work by repeatedly beating the Earth's surface. "I'm thinking about heading home after the Go-Devil drop," Mark commented.

Gus was silent.

"Nothing to say?" he asked his friend.

"I figured you'd tell me soon. The nitro and Go-Devil should be here today," Gus said.

"Remind me- what will happen once the Go-Devil is dropped?"

They had been through this many times. "There'll be an explosion, the ground will rumble and, if oil is there, it'll come gushing out."

The nitro had yet to be delivered and, right now, the weather was what was on Mark's mind. "It's hot," he said.

"Gonna get hotter as the summer goes on. Are you thinking of going somewhere cooler?" Gus asked, thinking the heat wasn't so bad. He'd lived in Texas, Oklahoma, and Arizona most of his life. He wasn't sure he wanted cooler temperatures.

"I have some thoughts, but if you don't like it cool, then you won't like it where I'm thinking," he commented. Gus started to ask where when carriages pulled up. There must have been fifty people getting out. They started to move toward the rig.

Today's the day, Mark thought. They had spent their evening practicing on new rigs, dropping pans of water to get ready. It would take patience but would be handled safely. *How much oil?* he wondered as he studied. His eyes moved to the lines of barrels. They stretched at least a mile long. *They must be expecting a lot of oil*, he thought. They'd been delivered over the past weeks; the men had rolled them out with the expectation of oil.

Joe walked to the group of people. He called to Gus, "We need you!"

Gus stood and walked over. Joe said something low into his ear. Gus nodded and waved to Mark.

He ran over. "What's up?"

"The nitro's been delivered."

"Oh." Mark followed both men to the wagon. Two additional men stood at the back with a heavily fortified box.

"Is that it?" asked Mark in a low voice.

"It is."

One of the two men got a small pry bar and opened the box

by loosening each side. Once that was completed, each man took a side and lifted it off.

Gus muttered to Mark, "It's an explosive. We have to manage it very carefully."

Mark observed and stayed where he was. Gus climbed up in the wagon and examined the container. The delivery men wanted to release custody of the material to him. *Shouldn't they stay?* Mark wondered.

Joe and Gus asked them to put the nitro back into the box for the move to the well. They nodded and secured the lid.

Gus called, "Mark, we'll need to go to the well. Come with us. I'll need some help once we get there." Mark nodded and they followed the slow-moving wagon to the derrick. Once they got there, the men were given instructions for their jobs during the drop. Gus had instructed them to remove the drill in preparation.

Gus gave last minute directions to the crew. "Okay, what'll happen is that I'll pour the nitro into a pan and then lower it into the well. At that time, once we're stable, George Keeler's stepdaughter will be putting in the Go-Devil ." George and his family were the owners of the land.

Gus said to Joe, "Keep everyone quiet and away from the area."

He nodded and headed over to the guests. Gus trusted him to keep them away from the derrick. He looked over at his men. "I need you to clear back and, once the nitro is in place, return." They nodded and started to move away. Mark stayed. Gus wore leather gloves and had the pan spotted by the well. It had ropes through the sides to allow them to lower it slowly.

Gus moved to the crate and waved to Mark to help him. They slowly removed the lid and placed it beside the box. Gus reached in and took out the container. He moved very slowly to the pan. Without looking up, he said to Mark, "Back up some." Mark followed his directions and watched.

The nitro was added to the pan and Mark returned to his side. Each took a rope and slowly moved it into the hole and lowered it in. The process took time to reach the required depth. Gus had measured the rope and knew when to secure it. He motioned to Mark and they tied it off.

Gus went over and waved at Joe. He waved back and a small group and a little girl started toward them. "They're on the way over with the charge," Gus said.

The little girl walked over with her father and his partner. They carried the Go-Devil. Joe called out to the crowd, "Once it goes in, an explosion will occur, and we expect oil will come gushing out."

A cheer went up from the crowd.

Gus called to his workers, "That's when the work starts for us. Oil will be shooting up and over our heads. Our owners will want pictures, but we need to be ready to get that pipe in and capture that oil. Does everyone understand their roles?" Each man nodded. "Good. Let's get to it."

Mark eyed the crowd. The guests looked hot; there was no shade out in the oil fields. The women looked like wilted flowers and the men were fanning themselves with their hats.

"They do look awfully pretty," said one of the helpers.

"Not for long," said another. Everyone laughed.

Mark had never seen a gusher, but he'd take their word for it. It would be a sight to see.

There was a platform set up so the young girl could drop the Go-Devil. She was a pretty thing with dark hair and a large hat. Speeches were made. She and her father were handed the Go-Devil and dropped it into the well. They quickly left the area. The ground started to rumble. Gus yelled to the men, "Out!"

They ran away as the pressure of the explosion released the oil buried deep into the ground. It shot up and rained down on everything and everyone in the area. Gus and his men weren't concerned about anything but getting the oil into the piping.

They struggled to get it under control. In time, they were able to stop the spray.

Mark noticed the people were still there watching the operation. He grinned at Gus. "You're covered."

"I wouldn't talk. You look like a walking oil spill."

There weren't many of them not covered in oil from their head to their feet. Mark rubbed his face and absently pulled out his handkerchief; he didn't look at it. Gus started to laugh. "I'm not sure how much that's going to help you."

Mark looked down at his handkerchief and noticed he'd been rubbing more oil onto his face. "I guess you're right. What'll happen now?"

"We continue to drum the material up."

"And then?"

"We do that until we run out of ways to store it."

Joe walked up with his photographer. "Let's get a shot of you two." They grinned and put their arms over each other's shoulders for the picture. It was taken and the crew was called in for a wider shot.

They watched the photographer walk off and Joe said, "It has been a good day."

"Yes, it has," Gus said with a long sigh.

Mark asked, "Where will you sell the oil?"

"Mostly local markets initially."

"Will they be able to take all of it?"

"That, my boy, is the biggest concern we have. The oil can be transported by barrel locally."

"But long distance is the problem," supplied Gus.

"You got it. If we don't figure something out soon, we may have to cap it until we can figure out a way to transport it."

"How do you think the pictures will look?" Mark asked.

Joe grinned. "Amazing. I'll have copies made for you."

"Great."

Joe looked over at Gus. "Planning to stick around for a little while?"

"Yeah, for a little while."

Joe nodded; he'd expected that answer. The owners called him over and he walked to them.

"What was that about?" Mark asked.

"He knows me," Gus said simply. "I don't stick around long after the oil comes in."

Mark knew better than to ask why; he already knew the answer.

Mark worked the rest of the day, and at the end of it, they were happy to see their relief show up. Showers were their first priority. They ran through most of their water trying to get the oil off. Mark still didn't feel clean at the end of it.

"I still feel oily," he commented.

"It'll take a few more showers to get the oil completely off," Gus said.

They went to dinner. Mark was tired, but he wanted to document the day for his article. It was exciting and he wanted the readers to understand what he'd seen. Before long, he put his pen down, happy with the article. It would need another review before he sent it off. Gus had already gone to bed when he extinguished his lantern.

A week later, Mark and Gus were working on the rig when the mail call came. Mark looked longingly at the mail bag but knew he had to wait until the shift was over to retrieve it.

They finished their day and headed to the dinner tent. The mail bag was there and the mail was being passed around. Mark's name came up and he went over quickly to retrieve it. It was from his editor and he hoped it was the news he'd been waiting for. He tore it open and read through it quickly. "Hot damn!"

"What is it?" asked Gus, laying down his sandwich.

"Yukon!"

"Yukon, as in *there's gold in them thar hills?*"

"Definitely!"

Gus frowned. "Isn't that in Alaska?"

"A lot of people think so, but it is actually in Canada," Mark said absently as he reread the letter.

"Don't you have to go through Alaska?"

"My research indicates there are three ways to go. One is over water, also known as the 'rich man's path'. So, probably not the method I might take to get there. The second is by steamer and then over land and the pass, still very hard. Especially if winter's setting in. Lastly, over land through the back way. That one is used more by Canadians than by people from the States."

"And that says you're going?" Gus asked, nodding at the letter.

"Yeah," he said as he held out the letter. "Trip approved to Yukon! Funding has been found. Get home so we can get organized."

"Well, that does it then," said Gus. He looked down at the news.

Mark studied him. "Do you know where you're headed to next?" He didn't ask about home.

Gus didn't look up. "Not yet."

"If you want another adventure with me, you could join me in the Yukon," he suggested.

Gus looked up. "I might consider it. Will you go for gold?"

"If there is an opportunity, maybe," he said with a grin. "I am going more for the story. I want to see it, through. I've read so much about the California gold rush. I want to experience the Yukon rush."

Mark thought about the details as they returned to their tent. He started to pull out his clothes and fill his bag. His reading material was next, then books and journals. When he got to the last one, he looked over at Gus and tossed it to him. "Hey, read through this and, if you change your mind, you can meet me there." It was the journal he'd carried around for years, *The Old California Prospector*. It contained the recollections of gold prospectors from the 1850s and 1860s.

Gus caught it and sat up. As he flipped pages, Mark said, "Look at the folded pages."

He flipped to those sections and started to read. He was engrossed and, when Mark called, "Gus!" he had to shake his head to clear it.

"I'm going," Mark said. He stood, holding his bag.

"Now?"

"Yes, they're holding the wagon for me." He wanted to say more, but the men outside were calling for him.

"Let me know where you end up," Gus called to him.

That stopped Mark. "Will you open mail if I send it to you?"

"Send it by way of Joe; he'll get it to me. I'll open it." He got up and walked over to shake his friend's hand. "It's been fun."

"It has."

With that, Mark picked up his bag and headed out of the tent.

Gus watched the tent flap fall back down. He looked at the journal on his cot and picked it up again to read. *The Yukon. Maybe I am ready to go somewhere cooler.*

CHAPTER 9

*T*he trip back to Chicago was quieter than Mark liked. He had gotten used to Gus' constant conversation and missed him. To get his mind off of him, he turned his thoughts to the next trip. The Yukon! It was the realization of a dream; the California gold rush had fascinated him since he was a kid. He'd missed that opportunity and now it was a tourist attraction. This time, he wanted to be in on the adventure at the beginning. The Yukon would give him that. *If* he could get there.

Plans, he thought. *I'll need to be organized for this to work.* He'd heard about the supply list that was required but hadn't seen an actual copy. He'd try to find one first.

Once the train pulled into the Chicago station, he had a list of what he needed to check on. The first stop would be the newspaper. He wanted to find out more details of the trip. He took the trolley and then walked to the office. Once there, he strode determinedly to the editor's office and knocked.

"Come in," Galloway called from inside.

Mark stuck his head in. "Got time for me?"

"You're back!" Galloway said. "I'm glad to see you. We have a lot to talk about. Have a seat."

Mark sat in front of the desk. The leather in the chair squeaked loudly as he sat. Galloway started with, "We ran your Bartlesville series and got some great response to it." He picked up a pile of articles and handed them to Mark. "The pictures in particular did well. Thanks for including those."

"I was lucky to get them," commented Mark as he reviewed each article in the pile. He got to the final one and saw the pictures front and center. He was proud of the series. "May I keep these?"

"Of course."

He folded them in half and put them in his inside coat pocket. That was in the past, and he wanted to talk about his next assignment.

"You said I was approved for the Yukon story," he said eagerly.

"You are," Galloway cautioned, "with some limitations."

Did *something happen to change the plans?* He frowned. He hadn't expected this.

"I've researched it and there are requirements that need to be met. I'm concerned about how you'll get the items and how to transport them."

"You mean the supply list?" Mark asked.

"Yes, have you seen it yet?"

"No, just rumors at this point. Do you have a copy of it?"

"Yes. I was able to get hold of one." Galloway shifted papers on his desk, pulled out a packet, and handed it to the reporter. "It's more than we thought. The cost will be over 250 dollars just for the supplies. That is, if we're able to find everything. Then there's how you're going to move it all by yourself."

"I've filled out some at my last job and can carry more than I used to," Mark murmured, reviewing the list.

The editor looked at Mark. His arms did appear bigger than

when he'd left. But even the new muscles wouldn't help much. "The supplies would weigh over two tons."

Mark reviewed the list. There was heavy clothing and boots; nonperishable foods like smoked bacon, beans, rice, and dried fruit; personal items like soap and razor blades; and mining tools. "There's so much here. Why?"

"You've researched California?" Galloway knew Mark had been fixated on that period of history.

"Yes," he said, thinking of his journals.

"You know how the stampede was; there was no control on who went in and what supplies they had."

"Yes, it was pretty terrible," Mark conceded.

"Well, Canada is looking at that and the fact there will be long months where supplies won't be able to get through. People will die if they open the borders with no restrictions. I also heard there are small towns and settlements being emptied of supplies they need for themselves."

"All of this is required for entry into Canada?" Mark asked in disbelief. A stove was listed; he was supposed to take a stove!

"It was set up to be a year's worth of supplies. There may be some once you get there, but I'm not sure Dawson is set up as a town quite yet. You'll be getting there early in the rush. I'd suppose this is to make sure you don't starve to death." Galloway continued to explain how the trip would work. "We can meet the 250 dollars, but then we can't pay for your transportation to the Yukon."

"Do you have any idea how this might work?" Mark looked up from the list. The whole thing was confusing. He'd hoped he was stopping by for the final plans, but it sounded like things were still being set up. The papers were crushed in his hands as he gripped them tightly.

The editor sat back and pulled a cigar out of his desk drawer. "Would you like one?"

"No, thank you," Mark said, his voice taking on a rough tone.

Why is he drawing this out? Mark wanted to get the project confirmed.

"I have an idea that might work." Galloway looked at Mark. "But it would require you to have a job as well as continuing to write for us."

Mark sat forward eagerly and demanded, "Tell me!"

The editor took a long draw off his cigar and exhaled the smoke before he started. " A friend of mine, a rich friend," he quantified, "lives in Seattle. That area more than anywhere is getting swept up in the gold rush fever."

"Yes, I could see that. They're seeing people coming back from the Yukon with gold. It's not just stories to them; it's real." Mark knew that stories of gold being found started a stampede. People in the city had firsthand knowledge that there was gold to be found. They would leave anything behind to get it.

"Exactly."

"You mentioned your friend lives there and is ready to go to the Yukon?"

"The person I have contacted is more than a friend. He's my brother-in-law, Henry White. He lives and works in Seattle. He got there when it first started to build and became a lumber baron."

"Your sister's there also?" Mark inquired.

The smile dropped off Galloway's face and he looked away. "No, she passed a while back."

"I'm sorry," Mark said.

"Thank you. I wasn't able to get to her before she passed."

Mark tried to get the editor away from bad memories. He asked, "Have you talked to him? Does he want to go?"

"I haven't seen Henry in years," Galloway admitted.

Mark sighed and sat back in his chair.

"But I did contact him and what came back was this." He handed the telegram over to Mark.

Mark grabbed the note before he could release it, and a

tearing sounded loudly in the room. Galloway looked at the piece still in his hand and asked dryly, "Would you like to read this part, too?"

"Yes, please, sorry about that." Mark's face was red as he took the torn paper from the editor's hands.

Galloway smiled and watched Mark put the two pieces of paper together to read.

"He wants to go!" Mark said in surprise.

"It appears that way. Read further down."

He did as directed. "He wants to meet me and he'll decide at that time if I'm the right person." He couldn't help but feel disappointed. "All of this for an interview?"

"Yes. And all of this may be for naught, but I don't think that will be the case. He just wants to meet you before he confirms that you're someone he wants with him. He's paying for the trip and wants to make sure he gets his money's worth."

"You're right. Is there anything I should know about him?"

"I haven't seen him in years, not since Sarah died," Galloway reminded him.

"Has he remarried?"

"No, he hasn't."

"Is he still working?"

"I believe he sold off the mills a few years ago."

"What'll he expect of me. What should I be prepared for?"

"He'll want you to already have studied the path your trip will take."

"There's three, do you know which one he wants to take?" Two of the three would take strong men to make it through. It would also require a plan to move over two tons of supplies.

"He didn't say, but I know he'd only take the one route by water. There was an accident years ago that impaired his left leg. I think that's why he might be willing to take you on."

An injury, Mark thought. *How is this supposed to work?* Men who were physically fit would have a hard time. How was he supposed to get him to the Yukon? "That route is the rich man's route, the only one that would work if he has an injury," Mark said consideringly. "The water route would allow us to go from Seattle to St. Michael, Alaska by steamship and then an additional trip to Dawson by barge."

"Yes, and he'll arrange to have your supplies transported with his."

"What's the next step?"

"Supplies. We'll outfit you here as much as possible and ship the items and you to Seattle. Though," Galloway cautioned, "it's not a done deal. You still have to convince him you'll be of help."

"What if he doesn't accept me?"

"We'll deal with that situation as it comes up."

"What kind of man is he?"

The editor shook his head. "I can only tell you what I saw when I went for the funeral."

Mark nodded, wanting anything that could help when he met the man.

"He was different."

"Different? How so?"

"I met Henry in Chicago when he first met my sister. At that time, he was friendly and open. He changed over time and, when I got to Seattle for the funeral, he didn't talk to me and didn't let me stay at his house."

"It could have been grief," Mark suggested.

"Maybe," Galloway said, still seeming doubtful.

"You still think I should go."

"It'll be your only chance. If he approves of you, he'll finance your trip." The editor sat forward, laid down his cigar, and pointed at the young man. "Mark, this is up to you. If you don't want to go, I can send a telegram to cancel."

Mark considered what Galloway said and the opportunity he'd been presented with. *The rich man's way,* he thought. It would get him to the Yukon well before winter set in. He'd convince the man of his worth. "I'll do it," he said firmly. Mark looked at his watch and saw it was already late in the day. "When do you expect me to leave?"

"As soon as possible." Galloway noticed the time and continued, "You'll need the supply list built before you leave. So, start first thing in the morning." He pulled out another list and handed it to him. "These are the stores that have gathered the items you'll need. Just get what's required."

"I will," Mark said.

The editor asked, "What're your thoughts on the articles?" This was still a newspaper, and Mark would be working for them while he was there.

"I think I'll handle it like the oil well, give you a day to day on what's happening and send them at various points on the trip. I can write one from here on the list, the next during the train trip, and then Seattle."

"That would be good. That way, we have some started before you get going to the Yukon. I'd assume there will be some delays in getting mail to and from there."

"What's the communication from there?"

"Dawson? Mail."

"Are there telegraphs?"

"You'll have to see when you arrive. I'd assume the mail will run through until the water ices over. Write what you can and we'll run the series as we receive it."

"I will."

As Mark stood, Galloway ask, "Are you sure you're ready for this? The physical hardships, the distance and time away from family and friends?"

Mark looked down at his calloused hands. "Yes, I'm ready." He'd been preparing for this since he was a kid. It was a true adventure to be there as the initial event was unfolding. "I'll start on the list in the morning."

"Have you told your family about your plans?" Galloway

asked idly as he picked up his cigar and watched his reporter's reaction.

Mark grimaced. That was the only part that would be painful. And not just for his mom and dad, but also Enzo. He hadn't received a letter from his friend since he'd gone to Dallas for the flying object story. "My family knows me and knows this is something I've always wanted to do."

"It won't be a short trip," the editor warned. "It could be a year or more."

"You're right," Mark said and thought of his mother and then Enzo. There was no wedding to prepare for, but he wanted to let Enzo know he'd be leaving soon. "I'll work it out."

They agreed to meet up in a few days to finalize the list and tickets to Seattle.

Mark walked to the trolley and then headed to the boarding house. It was after 4pm; the family would be arriving home soon from work. When he got there, he ran quickly up the stoop and into the house. All he could think of was a bath. He hadn't felt clean since he left for Dallas. *There's probably still oil in my hair*, he thought, reaching up to touch it. The house was quiet and he made it in without being stopped. *Bath first*, he thought and ran to get his towel. After running the water, he got in and scrubbed himself from top to bottom. Once he was clean, he drained the water and wrapped a towel around him before he pulled on his robe. Going back to his room, he was thinking about the upcoming trip. *There's a lot ahead of me*, he thought as he sat on the bed and dried his hair quickly. *Enzo*, he thought, *I need to find out what's going on with him. I wonder if he's back yet?* He reached for his clothes and dressed quickly.

Mark headed out of his room and found Mara in the hallway.

"Mark! You're back." She walked over and kissed him on the cheek. She stood back and said, "You certainly have some color now."

He had his sleeves rolled up, a habit developed in the oil fields. He looked down at his arms. "Yeah, Texas and Oklahoma are hot. More sun than anything else."

"It looks good on you," she commented.

"Thanks. Has Enzo gotten home yet?"

She looked pained and said, "Let's go to the sitting room."

"All right," he said and followed her downstairs. The sitting room was vacant and they sat.

Mara started with, "You know Ruth's left?"

"Yes, I had asked Clair to help her with a job."

"That's right and she left soon after you went to Dallas."

"How did Enzo take it?"

"Not well," she admitted.

"Is he still in Boston?"

"Yes, he said he'll stay until the start of the new subway. He wanted to be away."

From Ruth and me? thought Mark.

"Probably for the best," he said.

"You know they shouldn't marry if they don't know each other."

"Does Enzo blame me?"

"No, I don't think so. He was too wrapped up with Ruth. He kind of took her over."

"Do you have his address? I might not have the right one."

"Yes." She stood and went to the small table against the wall and opened a drawer. She pulled out a small back notebook and brought it over to him. He compared it with the one he had; it was the same. He just hadn't gotten any responses to his previous letters. He sighed.

"Are you back for a while?" Mara asked.

"No, I'm headed back out in a few days."

"Where to this time?" she asked curiously. Marco and her business were based in Chicago and they traveled occasionally for work.

"Seattle first," he said absently, still thinking about Enzo's silence.

"First…" She started to ask when a voice interrupted her.

"Mark! You're back!" exclaimed his father as he and Elizabeth entered the room. They rushed over to hug him.

"I certainly hope you're back for a while," his mom said as she put down her bag and reached up to take off her hat. She removed the pin and placed the hat on the table in front of them.

"Mom," he started. She heard the tone and saw the expression in his eyes.

"Where now?" Elizabeth asked, her tone low and her eyes dropped to her hands.

"Now, dear, you know Mark has always wanted adventure," George said.

"I know." She looked Mark in the eyes and said, "Okay, tell me, where's the next adventure going to take you?"

All three of them looked at him expectantly.

"The Yukon," he said and stopped, letting the word sink in.

George started. "That's a long trip and expensive. I'm not sure we have the money to help you."

"Dad," Mark assured him, "you don't have to. The paper's paying for the gear and they're setting up my travel from Seattle to the Yukon."

"That would take you away for months," his mother fretted.

"Not months," said his father.

Elizabeth looked hopeful until Mark said, "More like a year. I'll be writing a serialized story of my travels."

"A year?" his mother said faintly, putting a hand to her chest. George took her hand in his and squeezed it.

"Are you going for gold?" Mara asked.

Mark smiled slightly. "I'd like to experience everything: panning, building sluices, finding gold. Everything."

The dinner bell rang at that moment.

George looked up. "Why don't we go to dinner and we can discuss this calmly?" He put his hand on his wife's shoulder. She looked up at him with tears in her eyes.

He leaned down and said in her ear, "He isn't a boy any longer. We need to support his dreams."

Elizabeth nodded and quickly wiped the tears away. It was like her brother, Joseph, all over again. Once he was old enough, he'd left home. She'd lost him to traveling. Once he finally came home to them, he'd died before she could get to know him again. She shook herself; Mark was not Joseph. He would be back!

"Yes, let's go eat," she said, trying to put on a brave face.

Mark frowned, watching her. Mara took her elbow and escorted her into the dining room. His dad stayed close to them. He tried to reassure Mark with, "She'll be fine. And you'll be back."

He nodded, not wanting to correct George. It would be a long time before he'd be with his family again. He wanted to enjoy their time together.

There were other boarders already at the table. Mara and Marco sat together; the two engineers were talking business with Mark's family.

They settled down and Mark explained that he'd be leaving in two days. "I'll have to get as much of my gear here as I can."

"I'd expect that the items available in Seattle are drying up fast," George said.

"And what's there is probably very expensive," Elizabeth commented.

"What can we do to help?" Mara asked. The next day was Saturday and they were available.

He grinned at them. *Family*, he thought, *they'll always be here.* "I have the list of stores that carry the items I need."

George said, "If we work together, we can get it organized."

"Let's look at it after dinner," Mark said. "Eat first, then we'll split it up and work on where we need to go tomorrow."

With dinner complete, they helped clear the table and moved to the sitting room to get their assignments.

The group sat stunned at the number of items that would be required.

Marco asked, "Why so much?"

"It's a year's worth," Mark explained.

"A year," his mom mumbled and quickly wiped her eyes.

"A year is required by the Mounties for entering the Yukon. They don't want anyone to starve to death when searching for gold."

"It makes sense," said George, patting her hand.

Elizabeth nodded. "It is the safest way." She looked up and said in a firm voice, "We'll get you what you need for your trip."

The group agreed.

CHAPTER 10

$\mathcal{T}$he next day went by in a whirlwind as the group took their individual lists and separated. Hours later, Mark finished his assignment and returned home. He entered and dropped the gear he'd collected in the foyer.

A voice called from the stairs, "I hope you aren't planning to leave that there."

He looked up, seeing who it was. "Emma!" He ran up the stairs to meet her halfway. He hugged her tightly.

"Now, what's this I hear about the Yukon?" she teased, ruffling his hair lightly. She knew his fascination with the California gold rush and his regret that he'd missed it. Emma had a similar attitude to his about adventure and not doing things the traditional way.

"Do you have time to review my trip with me?" he asked. He wanted her input.

She started to answer when the others who had helped came in the door with additional gear. Mark looked at them and then back at Emma, torn as to who he should talk to first.

Emma saw the confusion and smiled. She tapped him lightly

on the arm and suggested, "Why don't you come over after dinner and we can review your plans."

"Perfect. I will."

Emma walked down ahead of him and warned him over her shoulder, "Dora won't be happy with this mess."

Mark came down behind her. "Not to worry, we need to get this boxed up and headed to Seattle on the train with me."

"When will you be leaving?" Emma asked, turning back to him.

"If I have everything," he said, looking over the items, "then Monday."

George said, "Mark, this isn't all of it. The food's being placed in a crate. We went to the bakery to get their contacts. They recommended having it moved from the warehouse directly to the train station."

"I will check with Galloway's men," he said thoughtfully.

Emma said lightly, "You were warned." She turned to the dining room, exiting by way of the kitchen door.

Mark got each person's list and they inventoried the items on the floor and in the warehouse.

"It's all here!" he said. "We did it! Thanks for all the help."

The group disbanded and moved into the kitchen and sitting room.

George nudged the pile with his foot. "This is a lot of gear; it'll be expensive to ship."

"Thank goodness Mr. Galloway said if I got it organized, he'd get it shipped for me."

George nodded. "We should send a note over today and let him know the items are ready."

"I'll get it done. He said he'd be at the paper and the men there can box it up."

His mom came back into the foyer with two plates containing sandwiches. "You need to eat," she directed and gave them each a plate. They did as they were told and picked up their sandwiches, all the while staring at the pile.

George said, "We should split out what you'll carry with you."

"Yes, the clothes and the coat for sure," commented Mark.

They finished their sandwiches and returned their plates to the kitchen. Once finished, they returned to the foyer and separated out the items that Mark could carry.

"I just hope the food stuffs don't get wet," fretted Elizabeth, looking at the list.

"I'll mention that to the guys who are packing for me," Mark promised.

With the items sorted, he sent a note over to the editor. Later, two men arrived to pick up the items in the foyer. "We'll move these back to the office and box them there," one of the movers said.

"This isn't all," said Mark.

The two men looked surprised. "We filled up the wagons. What's left?"

"Quite a bit actually. The rest is at Cousin's warehouse."

The driver rolled his eyes. "Okay, we'll take this over and then go pick up the rest of the supplies. When do you need this by?"

"I'm leaving on the train in two days," he confirmed.

"That's workable. We'll head off now."

"Would you mind if I go with you?"

"We could use the help."

"Great." Mark grabbed his hat and jacket and hurried down to the waiting wagons.

They dropped off the first two loads and then the men headed out to pick up the items at the warehouse.

Mark stayed at the paper as they headed out. Galloway had heard that Mark's gear had arrived to be packed. He whistled when he saw how much there was. He rubbed his neck and looked at Mark. "Write this up before you leave and get me a story in Seattle."

"I will," Mark promised. He already had an idea of what would be included in the article. The men returned, and everyone went to the dock to help unload the goods. Mark listened carefully to the instructions on food storage.

Once everything was boxed and preparations were made for shipping, Mark headed back home as the dinner hour approached. He arrived home and strode across the foyer to the stairs. His father called out, "Dinner is being moved to the table."

"Great, let me go up and change my clothes."

George noticed how dirty he'd gotten. "Go up, but hurry."

Mark changed quickly and went back downstairs. They ate and when they finished, he started to stand.

"Where are you headed?" Elizabeth asked. She hoped they'd have some time with him.

He hastened to reassure her. "Don't worry, Mom, I'll be here all day tomorrow and underfoot. I'll drive you crazy with attention."

She brightened. "I'll hold you to that."

He went over and kissed her on the cheek. She watched him go out to the foyer and front door.

Mark rushed over to the other boarding house on his right.

Before he could start up the stoop, a soft voice stopped him. "Looking for someone?"

"Emma!" Mark said when he saw her sitting on the second step.

"Mark!" she teased. "Have a seat," she said and patted the spot next to her. Once he sat, she prompted, "Tell me about your adventure in Oklahoma. I heard you were there for the oil strike."

"I was and it was amazing. Well, it wasn't before the strike. It was hard work, hot and a little boring." *Except for Gus,* he thought.

"And there was a flying object of some sort? I think your article alluded that it could have been from space?" she asked, sliding him a sideways glance.

He laughed slightly. "Yeah, that one didn't have much evidence, but I tried to write a fair article. Though, when we went back later that night, we did see a long scorch mark in the land and pieces of wood strewn about."

"Do you think it was a crash site?"

"Possibly," he admitted.

"It was well written and fair." Emma leaned back and observed, "Maybe one day we'll have the technology in the future to find out what did happen there."

He thought about that. "Would there be more answers later? Would time help prove what the witness claimed happened?"

"Could be," she murmured. "You're getting the adventures you always told me you wanted to go on," she said.

"Yes," he said simply.

"The Yukon."

"Yes, that's the trip I'm working on now."

"And all by yourself?" Emma asked. She did have concerns about his support system. In times of extreme risk, a person would need others to rely upon. It had taken her a while to accept she couldn't do everything on her own.

"No, I'm hoping to get with someone on this trip. He will be helping with the transportation."

"Good," she said, but a frown had settled on her face.

"What's wrong? Are you worried?"

She looked away from him to the street in front of her. "Partly, I'm a little jealous. Such a grand adventure. You'll be seeing parts of the country that no one's seen."

"I don't know. I hear the Mounties have things under control, so you might be a little bored."

She grinned. "That's probably true, and I have plenty to do as it is." Emma was an investigator working by herself and occasionally with the Pinkerton Detective Agency.

"Tell me all the details!" she demanded.

"The list is the hardest hurdle."

"Can I see it?"

He pulled it out of his pocket and handed it to her. It was already soft with the almost constant review.

She unfolded it, counting the pages. "Why so much?" she asked.

"The environment is tough and, once the ice sets in, there'll be little food or supplies available to the area," he explained. "The Mounties won't let you cross the border unless you can prove you have everything on that list."

She frowned again. "But you'll be going during the summer."

"This trip will take almost a month to get there, then I have to get settled. By that time, I expect winter will be setting in."

"You expect to be there for what, at least six months?"

"It could be longer, depending on how the spring thaw takes."

"So, the gear is to keep you alive for that time," she asked, looking at the things on the list.

"Yes."

"How will the gear be moved? It's too much to carry," Emma observed.

"You're right. I broke out things I'll carry: coat, long johns, things like that."

"Everything else?" *There was a stove on that list! How is he supposed to move that by himself?*

"The paper has crated it up for me and will get it to the train for shipping," he explained.

"Train first?"

"Yes, a train to Seattle. That's where I meet the man who'll hopefully help me get to the Yukon."

"How do you plan to get there? Aren't there multiple routes?" Mark had mentioned this over time to her.

"There's three. The first one is a ship to Dyea, Alaska, then hiking through the pass."

"On foot?" she asked incredulously.

"I think it's possible in the summer," he confirmed. *I don't expect that will work for me or the man I should be accompanying.* Mark thought of the man's injury.

"But not on your own," she said. No one could carry 2,000 lbs. of gear alone. "The second one?"

"Actually, kind of the same so still part of the first one. It starts with the same trip to Dyea, but from there we'll be building a boat or renting one."

"Building a boat?" Nothing about this sounded easy.

"As I understand it, the Mounties evaluate your build and you have to pass or start over."

"So, you could be stranded there building boats?"

"Exactly."

"Next one?"

"Over land. I think the Canadians are using this one and approaching without going through border points."

"So, some people are showing up without the necessary supplies?"

"Yes."

"You'll have to guard your supplies; things may get desperate."

He hadn't thought about that. His focus was on the trip. "There's one more. They call it a rich man's route; it's mostly a water pathway. A steamship from Seattle and then a barge from St. Michael to Dawson. The length will be based on the weather conditions."

"If you get the man to take you on, is the rich man's route the one you'll take?"

"That's my hope."

She was relieved. "How sure are you that he'll take you with him?"

"He's contemplating it. I'll have to sell myself."

"If you get there and he doesn't help you, will you come home?"

"No," he said emphatically. "I'm going to get there no matter what."

Emma reached to take his hand. "Mark, if you can't do this in a safe way, maybe you shouldn't go."

"The trip is something I want to do, something I have to do. I will find a path there," he said firmly, contemplating the alternatives if this one didn't work out. A sudden thought brought a twinkle to his eyes and he said lightly, "You're one to talk about taking the safe way to do anything!"

"You're right," she acknowledged. She gave him a long look. "I think I still see you as the nine-year-old boy I met years ago in New York City."

"I'm a bit taller now," he commented.

"You are." She laughed. They sat quietly and she leaned over and said, "We're here if you need help. Keep us informed."

"I will." They talked more and would have continued but a door opened behind them and a voice called, "Emma."

Emma placed her hand on Mark's and squeezed. She called back, "Coming, Jeremy."

Mark watched her walk up before he headed home and up to his room.

The article, he thought, *I can't put it off any longer.* He sat down at his desk and pulled out some paper. His typewriter sat on his desk, and as he put a piece of paper into it, he thought of the items he would miss. This would be one of them.

With his notebook opened, he started typing the article. *That list*, he thought. *If Canada wants to limit people, the list would do it.* The last key was hit and he pulled the completed article off the typewriter. He proofread it and placed it on the desk; he planned on taking it over to the newspaper the next day.

CHAPTER 11

*T*he sun streamed onto Mark's face the next morning. He turned toward it and thought, *It's going to be a good day*. He'd promised his mom some time, and he needed to finish compiling the gear he'd carry with him.

His thoughts were also on Enzo. He didn't want to leave without sending him a letter. He got up and went directly to his desk. This one, he hand wrote. It included where he was going and that he wanted Enzo to write to him. When finished, he folded it and placed it into an envelope. It would be placed in the mail to be picked up on Monday.

With all of his tasks completed, he went downstairs to spend the day with family. It would be a long while before he returned, and he wanted to store up memories for long days in the Yukon.

CHAPTER 12

The time went by quickly, and the morning of his trip arrived almost before Mark was ready. The feelings he had were a mix of nerves and excitement. On a regular trip, he'd have an idea of what would be happening, but this trip would be full of surprises.

The ticking of the clock reminded him he had someplace to be that morning. He turned his head toward the clock and saw his train ticket beside it. *It's time*, he thought. He moved to the side of the bed and stood. His clothes and gear were scattered around the room. *First things first.* He grabbed his robe and headed to the bathroom. After that was taken care of, he went back to his room and pulled on his clothes. The final button was done up on his shirt when a knock sounded on the door. He called, "Come in."

His dad entered. "Are you ready?" George looked at the bags and asked, "Will you be able to do this on your own?"

"I'll be able to carry two in one hand and one in the other."

Mark did a final review on what he was taking and thought about his books; they would be heavy. *Just one*, he thought and picked a book to take with him, slipping it into one of his bags.

George stood there, fighting a yawn. He hadn't slept; the worry about Mark and his trip had kept him up. It was the adventure Mark always wanted, but he'd be so far away. Though George would have liked to ask him not to go, he also wanted to support his son's dream. He stayed quiet and helped him with the bags.

As they went downstairs, Mark was surprised to see everyone in the foyer. Most were still in bed clothes, as the sun had yet to rise outside.

"Good luck!"

"We'll miss you!"

"Write us about your adventures!"

"Thanks! I will," Mark said. He walked over to his mom and tilted his head down to kiss her cheek.

"Stay safe," she murmured, touching his cheek.

"I will, I promise. I'll write along the way and let you know how things are going."

Elizabeth took a breath. "I love you."

"I love you, too."

"We have to go." His father nudged him.

"Yes." Mark looked around at everyone. "I'll see you soon!"

"Bye!" they called as he and George exited the front door and went down the stoop to the waiting carriage. The trip was rather quiet and, once they were at the train station, George said, "Write and let us know if you need anything." He wasn't looking at Mark when he said the words.

"Dad," said Mark, "I'll be back."

His dad wiped tears off of his cheeks. "Of course, you will; you know how women are, they worry. Be sure to let us know if you need anything."

"I will," Mark murmured, at a loss at what he should say. He hugged his dad and said, "Bye."

"Bye." George watched his son climb the stairs to the train.

Mark turned and waved before he took the final step. Once

on board, he found his seat in 2nd class. His bags were put in the storage rack above his head and another one at his feet. He already regretted having only the one book. *But there were sacrifices to be made,* he thought wryly.

The train jerked, signaling that the trip had started. Mark glanced out his window and was surprised to see his father still standing there. His form was so still that Mark worried he might need to get off and check on him. He raised his hand to the window and watched his father raise his in return. When George had faded from sight, Mark sat back and thought about where he was headed.

The first stop would be a train switch to the Great Northern Railroad. This would then be the last train that would go straight to Seattle, Washington.

Once they stopped a few days into the trip, the conductor walked down the aisle and told passengers to exit for the Great Northern Railway.

Mark tapped the man on his shoulder and, when he turned, asked, "Will my crates be moved?"

"That's happening now. Once you change over, everything should be in place."

"Thank you." Mark pulled his bags from the trays above his head and walked toward the exit.

He went straight to the next train and waited for the other passengers. Up to this point, the train had been mostly empty. When people started to load in, he realized most seats would be taken. More and more people boarded, carrying many bags. *Will they be headed to the Yukon?* he wondered. They walked down the aisle, filling up seats as they went. He continued to watch them sit and heard a voice, "Mind if I take this seat?"

Mark looked up and saw a man about his own age. His hair was blond and his eyes were a snapping blue. The lines that marked his face told Mark he was a man used to smiling. "Sure! Company would be nice."

"Great," the man said and shoved his gear overhead and put his two other bags around his feet.

"I'm Mark Sutherland."

"Ed Gantz." They shook hands.

"Looks like a delay," Mark said, glancing out the window.

"Supplies," commented Ed. "Mine are crated up."

"Headed to the Yukon?" asked Mark with interest.

"Eventually. Seattle first. What about you?"

"Same for me. Traveling on your own?"

"Yeah, just me. No family to speak of. What about you?"

Mark looked contemplative. "I'm hoping a friend I met on my last job joins me." He thought about Gus. His friend had been through so much. *Is he still avoiding his home?* He hoped there was a chance he still might come to the Yukon.

Their attention was drawn to two men boarding at the same stop. They were leaning toward a man seated a few seats in front of them.

"Something we should be worried about?" Mark asked in a low voice.

"Might be," Ed said in a similar tone. "I heard them at the station. The taller one with the dark beard is Jerry and the smaller man with him is Wade. They were hassling people while we were waiting at the station."

"Why?"

"They didn't have train tickets," said Ed.

"And now they do?" asked Mark.

"Yeah, I don't think they have any supplies or steamship tickets. I am sure they plan to get those items in the same way they got their train tickets."

They watched. The man they were talking to got up and moved away, giving up his seat. Ed caught his arm as he passed. "You don't have to move."

"No," the man said, gripping his bags tightly and nodding. "I- I want to move. I'm okay."

Jerry and Wade turned in their seats toward Ed. Wade sneered at them. "Yeah, he's okay."

Rather than create a bigger situation, Ed and Mark watched the man go toward the back. Once he found a seat, he looked relieved to be away from the two men.

"Should we do anything?" murmured Mark.

"Not now. That man didn't want to create a scene," Ed replied.

They settled in for the long trip. Both carried books and were interested in the scenery going by. "What're your thoughts about the Yukon? Are you going to try for gold?" Ed asked, voicing the familiar question.

"I'm going more as a reporter, and I may be working for a man who'll be involved in searching for gold. What about you?"

"I sold the family business. My father just died and we lost my mother years ago."

"I'm sorry," said Mark. "What was the business?"

"Mercantile; buying and selling is what I was raised doing. I'm thinking that the town we're going to will need a business like that. Of course," Ed chuckled, "I won't turn down any gold that's lying in the road."

"Agreed," said Mark. *Smart,* he thought. *Many people will be needed to build the support structures for all of the people showing up.*

"You're a reporter, but you'll also have a job? How will that work?"

Mark explained the details and, when he finished, Ed whistled. "You're taking an awfully big chance, what if he says no?"

"I don't know," Mark said honestly. He had his savings with him, but he had hoped to not use it.

They continued to discuss their plans as the train made its way through to Seattle. At each stop, they picked up people headed to the gold rush. By the end, there were no more seats and people were lying on their bags in the aisles.

"I heard there was gold just there for the taking," said one.

Another said, "I hear that men coming back can't carry the gold by themselves."

Mark heard bits of conversation. "I don't think they're being realistic about how hard it is to search for gold."

"Have you mined for gold before this?" Ed asked. He had fantasies similar to the ones being discussed.

"No, but I've read at length how hard the life is. Even in California, where the weather is easier, it was a hard life. The area where we're headed to will be covered in ice a large amount of time. I think this will be harder than we, or anyone, expect."

"I heard the size of the area is more limited than California."

"There's that. And there might not be any area left to claim."

Ed looked around and murmured, "I hope that isn't true. There will be a lot of disappointed people."

"I agree. What's the pathway you're taking?"

"Seattle to St. Michael to Dawson."

"That's what I'm hoping also."

Mark thought about the strike, and how it had begun quietly on August 17, 1896, when three miners found gold in the Klondike River, a tributary of the Yukon. It had begun slowly, by word of mouth. He looked around at the packed car and thought, *It didn't stay that way.* Seattle would be the first stop and an indication of what he could expect in the Yukon.

CHAPTER 13

*T*he train pulled in for their final stop in Seattle and the confusion began. Mark had kept his eyes on his bags during the trip, but some couldn't seem to remember what they brought with them and a brawl started. Mark wanted off the train. The trip had been more than a week and the smell was enough incentive for him to take his bags and move toward the men who were exiting.

The two men who'd been causing trouble throughout the trip were in the middle of the brawl. They'd pushed a man to the floor and were trying to pull the bags out of his hands.

Emma was right; supplies would be at risk for the entire trip. He tapped Ed and they moved to help. "Break it up, give the man back his bags," Mark said.

"Oh, yeah? Why should we?" Jerry said belligerently.

Wade said, "Yeah, Jerry's right. These're ours."

"Are they?" Ed questioned.

"Yeah," Wade said with bravado.

Ed and Mark stepped closer to them.

"Who're you tellen us what to do?" Jerry asked.

"Just somebody who wants off this train," Mark said. Finally, he'd had enough and pushed his way through, using his bags to force Jerry and Wade back into their seats.

They hadn't expected the move and yelled out, "What're you doing? Hey!!"

Mark ignored them and exited the train. Ed held out his hand to the man on the floor and made sure he exited with his bags intact.

"Thanks," the man said gratefully.

"No problem. Stay in front of me."

As they got off the train, the man Ed had helped started to run away as soon as he hit the platform. He shook his head and walked at a slower pace toward the crowds making their way to town. He spotted Mark in front of him and he called out, "Mark! Wait up." He caught up with him. "Where're you headed?"

"Through town for now and up to see the man about a job."

"Mind if I tag along?"

"Nowhere to stay?" Mark inquired.

"Not really. I'm hoping to find something in town."

"You might as well come with me. Though I have no idea what's going to happen once we get there."

Jerry and Wade descended the train stairs.

"We didn't get them bags," Wade complained.

"We'll get more. There's plenty of people in town," Jerry commented, watching the two men who'd stopped them on the train.

"What about them?" Wade asked, gesturing to Mark and Ed.

"We'll see to them later. Now, how 'bout we see about supplies and steam tickets?"

Wade grinned and rubbed his hands. "This should be fun."

Mark and Ed went to where the carriages and wagons were normally parked. Ed called to a boy sitting with a knife and a piece of wood. "Where's all the carriages?"

The boy snickered. "Man, there's no transportation available.

Don't you know how many people are going through Seattle to get gold? Even our mayor and councilmen have gone."

Mark looked over to Ed. "I think we should make sure our gear's taken off the train and secured before we leave."

"Over there." The boy indicated to the clerk's office with his knife.

"Thanks," said Mark. He and Ed walked to the office. There was no line. They stood and waited patiently for the man to turn toward them.

The clerk walked to the counter. "Yes, can I help you?"

"We both have boxes of gear that arrived with the last train," Mark said.

He got a pencil. "Your names and number of crates?" After he got the information he said, "We'll have them taken to storage but, after two days, you must make arrangements to move them out."

Mark and Ed started to walk off and Mark ran back. "Can you tell me how to get to this address?" he asked, handing the clerk a folded piece of paper.

The clerk took it and unfolded it. When he saw the address, he whistled, "High class area!"

Mark didn't comment.

"It's going to be a bit of a walk, through town and, then past that, you'll see the large mansions. This one is the biggest. You can't miss it."

Mark and Ed picked up their bags and followed the clerk's directions. As they approached Main Street, they found it teaming with people.

"I guess that's it. This doesn't look good for me to have a place to sleep tonight," Ed muttered as he followed Mark into the crowd of people.

Mark said loudly over his shoulder, "Yeah, let's stay together and get through this crowd."

They moved forward slowly, when suddenly the group

surged forward to surround two men fighting in the street. The momentum knocked Mark to the ground. He pulled himself off the dirty ground and tried to push his way back in. Again, he was forcibly pushed out and fell back into the street. The two men fighting barely missed stomping on him in their zeal to be the owner of a winter coat.

"It is mine, let it go!"

"I saw it first!"

Another man in an apron ran into the street screaming, "You're damaging my wares! Let it go!" He reached for the jacket and the three of them pulled on it at the same time. The jacket separated abruptly and each man ended up on their bottoms holding a part of the coat.

The clerk was the first to recover. He stood and yelled, "What did you do! You'll both pay for this! Do you know how much this is worth?"

A voice yelled, "Make room!" The crowd begrudgingly split to allow a policeman through. He took each man by the collar and pulled them back through the crowds and into the store.

The crowd started to disperse some. Ed walked over to Mark and offered him a hand up and helped him dust off.

"What's going on around here?" Mark muttered.

A man near them commented, "Supplies are running low and people are nervous." The man next to him nodded.

Mark looked around at the people in line to get into the store and was glad he had everything on the list. He was going for a story, not gold, but the difference wouldn't matter to the Mounties.

"Even if they get onto a ship, without supplies, they won't make it over the border," said Ed.

"I actually heard the items will be checked for two of the routes in Alaska," Mark replied.

"The US and Canada worked that out?" Ed asked. Normally, this would be handled at the Canadian border.

"Both sides want the supply lines to stay in place. Some of the men who got in on the first run for gold didn't have the needed supplies and relied upon local communities. Unfortunately, they left nothing for people living in the areas. The Royal Canadian Mounted Police quickly set up checkpoints on the routes to Dawson City."

"You've been studying."

"I wanted to be ready when the opportunity showed up."

"Yeah, I get that they wanted to protect their people, but it does limit the miners to only those who can afford the list. I'm not sure that's right." Ed looked at the people around and said, "But if it'll keep people from dying up there..." His voice trailed off.

"I would rather they were in place; they're trying to learn from the California rush. They want this orderly and crime free."

"Relatively," Mark said, thinking again of those men on the train.

Ed distracted him with a question. "Did you see the price on that coat?"

"I did." It was four times what he paid in Chicago. He pulled his bags closer to him as he and Ed continued on through the crowd.

"The cost of the ship tickets will go up with every load. You can bet on that."

"You know those two troublemakers, Jerry and Wade? They said they didn't have steamship tickets."

Ed grinned suddenly. "Now that is good news! I'm glad I purchased mine in advance."

I hope I have tickets, thought Mark.

"If those two guys from the train are examples of who we're going to be traveling with, it's going to be dangerous up there. "

"Agreed." Mark looked at the other man. "Ed, why don't we look out for one another?"

Ed extended his hand. "That's a plan."

Mark took the offered hand, grinning as he shook it. "Let's get through this crowd and find my new boss."

"Will your new boss be angry that I'm with you?" Ed asked, removing his hat and running his hand through his hair.

"I'm not sure," Mark said thoughtfully. "We can figure out the next steps as we go."

Ed put his hat back on his head and nodded.

They continued the long walk, each thinking of what would be happening next.

Jerry and Wade looked at that same store line. Jerry tapped Wade and motioned to a man on his own, carrying supplies. Jerry followed after him, Wade grinned and followed his lead.

The further Mark and Ed got from the city center, the fewer people were around. Mark took a deep breath; he hadn't realized how tense the crowds had made him.

They walked through different neighborhoods and Mark glanced down at his directions. "No, I don't think this is it."

"Keep going?"

"We've made it this far."

The houses got nicer the further they went and, when they saw mansions, Mark commented , "I think we're here."

"What's the number?"

He showed it to him and Ed looked around at the house numbers. He pointed down the street. "I think it's that one."

Mark looked in awe and said, his voice hoarse, "It must be." It was the biggest on the hill. It was stone, which seemed unusual for a man in the lumber business. It was also very grand, two stories with tall white columns in the front surrounding a porch.

Mark tried to remember what he knew about the benefactor he was headed to see. Henry White had moved to Seattle when it was mostly wilderness and set up a lumber business. Mark took a deep breath and looked at his friend. "Ready?"

Ed looked at the mansion, then back at Mark. "I guess."

They walked up to the house and then to the stacked stairs leading to the front door. Mark set down one of his bags to allow him to knock on it.

Ed said with a sudden stutter, "Wait, why don't I stay out here, in case it doesn't work out?"

Mark started to say something to him when the door opened.

A tall, solid man in a dark suit was there. He seemed as wide as he was tall, and he took up the entire doorway.

"Can I help you?" he asked.

Mark didn't know what he expected, but this man wasn't it. "I'm here to see Mr. White."

"Do you have an appointment?" the man asked and wrinkled his nose at both men's appearances.

"I do. I'm Mark Sutherland. I also have a letter of introduction," Mark said and set down his other bags to search through his jacket. "Here it is." He pulled out the letter to hand to the man.

He took it and looked over at Ed. "What about you?"

Ed hurriedly explained, "I just accompanied him here."

"You go around to the kitchen and wait there," he directed.

"Yes, sir," Ed said and turned to the left.

"To the right," commented the man, his voice dry.

"Oh, okay." Ed made the correction and walked to the right and around the house. "Thanks!"

The man nodded and turned back to Mark. "You wait here."

Before Mark could answer, the door was closed in his face. He stared at it for a long moment, then the door swung open to reveal another man, this one rather average in height and wearing a blue suit. "Mark! You made it! I'm Henry White. Come in, come in." He turned and headed back into the house.

Mark picked up his bags and followed him in. Mr. White called to the man who'd answered the door. "This is my butler, Tait." He looked at Tait and directed, "Take Mr. Sutherland's bags."

Mark handed the bags to Tait, who nodded his head toward Mr. White who had already started to move toward a room across the foyer.

Mark nodded and followed his direction. The doors opened to a large room that looked both like an office and a study. As he entered the room, his eyes went to Mr. White. The man's physical demeanor was different than he was led to believe, and he looked older than the description Don Galloway had given. He also looked like he didn't go outside. His pallor matched his white shirt.

If this man worked outside, it has been a while. The Yukon will require strong men. Could this man survive that environment? Mark watched Mr. White move around. His movements were jerky, like something had affected his gait. It looked worse than his editor had mentioned.

White sat in the large leather chair behind the desk. "You're here to accompany me to the Yukon?"

"Yes, sir," Mark said tentatively and wondered if he should be the one to turn him down. *How can this be successful at all?*

"Don mentioned you'd bring your gear with you?"

"Yes, I have it stored at the train station."

"I'll have my men get it and place it with mine. Tait!" White called.

"Yes, sir," Tait said, appearing in the doorway.

"Mr. Sutherland's gear is in storage at the rail station. See to it that it gets moved out of the storage location."

No please or thank you, thought Mark.

"Yes, sir." Tait turned and disappeared from their view.

White turned back to Mark. "Do you know the routes to the Yukon?"

"I've investigated several different ways to get there; some are more arduous than the rest," he answered.

White stood and walked to a table on his right, dragging his left leg behind him. Mark followed him and again wondered how the older man could stand up to the travel required to get to the Yukon.

White was concentrating on the map in front of him. "We'll be taking the water route."

The rich man's route is confirmed, thought Mark. It would be the only way White could survive that distance.

"Look here," White directed and pointed to the map. "We'll travel by sea up the coast to the port of St. Michael in Alaska. From there, we'll take a barge, which will take us the rest of the way up the river to Dawson. That will allow us to reach Dawson with little to no land travel."

"Won't it be a longer trip? Going by all water?" Mark asked, studying the route.

"Yes, but it will be easier to go by water than by land."

Mark nodded, not mentioning the man's physical restrictions. "We'll also have to get moving quickly. The timing is important; the water routes will start to freeze in October. We must be settled by then and hopefully mining for gold." Mark frowned, the cost of the tickets would probably be expensive. How would he be expected to repay something like that?

"I'll cover your $150.00 fee to go on the steamship and the additional $100.00 for the barge from St. Michael," White said, reading the young man's thoughts.

Mark's eyes opened wide at the amount.

"I will, however," White cautioned, "expect you to assist me in this adventure."

"Assist, sir? What type of assistance will you need?" *Finally. We're down to* what's *expected of me.*

Mr. White looked at Mark and then walked to a nearby chair, pulling up his twisted leg and placing it on a stool. He took a long moment to take a cigar out of his pocket. "My boy, this is my last adventure. I want to see the country and make some money at the same time. I did that here in Seattle. I was here when there was nothing. I started small in the timber business and I worked to make the business grow." He looked around the room. "I think I have done well with my time here."

Mark followed his eyes around the spacious room. The walls were covered in books, the wood floor draped with rich rugs and heavy furniture. Mark's eyes settled back on the books and he thought of the ones he'd left behind.

White noticed Mark's interest. "If you agree, I'll let you bring books from my library with us."

Another incentive, thought Mark. He wanted more information before he would agree. "You want an adventure?"

"Yes, I want the same experience I had here, a mostly unsettled land with business opportunities; I believe I'll find that in the Yukon."

"Do you plan to mine for gold?" asked Mark, letting some of his doubt enter his voice.

"My plan is to have you investigate claims for me and return with research so that I can purchase those claims. At that point, you can run the men for me."

Mark frowned heavily. "Sir, I have to be honest, I don't know much about mining. I've only read about it."

"You can learn; you're an educated man?"

"Yes, I am."

"Then you'll pick up the skills as we go," White said bracingly. "That will allow you to earn your tickets back. Think you're still up to the challenge?"

Mark thought about all of his reading, the journals and news articles about the gold rush. He looked White in the eye and said, "Yes, sir. I've dreamed about this for years. I'll do anything to go and search for gold. I'll learn and help you with this trip."

"Good," White said quietly and leaned back, watching him.

Mark pulled on his collar and asked nervously, "Sir?"

"Yes?" White said as he puffed out some smoke.

"I was hoping I could stay here. The crowds in the streets and signs on the buildings say no rooms available." Mark hoped he wouldn't be sleeping in the streets. There was also Ed, but he didn't think Mr. White be open to having another man with them.

"Of course my boy, we have a lot to do before we leave." *I can't take the chance you'll leave me behind,* he thought. He could see Mark was concerned with his physical limitations.

Mark let out the breath he was holding. "Thank you, sir."

"Tait!" White called.

The butler appeared in the door again. "Yes, sir?"

"Take Mr. Sutherland to his room and get him settled. We'll be sailing by the weekend," White dictated.

Mark nodded toward Mr. White and followed Tait out. At the base of the stairs, he picked up his bags.

Tait didn't offer any help and Mark started upstairs.

"Not that way," the butler said.

Mark looked over at him and saw Tait was headed across the foyer. He glanced upstairs and wondered where he'd end up. "Oh, okay," he said and hurried after him. They went through several rooms and finally into the kitchen. They found Ed there enjoying a sandwich and a glass of milk.

"Mark," his friend said as he put down his glass and wiped his mouth on his sleeve. "How did you make out?"

"I'm going to the Yukon," he confirmed.

Ed grinned. "Great! Steamship?"

"Looks like the same one as you," he confirmed. "Ed, I…" He started to explain that he hadn't asked Mr. White about him staying there.

"Don't worry," Tait said quietly behind them. "We have room."

"But Mr. White…" Mark started.

"What he doesn't know won't hurt him."

He and Ed stared at him. He smiled; these were good people.

"Would you like a sandwich?" asked the cook.

"Please," Mark said gratefully. He sat with Ed and watched her make the sandwich. She put it on a plate and handed it and a drink to him. "Thank you," he said and ate it quickly.

"We should get you both settled," Tait stated, as he had other duties to attend to.

"Yes, of course," said Mark.

Both men stood, took their bags, and followed Tait into the hallway. He stopped suddenly and seemed to disappear into a wall. As they got closer to it, they saw there was a mechanism to slide the door open. It slid seamlessly into the wall panel and, once they entered, it closed behind them. They hurried down the stairs after Tait. *Must be the servant's quarters*, thought Mark. *I guess I'm being put in my place. It does put me with a better quality of people, though.*

The three of them walked down two levels and followed Tait when he opened the door into a long hallway. He stopped at one of the doors and inserted a key. He pushed the door open and turned to Ed. "You'll stay here until your trip. And you, young man, will stay in the room across the hall." He walked to that door to open it.

Mark stepped into the room. There wasn't a lot of space to move around. He saw there was a desk on the left and a small bed on the right.

"The bathroom is shared down the hall. We have a schedule posted," Tait said.

"Thank you. I would like a bath. It was a dusty trip here."

"You'll have time before dinner."

The butler started to leave and Mark asked, "Where do we eat in the evening?"

"Both of you will go to the kitchen and eat with the staff. Use the path I took you through today. Dinner will be at 7pm."

"Thank you."

Tait nodded and left the room.

Mark sat and looked around. A knock sounded at the door. He called, "Come in."

Ed stuck his head in. "Thanks for this!"

"Come in."

Ed moved to the bed and sat down.

"We were both lucky. They're taking a chance letting us stay here," said Mark.

"Do you think we'll get them into trouble?"

"If something happens, I'll take the responsibility."

"We both will. What was Mr. White like?"

"Older than I thought. He's the brother-in-law of my editor. I expected him to be about the same age."

"What else? You seem worried."

"His injury's worse than I expected. He's reliant on a cane."

"Will he be able to make the trip?"

"I hope so." He looked at Ed and asked, "How were you able to afford this route? I heard the tickets are very expensive."

"They are," he agreed. "I sold everything for that steamship ticket. But I won't be going on by barge."

"No? What's your plan?"

"Take a boat upstream and meet the barge in Dawson."

"What about your gear? There's too much to carry."

"I've made arrangements for the gear to continue on. Otherwise, it could take me years to go back and forth."

"Yes. I'll watch out for it."

"Thanks. Well, for now, I need to get cleaned up."

"The bath is down the hall. You go first. I need to make some notes for an article about the trip here and another about Seattle." Ed stood and headed that way.

Mark pulled out some paper and started to outline an article about the train trip and a second about his first impressions of Seattle. The adventure was already starting differently than he expected. His thoughts turned to Emma. Her influence allowed him to discover a loved of reading and writing that helped direct him to the career he had now. Without her, he wouldn't even be in Chicago, much less the Yukon. Maybe the direction of his articles should be life changes—big decisions leading to bigger adventures.

A short time later, Ed knocked and stuck his wet head in. "It's all yours."

"On my way now." He pulled the paper out of his notebook and laid it on the desk. Next, he grabbed his bag and walked down to the bathroom. There, he found a clean towel and soap. He filled the tub and soaked for a few minutes before using the soap to get clean. He dressed quickly and walked back to his room. The energy that the trip had drained from him had returned.

He took his outlines and fleshed them out into articles. The clock pinged the hour and he realized it was time to pick up Ed for dinner. He pulled on his coat, left his room, and went to Ed's door. Knocking lightly, he waited.

"Come in," Ed called.

Mark went in and saw Ed sitting on the bed.

"Sorry, I nodded off," his friend said groggily shaking his head.

"No problem. Are you ready to go down to dinner?"

"Oh yeah, I'm always up for food." He jumped up and walked to the door.

Mark looked down. "Um. I think shoes are required."

"Wow, I must have been more tired than I thought." Ed

laughed and walked back to the bed. As he put on his shoes, he asked, "Did you get any rest?"

"No," Mark admitted, "but I did get my articles drafted."

Ed stood. "Better?"

Mark grinned and they exited the room and headed down the hallway to the stairs and to the kitchen. When they got there, a number of people sat around a large wood table. *Rather like home*, Mark thought.

One of the footmen spotted them and called, "Come, sit."

Mark and Ed went to join him. They pulled the heavy wood chairs out and were happy to be included. The food was brought in from the kitchen. "Can we help?" asked Mark.

The woman bringing in the platter said, "No, sit. You both need to eat." Others came out with additional platters and joined them. Mark noticed Tait was not in the room with them.

"Where's Tait?" Mark asked the people at the table as he tore a roll in half.

The footman who told them they could sit down responded. "Oh, he stays upstairs with Mr. White and will eat after us."

"Hmm," Mark said, wondering about the two men's relationship. The smell of the food distracted him and he took his share as the platters were passed around the table. The conversation flowed, most of it about the people streaming into and out of Seattle.

After dinner, he and Ed grabbed the platters and carried them back to the kitchen. Some staff stayed and were speaking in low tones to one another. The others went back to their jobs or to their rooms. They carried their deserts back to the table and Ed ate it, savoring its sweetness. Mark sat next to him at the table and pulled out his folded papers. They needed to be mailed before leaving the area. He reviewed them one last time—the description of the trip from Chicago, the increased level of discomfort with less and less space and more and more people. The train also didn't have enough food to feed all of the hungry would-be miners. He wanted to include the level of excitement and hopefulness they found in the people traveling with him to Seattle.

Next, he looked at his article detailing his arrival in Seattle. The description included streets full of people and the fight over supplies.

"How long has Seattle been so full of people?" Mark asked.

One of the maids at the end of the table answered, "As soon as that first gold was reported, the area's been getting busier."

"Yeah, it's odd," said another man near her. "Everyone's leaving that's from here, but with so many people coming in every day, it just doesn't seem like the numbers change at all."

"Can you tell us something about the area?" Mark asked, holding his pencil and looking toward the group.

The man continued. "Seattle's Pioneer Square, the area of the town's first settlement, welcomes multicultural people from many countries. We love visitors, but this has been too much for us. The stampeders don't respect the people who live here and are using us as a pass through to get to the Yukon. The merchants and ticket agents are being pressured to provide the wanted transportation. The shops quickly stocked up with items on that list everyone is carrying around."

"The prices on supplies, I noticed they were significantly higher than I paid back home," Mark commented.

"Supply and demand," the man said and shrugged. "Can't blame them for taking advantage, especially when the buyers aren't only willing but eager to pay the higher prices."

Ed interjected. "What'll happen to the people who can't get transportation?"

"That's the question. We may have a large number of people with nowhere to live. Seattle has become a temporary home to thousands as they feverishly plan their trip north."

"It's not only that," Ed continued, thinking of Jerry and

Wade. "I wonder about people's tickets. Have there been reports of theft?"

"Unfortunately, yes. There's been cases where men have been found stripped of their gear."

"I heard about one this afternoon," said the cook from the kitchen doorway.

"What happened?" asked Mark.

"Just what was described by John," she said, referencing the man who had been talking. "Only, this time, the person didn't survive."

The room went quiet. Had their desperation to get to the Yukon turned men into killers?

"When do you leave?" the cook asked, directing her question at Ed and Mark.

"The steamer will be leaving in two days," Ed said, absently patting the ticket in his jacket pocket.

John said, "Be careful there. I heard rumors that the steamers taking passengers to Alaska are overbooked and often dangerously overcrowded."

Mark looked over at Ed. His friend was tapping the table and looking down.

"Hey, we'll make it onto the steamer."

Ed didn't look up. "What if they oversold and there's no place for us?"

"We'll be fine," Mark said bracingly, though he was unsure if they'd have a place. He stood and carried his plate to the kitchen. Ed followed, his mood improved.

The cook followed them in and stated warmly, "You were raised right."

Mark smiled slightly. "I live in a boarding house where they wouldn't tolerate people not pitching in."

"Good for you. Just come here for your meals until you leave. And I'll pack you food for the trip," she promised.

"Won't they feed us?" asked Ed, suddenly worried again.

The cook moved over to the table. "From what I hear, you'll need additional food with you. And mine is better."

"We'll take it," said Mark. The last thing he wanted was to be stuck with no food.

"Count me in on that," Ed replied.

The cook nodded. "I'll have it ready for you." Pans banged behind them and the cook stood and left to help with the dishes.

"Want to take a walk?" Ed asked Mark.

He pulled the papers out of his pocket. "Yeah, but I need to finish my articles quickly. Would you mind?"

"I can wait," he said, walking back into the dining area.

The articles were completed and Mark folded each up and put them into envelopes. At that moment, Tait came into the room. He stopped abruptly when he saw Mark at the table. He frowned but continued through to the kitchen.

"Mr...?" started Mark, stopping the man mid stride.

"Tait is fine," he said and slowly turned toward him.

"Tait, I was wondering if you could tell me where the post office is located. I need to get these off," he said, tapping the envelopes on his hand.

The butler answered brusquely. "Just leave them there and I'll have them taken over later. Letters to family?"

"No, though I may need to send one before we leave. I'm a reporter, and this is my assignment. I have to send in at least two articles before we leave for the Yukon."

Tait nodded and headed into the kitchen.

Mark did as he was asked and left the letters on the side table. Tait came back into the room, carrying his dinner. Mark and Ed left the room to give him some time alone.

Tait called after them, "Try not to be seen from the front."

They understood. Mr. White was not aware Ed was staying there. Mark called back, "We won't, thank you."

As he and Ed walked to the back door, Mark wondered about Tait. He seemed to spend much of his time with Mr.

White. *What is their relationship like? I wonder why he isn't coming with us to the Yukon?*

The cool air hit them in the face. "Brr," Ed said as he pulled his jacket closer.

They went down the back steps and into the large wooded backyard. There were gas lamps set up on the marked pathway.

"This is just a breeze compared to what we'll experience further north," Mark told his friend.

"Don't I know it. The trip will start soon. Are you ready?"

"It's been a long trip here, and we still have so much in front of us."

"Do you think we'll make it there?" Ed's doubt was sneaking back in.

"To Dawson?"

"Yes."

"We'll just have to keep going and not let it overwhelm us. You mentioned you'd go by boat once we reach St. Michael?" Mark hoped that the plans would help reassure his friend.

"Yeah. As far as I understand, I can either hire a boat or build one."

Mark laughed and asked, "Do you know how to build a boat?"

"No," Ed replied. "I'm a shopkeeper by trade, but I can use a hammer and nails."

Mark stopped in his tracks, *"What if things don't work out?" Is this where Ed's doubts come from?*

"I'll find my path, don't worry," Ed said, sounding more sure than he had earlier.

Mark watched his friend and wondered what he meant. He thought about Ed's words as they went back into the house, each relieved that they had a bed to sleep in that night.

CHAPTER 14

*T*he next day, Mark and Ed accompanied Tait to the rail station. When the butler walked into the kitchen, the duo almost didn't recognize him. Tait had changed into jeans, a button up shirt and a thick jacket.

"I can't wear the suit to town, otherwise it will draw too much interest," he commented, seeing their looks.

They nodded and accompanied him to the carriage house. Their gear would need to be relocated to the steamship. The roads were still impassable because of all the people, so their carriage dropped them outside the city. "Stay together," he cautioned them.

They followed his lead and pulled their hats down. Tait's size helped to push their way through the crowds. They heard the same rumbling of men wanting tickets, food, and gear. Are the killers in this mix? Will they be on our ship?

They eventually made their way to the rail station and approached the same clerk who had helped Mark and Ed before. The matter of moving their supplies to the right dock was arranged quickly. Ed tapped Tait's arm. "Thank you for helping. I don't know how I would've accomplished this."

Tait nodded and completed the transaction. They started back to the city and to the house.

That evening, Ed and Mark were relaxing on benches on the path after dinner. The trip would start tomorrow morning; preparations had been made and it was just a waiting game now. All of their items had been inventoried and taken to the ship. Guards had been set up to watch the goods. With so many people in Seattle, especially by the docks, it was important that the goods not be stolen before they left. There would be no way to replenish their supplies on the way there.

Men's voices could be heard coming closer to where Mark and Ed were sitting. It was tight and the carriage driver, Pete. They were both holding lit cigars.

"Like one?" Pete asked, holding out a couple of cigars.

Ed and Mark nodded, and he handed them each one. Mark took out his knife and snipped the end off; Ed borrowed it and did the same. Once lit, the four watched the smoke settle around them.

Tait stared up at the night sky. The stars seemed so close. "You'll have to watch your back with Mr. White," he commented, breaking the silence.

"What do you mean?" Mark asked, startled at the topic of conversation.

"What he means is he'll turn on you in a minute if it benefits him," Pete said.

Mark frowned. Up until now, he'd only heard good things about Mr. White. First from Galloway, then the house members who never gossiped when they were together.

Tait continued. "We decided, Pete and I, that you needed to be told a few things before your trip. You'll need to know what kind of man he is."

Mark waited, listening intently. Ed watched and stayed silent.

"We came to Seattle," the butler started, "when the lumber

mills were just getting a foothold. We—Pete, myself, and Hank White—worked together cutting trees, making boards, etcetera. We saw it all the way through from start to finish." He saw Mark's confusion and explained, "Back then, he wasn't Mr. Henry White. He was just Hank. But Hank saw an opportunity for himself. He did this by going back east to find a rich wife. He brought her here and used her money to start a business."

"What happened to you both? He got rich, but you work for him?" Mark asked, confused.

Pete filled in some of the gaps. "At first, we were partners with him, building and helping. We thought we had a grand future ahead. We thought the changes would benefit all of us."

"What happened?" Ed asked, fascinated with the story.

Tait took it from there. "Once the money started coming in, we were informed that there was no paperwork spelling out our part of the business. He used the courts to cut us out."

Mark asked incredulously, "Then why are you still with him?"

"We moved on to other businesses and, when we got too old, we asked him for help. What he offered was for us to be servants in his mausoleum," Pete said, his voice taking on an angry edge.

"It is that," Mark replied, looking back at the house. It loomed over them.

"And you just took this treatment from him?" asked Ed.

"We didn't want to, but he was in control of the whole area and he prevented us from getting other jobs," Tait said.

"And there was another reason..." Pete said and looked at Tait.

Tait nodded. "There was Sarah." He saw their questioning looks and explained, "Hank's wife. I cared for her and didn't want to leave him alone with her."

"Was he abusive?" Mark asked tentatively. *Did Galloway know his sister needed help?*

"No, just absent. He ignored her until she just faded away."

"You stayed also?" Mark asked Pete.

"At my age, I had nowhere to go and no money. He cheated us, then locked us up here."

"What'll you do when he goes with me to the Yukon?" Mark asked.

Tait took a long draw on his cigar and let out a stream of smoke. He said idly, "Now, that's something we're thinking about." Mark got the idea there were plans in place that would be activated once Mr. White was out of the way.

"Do you think he could turn on me?" Mark asked.

"It's possible. Don't be surprised if things change when he doesn't think he needs you anymore."

"I'll remember that," he promised. "Thank you."

They sat outside a while longer, then Ed said, "Early day tomorrow."

Mark nodded. "Yeah, we should head back in." He looked over at the two men. "I look forward to checking in with you when I return."

Pete and Tait looked at each other and nodded.

Ed and Mark strolled silently back to their room. Ed stopped at his door and pulled out a key. He looked over at Mark and suggested, "Mark, you could join me in my business plans once we get to Dawson." The warning had worried him.

"For now, no. I made a commitment with Mr. White and I want to see it through."

"And if he does do something behind your back?"

"It sounds like not an "if" but a "when", and then I'll take steps to correct the situation."

They parted for the evening, each lost in their thoughts.

CHAPTER 15

*S*teamer Day
The next morning. A knock sounded on his door. Mark looked over and called, "Come in." As the door opened, he put his bag on the floor with the others.

Ed stood in the doorway, loaded down with his bags. "Ready?"

"I am." Mark had slept well and woken early, ready to start the trip. "You seem more chipper this morning," he observed.

"I am. We have tickets and we'll get on the ship and start our adventure."

Mark grinned. "Now, that's the mood we need to start the trip." He picked up his bags and followed Ed down the hallway. "What's the ship's name?" he asked.

"*The City of Seattle*, owned by the Washington and Alaska Steamship Company."

They continued up the narrow servant's staircase and exited into the hallway. Mark looked around and said, "Let's go to the kitchen first."

Ed nodded. He was still unsure of how he'd get to the ship; for now, he'd stick to Mark.

Mark hadn't been told where to meet, but the kitchen seemed like a good place to start. The dining room was empty; the servants would start their work day in the next hour. He pushed open the kitchen door and saw Tait coming through.

"Good, you're awake and packed. I have the wagons and carriage in the front," he said.

Mark and Tait started that way and Ed asked tentatively, "What about me?"

"Yes, come along."

Ed grinned and followed them. They exited the front door and saw the wagons and a carriage staged there. Mark started toward the carriage and a footman tugged his sleeve and said, "No that one is for you both." He pointed to the box-filled wagon. Mark nodded and gestured to Ed to move to the it. It was a relief to know he wouldn't have to travel in such close proximity to Mr. White.

Mr. White came out of the house slowly, leaning on his cane. He made his way over and stopped to speak to Tait. It must have been a contentious conversation; Mr. White raised his cane and waved it in response. They seemed to come to an agreement and he finally walked to the carriage.

Tait stayed behind and, as they pulled away, Mark watched him. His normally stern expression changed to a smile. It was an actual wide smile that took over the butler's whole face. Mark pointed this out to Ed. They both grinned back and waved.

The carriage and wagon made slow progress to the ship. Several men were brought along to clear the roads in front of them. The closer they got to the water, the slower the carriage and wagon moved. Mark looked at all the people surrounding them; the area was overrun, the people desperate to get onto the ships. Mark saw Jerry and Wade; they looked like they were going to board. He leaned over to Ed and muttered, "Hang on to your ticket. We have to get on board." Tait had given him his ticket that morning, and he tapped his coat pocket.

The driver stopped and called back to Mark and Ed. "There's your ship." It was a large white steamer and it hadn't started to load. "Don't forget to take the basket the cook sent!"

"I'll take it," Ed said and grabbed the basket and jumped off. He didn't want to create any trouble with Mr. White. "I'll see you on the ship," he said to Mark and ran off.

Mark shook his head and looked toward White's carriage. Pete jumped down and went to the ship and, within moments, returned with a man dressed in a suit. They hurried toward the carriage. Pete leaned in and then White stepped out, and after a short conversation he accompanied the man to the ship. Mark trailed behind them with one of the footmen carrying Mr. White's bags.

As the line was separated in front of them, the comments got progressively louder. "Why is he going on before us? What makes him so special? Why him and not us?" Mark kept his head down and slowed his pace. This was not a happy group; he didn't want to anger people he'd be sharing a ship with.

The wagon driver heard them and said in a low voice to Mark, "Money. You see all of these people? They'll work and sweat to get to their dream." He shook his head and said, "And people like Mr. White will pay and get the best treatment. He won't suffer at all."

Mark nodded, understanding a little more about the man he'd be accompanying. Money seemed to be his tool and his motivation. "What do I do? Do I go now?" asked Mark, not wanting to have the crowd go after him.

"Yes, follow and let them know you work for him," the driver suggested. "Don't worry about them. This is about getting on a ship that may be oversold."

"You're right." Mark's goal was to make it to the Yukon, and this was where it all started. He nodded and quickly grabbed his bags. He ran up to the gangplank. A man guarding the area stopped him and said, "We aren't loading as yet; you need to wait with them."

"I work for Mr. White. I'm accompanying him on this trip."

The man looked him over and then nodded to the young man at the access point to the ship. "Let him through."

Mark said, "Thank you." He hurried onto the ship.

There was a roar behind him.

"Why is he going up!"

"None of your business! Stay where you are! We'll be boarding soon!" a crewman called.

Mark didn't look back and entered the ship. A man at the deck office at the entrance greeted him and asked his name. Mark gave it. He looked at a list and said, "You'll be grouped with four other men."

Mark looked back at the crowd. "There must be 3,000 people out there. Are all of them passengers?"

"Most of them will try to get on."

"Will they all fit?"

"No, most don't have tickets. We can only safely hold 275 passengers. "

"How long will they wait for a ship that will take them?"

"Some could be waiting three weeks. There are other steamers that will be in port later."

"You said 275, does that include the gear we're required to bring?"

"It does."

"It's keeping you busy."

"Yes," the officer muttered. He directed Mark to his room. "Find yourself a space and stay there until we get everyone on board. Not everyone will get a bed."

"How is that possible?" he asked. This confirmed the over-booking. Selling spots with no beds.

"Your room is located on the lower deck, 3B." The office

pointed him in the direction to go. Mark found the room quickly, as the ship was mostly empty. He opened the door and saw there were two sets of bunk beds. He took a lower bunk and waited. He didn't want to be the one that ended up in a hammock or sleeping on the floor.

Mark continued to study the room and looked at his bags. He shoved them under one of the lower bunks and hoped they'd be safe there. The door opened suddenly and Ed entered.

"Hey!" he said. He was happy to see Mark.

"You're in here also? Great! Hurry and grab a bed. I heard one person will be sleeping on the floor." Ed took the upper bunk where Mark had the lower.

It wasn't long before feet sounding like a stampede could be heard in the hallways. Mark sat down quickly on the lower bunk. The door swung open and hit the wall violently as another man came in. He was large. He nodded to Mark and Ed and took the other lower bunk. They heard the next set of passing men before they saw them. Mark rolled his eyes, and tapped Ed on his leg that was dangling from the upper bunk.

"Yeah?"

He nodded to the door. Ed heard the voices and tensed. It was Jerry and Wade. The door slammed in again as they entered.

"I get a bed!" Wade called.

Jerry pulled him back. "Not if I get it first!"

"There's only one bed left," Mark commented.

"Sez who?" Jerry asked, his tone belligerent.

Mark started to respond when the large man on the other bottom bunk stood up. At his full height, he towered over the two newcomers. "You got something to say?" he challenged.

Their eyes widened at the implied threat and Jerry stuttered, "N-n-no."

"Where am I gonna sleep?" Wade whined when his friend took the top bunk.

"I think there's blankets and pillows for the floor," Mark commented.

"That ain't fair a'tall!" Wade complained.

Jerry tapped the bed he sat on. "I reckon I deserve the bed. I'm very important, you know. My brother's found gold in the Yukon and I'm joining him."

"How long has he been there?" Mark asked with interest.

"Since last year. I'm gonna take over running it for him."

"Did he ask you to come?"

"He didn't have to. We're brothers and what's his is mine," Jerry said with what sounded like false bravado.

"Hmm," Mark said noncommittally. It sounded like Jerry's brother was in for a rude surprise.

The room went quiet as each considered the trip in front of them.

The ship finally got loaded. Mark could have sworn he felt the ship lowering further in the water. He prayed it wouldn't sink with all of them aboard. They stood to leave the cabin to watch the departure.

The large man leaned very close to Jerry and Wade. "I'll know if anything goes missing," he said threateningly, "and guess who I'm going to come looking for? Do we understand each other?"

The two men nodded nervously and shared a look.

Mark, Ed, and their large roommate joined the people in the crowded hallway and followed them upstairs to the deck. The people standing on the docks and watching them leave Seattle were quiet. *Did we make the right decision to uproot our lives to make this trip?*

Mark looked around and realized it wasn't just men; there were women and even families. He took note of this and wondered how many would be willing to stay in Dawson. The ship moved out and everyone stayed on deck. That evening the meal was a simple affair of soup and hard bread. The mood in the dining room was the same as the deck, silent and serious. Few people made jokes or created the festive atmosphere he'd expected after reading about the California gold rush.

Who are these people? All competitors for gold? The ages appeared to be neither young nor old. He thought two-thirds appeared to be from the States, listening to their speech patterns. The last third were from different parts of the world, Sweden seemingly the most prevalent.

Mark sat with Ed at the long table, nursing his soup and listening intently to those around him. Many had mining experience, but many were like him, unsure of what was ahead.

CHAPTER 16

The days turned into a routine, starting with waking early to go get breakfast with Ed. It was rather hard to exit the room with Wade drunkenly sprawled on the floor. They maneuvered around him to make their way out for a simple breakfast of gruel to start their day.

After breakfast, Ed said, "I'm going to walk around the decks, see if anyone's awake yet."

Mark nodded absently as he noticed a petite woman in one of the deck chairs. Her dark black hair was down and she hadn't yet woken. *Who is she?* "I think I'll stay here for a little while," he said in a distracted voice as he continued to watch her.

"I'll catch up with you later," Ed said cheerfully. His attitude had been upbeat since they boarded the steamship. His worries seemed to have melted away.

Mark turned to watch him go, *There must be a card game somewhere.*

The ocean pulled his attention and he watched it flow by. They moved through the settled waves. He hoped that would continue; he didn't want to be sick.

"Are you sick?" asked a female voice behind him. He turned

toward the sound of the voice and saw that it was one of the women he had seen during his previous walks. Her dress was a bright blue and her brown hair was tied back in a bun. She looked confident and happy. She was a lovely woman and looked about his age.

"No, I'm okay. Just watching the scenery."

"I'm Jenny Taylor."

"I'm Mark Sutherland, nice to meet you."

"You too."

"Where are you from?"

"New York," she commented.

"You're a long way from home."

"Yes, I needed a new start and this was the opportunity I wanted."

"Are you alone?"

"I am," Jenny confirmed. "What about you?"

"Me also."

"You know, all anyone can talk about is how they'll spend the gold they find."

Mark laughed shortly. "Gold that hasn't been found?"

"Yes. People are already dreaming, I guess," she said and looked out toward the horizon. "What about you? Are you going for gold?"

"Maybe. But first I'm here to write about the gold rush."

"You're a reporter? Are you with a newspaper?"

"I'm with the *Chicago Tribune*. I travel for them and send stories back."

"What type of travels?"

"Lately, I went to Texas for a story on space and a possible crash and then worked at an oil well in Oklahoma."

"Adventures!" She laughed.

"They have been," he acknowledged. "What about you, will you be going for gold?"

"Oh, I'm going for gold," she said, but didn't offer any details.

Mark wondered what she meant but, instead of asking, he looked over at the other girl still asleep in the deck chair. "What about her?" he asked.

Jenny hid her disappointment that his eyes were already on another girl. She commented, "That's my roommate, Helen Campbell."

"What's she here for?" Mark thought she looked like a refined woman who didn't work.

"What else? Gold," she said, with no intonation.

How? he thought. *Surely these ladies won't work the mines.* He was curious about that. Mark pulled his gaze away from the girl and asked, "How is it possible for all these people to get a year's worth of supplies?"

"For me, I had money I needed to invest," Jenny said quietly. "And Helen, I believe her father died and left her some money."

He was looking toward Helen again. When he saw her shiver, he said, "I'll be right back."

Jenny shook her head; she just wouldn't play that game. That woman was here for a man, and not a poor one. She wanted her gold and would do anything to get it.

He headed directly over to Helen and picked up the blanket that had fallen on the deck. "Here, let me help you with that." He put the blanket on her.

"Thank you," she said, looking up at him through her lashes. He was struck by her beauty.

"I'm Helen Campbell."

"I'm Mark Sutherland."

"I saw you talking to Jenny."

"Yes," he said, looking back at the other woman. She'd turned away from them and was staring out at the water. The sun caught her hair and it seemed to have gold running through it.

"Are you friends?" Helen asked, watching him closely.

His eyes moved back to her. "More like acquaintances. We just met."

Good, she thought. She smiled sweetly. "That's nice." She looked at him and saw, on closer review, that his clothes weren't as fine as she'd thought when she spotted him at the rail. Though he was handsome. She gave him a long look and asked, "Do you have a claim to get to?"

"A claim?" Mark laughed suddenly and said, "No, I'm no gold seeker. I'm a reporter."

"A reporter!" she exclaimed. She stopped herself abruptly to say again as a question, "A reporter? Didn't I see you with Mr. Henry White?" She'd spotted him in the cabin down from hers. She knew Mr. White had money, as the stewards were eager to help him.

"Oh, yes. I'm working for him in exchange for the trip," Mark explained.

Working, she thought. Helen looked at him consideringly and thought he'd be a fun distraction, but she would settle down with someone who was well off. "Where is Mr. White?" she asked, looking around.

"He isn't tolerating the ship that well and is lying down. I suspect he'll stay in his cabin for the duration." He'd inquired earlier that day and found that Mr. White was being served meals in his *private* cabin.

"Will you and Mr. White be on the barge in St. Michael?"

"Yes. We can't go over land this trip. He has an injured leg," he explained.

"Is he healthy other than that?"

"He seems to be. We probably won't see him until we reach St. Michael."

That's fine by me, she thought. *I'll spend time with Mark for now.*

They spent that day together and the next and the next. In the evenings, Mark escorted Helen back to her room. "Will you turn in also?" she asked and leaned toward him.

He took the opportunity and kissed her for the first time. Pulling back reluctantly, he said, "I'll probably read first."

"Good. I'll see you in the morning." She stepped back and closed her door, a soft smile on her face.

He stood there for a moment, staring at that door. He had told her he would go to his cabin, but it was still early and he needed to start gathering information about the mines. Turning from the door, he followed the corridor and found the stairs. The boat was teaming with people; they'd found something they had in common and were in small groups. Right now, he was looking for the men Ed hung out with.

He found them on the far side of the deck, playing cards. To his surprise, Jenny was there also, and she wasn't just watching. She was playing cards. She grinned as she laid down a hand of cards. "Read 'em and weep, boys."

The men groaned when they viewed her cards; she had a full house. She leaned in and scooped up their coins.

"You couldn't go easy on us tonight?" one complained good-naturedly.

Jenny grinned and said, "Yeah, I can do that," and flipped each a coin from her pile. It didn't look like they were playing for big stakes. She glanced toward Mark's direction. "Going to spend some time out tonight? Won't the missus be upset?" she asked, laughing. The men laughed along with her.

Mark laughed also. It wasn't something said with malice. "Yeah, I wanted to see what was happening at night."

Will Black, one of the men playing, shuffled the cards and said, "Not a lot, but it is nice out here."

The breeze came off the water and it was refreshing. It was getting cooler as they moved north.

"Do you want me to add you?" Will asked.

Mark looked around; he didn't want to take someone's place. "No, I'll just watch."

As Mark stood there, he studied the group. They were a mix

of younger and older men, as well as Jenny and Ed. He watched how Jenny handled herself, and how they handled her. They seemed to be friends, with no one overstepping that boundary.

She and Ed sat together, sharing low conversations. Are *they a couple now?* Somehow, he didn't think so. He moved to brace his back on the steamship and the man next to him asked, "Do you expect to find gold in the Yukon?"

"I don't know," Mark replied. "I do have a job, so I guess I want to find gold for my boss."

The man nodded. "Better to go with a job."

"Why is that?" He wanted the man's opinion of what they could expect.

"I hear that the Yukon rush is smaller than the one in California. Less land, fewer men to find gold."

"I've read about the California rush," said Mark, ready to bring up the facts he knew from his reading.

"You might as well throw all of that away; this mining will be different."

Mark sat forward, eager to learn. "How so?"

The man said shortly, "Ice."

"Ice? But it's still summer. Won't we be there before it sets in?"

That statement made the man laugh out loud. "Son, the ice only melts two feet in the summer. We'll have to build fires in the ground to excavate and retrieve the soil."

"Won't there also be panning in the rivers and streams to find the best areas?"

"Yeah, but I think the bigger strikes will be deeper."

"Hmm. So many things to learn for everyone."

"Yes," the man commented. "One of the main differences is that family's won't look to settle in that area. My wife refused to leave California; she says Dawson is too cold."

"Won't it be a long time before you see them again?" Mark

wondered if a year would be enough time, but if ice was an issue… He had to think about that.

"Yeah, but that's the life of a miner; you move with the new discoveries."

"How will you know where to start?" Mark asked, thinking about the job he'd agreed to do for Mr. White.

"The Klondike is better than California in that way," the man commented.

"How so?"

"Well, for one thing, anyone who has struck gold will tell you. They're open about it. Nothing hidden up there."

"Wow, really? Why would they do that?"

"Don't know. But I heard from a man who'd come back from there. It's a different environment."

"What about the claims, will they resent us coming in and potentially shrinking their claims?"

"You're thinking California again. This is the Klondike; the rules are different. Once the miner's made his claim, then the areas around him are up for grabs."

"What about abandoned claims?"

"That's the same as California. If it's abandoned, you can take it up. But you have to be careful with relatives of the miners."

Mark thought about Jerry and Wade. Jerry had said that his brother had struck it rich and he expected his fair share. "How can they police the area? And keep people honest?"

"It isn't as big as the California strike and I hear the Canadian police don't put up with much."

"Will we all find gold?"

"I bet when we get there a large majority will either head back home due to the conditions or work the mines for someone else, like they did at their previous sites." He puffed on his pipe and asked, "Have you heard the gold isn't as pure as that in California? I hear they were getting a dollar less than we got in California."

"How so?"

"Different bases: iron, silver, and lead."

"Will that make a difference?"

"Makes it less pure."

Mark remembered as much as he could. He'd need to scout claims and interview prospectors for locations before filing for one, panning, and then mining. He didn't think Mr. White understood this would be hard work. It also looked like they'd need to hire people once they got their claims set up. He couldn't do this on his own. This would be a business.

Mark had seen the footprint for the area and had wondered the same thing. Is *there enough to go around?* "Have you found gold?"

"I have." The man saw the look on Mark's face and added, "It didn't make me rich; it just got me a few nicer things."

"So, on to the next mine?"

"I'm hoping this is my last, that I can settle there."

"I heard the climate is rather harsh," Mark said tentatively.

The man laughed. "I heard that, too."

"And you still think you might stay? Even without your wife?"

"She didn't want to come with me. I'm planning this as my last move. If I can find a claim that puts out enough to live on, not make me rich, I'll stay."

Mark stuck out his hand. "I'm Mark Sutherland."

"Ben Jones," the man said, taking Mark's hand in a firm shake.

"Can you share some more information about mining with me?"

Ben pulled out his pipe and packed it. Lighting it, he sat back and puffed. "Ask your questions."

"The mining you mentioned, how's it different? You mentioned ice?"

"Yes, it will change how we get to the gold. The sluices will be used on the streams as they flow and the soil you dig up. I expect the weather will limit the time we have to use them, though."

"The ice should set in around October, and that would be when we're using fires," Mark commented. He'd studied the weather patterns.

"Yeah, and once the water stops moving, we have to look elsewhere."

"It'll get too cold to be outside. The months could be long with no income."

"That, my boy, is what I'm thinking about. We're getting there in time to set things up, but are we going to have time to mine?"

Mark nodded. "What about Dawson? Do you know anything about it?"

"Not really. I don't think it's developed much. California started that way and grew to where it is today. I expect, if the gold rush lasts, then Dawson will be the same."

"With all these people coming, what'll happen to them?" Mark asked.

"I don't think all will stay. It takes a certain kind of person to work that kind of life. It's hard and dirty and with little reward."

"But some will find gold and get rich?"

"Some," Ben allowed, then looked at the men around them. "Most won't."

Mark mulled that over and shifted his gaze to the card game. It was friendly, with each person winning a hand over time.

Mark was lulled into a slumber by the moving of the ship. He heard a soft voice float around him; when he didn't stir, another voice said, "Mark, you need to get up."

He opened his eyes and saw Jenny and Ed kneeling in front

of him. He looked behind them and saw people had settled down for the night. "Is it late?" he asked with a yawn.

"It's getting there," said Jenny.

"Would you like some help up?" Ed offered.

"Please," Mark said, still feeling groggy. Jenny took one hand and Ed another and pulled him up.

They walked together to the rail and Mark commented, "I didn't know you knew each other."

Ed and Jenny glanced at each other and smiled. Ed responded first. "We just struck up a conversation."

"The card games didn't hurt," she teased.

"That's true, she's improved my game."

They don't seem to be romantic, but they do seem to be friends, Mark thought.

The night air was refreshing; the three strolled together around the ship. They talked about everything. He realized he felt better than he had in days. "I should've been doing this a few days ago."

Jenny knew what he was referencing and commented with a sideways glance, "Just come up after she turns in."

"I'll do that," he promised. That shouldn't be a problem; Helen retired early each evening.

As they continued to walk, she asked, "Will you tell Helen about the nightly activities?"

"I'm not sure," he admitted. He'd noticed Helen wanted to know where he was most of the time. That was fine for the day, but at night he wanted to spend time with Ed and Jenny.

They had to step over people as they walked. Ed asked, "With so many people, will there be gold for everyone?"

"No, I don't think so," Mark said, thinking of Ben's responses to his questions. "I worry about that also. Ben Jones said Dawson's barely a town and that people may be surprised when they get there."

"That's exactly why I'm going," Jenny said.

"What do you mean?"

"If the town's just forming, there's opportunity for other ways to get some gold."

Ed nodded. Evidently, it was a topic they'd discussed at length. "I agree, maybe the gold we want doesn't have to have us digging in streams."

Mark was confused. "How would you get it without digging for it?"

"Merchants," Ed said and Jenny nodded. "Stores, restaurants, and others."

"Others?" Mark asked.

"Gambling establishments," she commented wryly.

"Definitely gambling establishments. The miners will have money to spend," said Ed.

Mark had heard about towns taking all of the miners money so that they worked and spent it all without taking anything home. "Will you cheat them?"

"No!" They both hastened to assure him. "But," Jenny continued, "businesses are set up to make money. There are ways to do it without cheating people."

Mark turned to Ed. "You mentioned a store?"

"Mercantile. I'll look for opportunities around the area. I've enough money put away for some land and building." He frowned and stopped talking.

Mark saw his hesitation and asked, "What's wrong?"

"Well, I may come up short on the money for supplies. I may need extra funding when I get there."

Mark watched him and hoped his dreams would come true. "What about you?" he asked Jenny.

"Oh, I have plans and a few business opportunities already set up."

"Will you share what those are?" asked Mark.

"Not now, but once we get there," she promised. Her contact was already in Dawson, getting things organized. "What about you? You aren't going for the gold directly either; you'll be working for Mr. White."

"Yes," said Mark, his voice going flat. He wished he had more of a say in what he'd be doing in Dawson. He envied their independent plans.

"Any idea what that entails?" she asked.

"Finding a claim first and foremost."

"Do you know where to start?" Ed inquired.

"Not really," he admitted. "I'll have to find out as I go."

That evening started a nightly occurrence, and the three would spend their late evenings together. Mark and Jenny also started to meet in the early mornings.

"I'm seeing you more," Jenny commented, pulling her coat closer to her.

"Yeah," replied Mark. Jenny was easy to talk to and he enjoyed their morning walks.

"Why her?" *And why not me?* she wondered.

"Helen? I don't know. I feel protective of her. And I guess love."

"You guess?"

"I'm not sure. I've never experienced this before."

"Never?" she teased. "Then it may not be real."

"Have you..."

"Been in love?" she supplied the words for him.

He nodded and thought about other questions he wanted to ask.

"I have, when I was in school. He was similar to Helen."

"What happened?"

"What happens to users?"

"No, she isn't that," he protested.

A soft voice called him. It was Helen.

"I think you're being summoned," Jenny commented, her eyebrows raised.

"You're wrong about her," he said, walking backwards, looking as if an invisible rope was pulling him away.

"Am I," she murmured as she watched him join Helen. Jenny saw her smile up at him. *Why do I continue to talk to him?* She answered herself with, *He's my friend, and that's what I need right now.* She walked over to the side of the steamship to watch the scenery.

Mark allowed Helen to pull him to the deck chairs. "Tell me your plans again," she said. She made the same request every day.

"Work with Mr. White and write columns for the paper I work for."

"You'll look for gold, once we get there?"

"I won't kick it away if I find it," teased Mark.

She smiled brightly and took his hand in hers. The trip was turning out wonderfully. She had everything she wanted.

CHAPTER 17

*S*t. *Michael, Alaska*

The next morning, they arrived at the Bay of St. Michael. The decks were crowded with people, moving this way and that to get their first view of Alaska. Mark, Jenny, and Ed had been waiting since the early hours and were at the ship's rails.

"Not much to see," said Mark, looking toward the shore. The land in front of them was covered in what appeared to be clumps of moss and the air hung heavily. It was dreary and only a few house rooftops could be seen from their vantage point.

"There must be twenty vessels, two deep already here," Jenny muttered, looking at the ships piled up around them.

"From what I read," Mark said, "St. Michael is a trading post for Alaska Natives to trade their goods for Western supplies."

"And this is just St. Michael and not Dawson. We haven't even reached Canada yet. What are we in for when we finally get there?" commented Jenny.

"What? This is what it looks like up here? You said it would be nice! You said we could be happy here!" called out an older woman. She towered over her husband and he didn't move when she grabbed the hat off his head and slapped him on the ass with it.

Mark grinned as he observed their antics. That smile turned down as he turned back to the ships. "With so many ships, how can we get through?"

"We're still moving," Ed commented. The group stilled as the ship tried to move into a space that didn't seem big enough for them.

"How are we going to offload all of these people into this tiny place? Will we have to wait here?" Mark asked, thinking ahead.

A member of the crew called out, "Give me access to the rail."

The people split to allow him to move toward it. Mark, Ed, and Jenny moved out of his way. The man got a good look and said, "The people will either stay here and wait for the barges or leave and get separate boats. There's only one hotel in St. Michael and no one will go to that."

Mark's mouth fell open and he said, "But, but there are so many people!"

"And people waiting on the shoreline," said the crewman. "I assume they're camping out there."

Jenny said, "That would be thousands of people waiting. The steamships, the people in St. Michael... Will there be enough room on the barges for everyone?"

Before the man could answer, Jenny made a sudden move and swatted Mark's arm violently.

"Ow! What did I do to deserve that?" he asked, rubbing his arm.

"It was some sort of bug," she said and pried the body of the bug off his sleeve. "What's this?"

The crewman said behind them, "That's the Alaskan mosquito."

They turned to him in disbelief. "A mosquito! But this is

huge!" she said, holding up the body for him to see. It was at least twice as large as the ones they had seen at home.

"Oh yeah, and they can get through a kid glove. They're attracted to the water, so once you get off, try to get some space between you and the shore. They'll be swarming the area."

"Now there's bugs?" asked the woman who'd hit her husband with his hat.

"Yes," commented the crewman.

A loud slap could be heard. They turned toward the woman. She looked shocked and put her hands on her backside. "What – did — you — do?" she asked.

"There was a bug," her husband said innocently.

"A bug!" she yelled. "You better have it in your hand or you better start running!"

He took the latter option and raced away from her. She chased him around the deck. Everyone watched, enjoying the distraction. It ended after a few rounds when he stopped to catch his breath. She caught up to him and the audience was riveted. What would she do when she caught him?

That was answered moments later when she picked him up by the shoulders and kissed him. He seemed to be enjoying it and the crowd turned away to give them privacy.

Mark shook his head and turned to Jenny. "Will you be on the *Leah*?" The *Leah* was the barge taking them to Dawson.

"Yes, I have my ticket."

Ed said to both of them, "Since I don't have a ticket, I need to get a boat into port." He left them with a bright smile.

"Will he be okay?" asked Jenny. "Will he be able to get transportation?"

"I hope so."

Jenny looked around. "Is our barge here? Will we be able to board soon or will we have to go to St. Michael first?"

"I assume we'll get off here and then move to the *Leah*."

"You'll be staying on the ship," the crewman said over his

shoulder. He finished reviewing the perimeter and then turned back to them. "It'll be just under two weeks, depending on available barges and then moving your supplies off the ship."

The people around them groaned. They were already worn out with ship travel and the delay was fraying tempers.

"Can we go into town?" asked Mark, hoping he could see something of the place. He also needed information for an article.

"Yeah, the town will start running boats for a dollar. But be aware, if you think the mosquitoes are bad here, they will be worse as you get closer to land," he warned.

That gave them all pause.

Mark hated to think he'd made it to Alaska and wouldn't take the opportunity to leave the ship. He looked over at Jenny and asked, "Want to take a chance?"

She looked at the shore and back at him. "Sure, let's do it."

"Okay then," he said. "Do you think any of the townspeople would mind taking me over to other ships so I can make some inquiries?"

"They can row you over. It's pretty sociable. What'll you ask them?" the crewman asked, intrigued.

"I'm curious about why they're here and where they're from."

"Hmm," the crewman said. He turned away to address another crewman who called to him. He said over his shoulder as he left to join the other steamship employees. "The boats should be around soon if you want to go to the shore."

"Thanks!" Mark called back. "I hope our jackets are thick enough against the mosquitos," he said to Jenny.

"What about Helen?" asked Jenny. "Is she going to come with us?"

"I haven't seen her to ask," he said, shrugging his shoulders. "Before I saw you this morning, I went by the room you shared. One of your other roommates told me she wasn't there."

Jenny nodded, unsure what to tell Mark. Helen had been

gone when she woke up. She wasn't there when she went to sleep and she didn't think she'd returned. *Should I tell him?* This was a dangerous area. They were friends, and she didn't want to jeopardize that, but she also didn't want to lie to him. "Mark..." she started.

Mark leaned over the rail and called to the men in the boats, "Hey, we'd like to go to the shore!"

"That'll be a dollar each!" the man rowing the boat nearest to him called back.

Jenny leaned over and saw the boat. "The rope ladder is over there." She motioned to it.

"Let's go." They made their way over. He looked at her long skirt with worry and said, "How are we going to do this?"

She chuckled and reached down, bundled her skirt between her legs, then pulled it up to tuck into her belt. She created pants that would preserve her modesty and his nerves as she descended the latter.

"Well, okay then." He went down first and had her follow him so he could help if needed.

They got settled in the boat. Business was conducted first and their dollars were given to the boatman. "Will that also take care of the return?" Mark asked.

"Yeah, just make sure you get me," the boatman replied. "Anyone else will charge you to return."

They nodded and watched as the man rowed them to the shore. As they got closer, the mosquitoes were swarming. "Pull your coats up over your head," the boatman said and batted the monsters from him as he moved them to the shore.

They did as he said and swatted at them until they were able to disembark. Mark climbed up the ladder and helped Jenny. They kept their jackets over their heads and started to make their way down the wharf. "What's all of this?" he asked one of the many men standing around large mounds of boxes and bags.

The man pushed back his hat, swatting at the mosquitoes. "Our supplies. We have them here until we can get transport on the barges or pay local people to take us on to Dawson."

Mark looked at the number of people and supplies waiting. *What would Ed do? Will he be able to make his way to Dawson?* The area had mounds of supplies; they'd all done as they were told but the amount was overwhelming. "What'll you do?" he asked the man, glad that Ed's supplies would go on with them aboard the *Leah*.

"I only had enough money for supplies and a ticket to get me here. I'll have to find alternate transportation. I'm not the only one; there are a few of us."

More than a few, thought Mark as he looked around at the men standing by their supplies, guarding them. He knew he was lucky to have his supplies being transported for him. "Can you build a boat?" asked Mark, thinking of Ed's plans.

"No trees," the man said simply. "You're thinking of Dysen, the alternative pathway to Dawson. There, trees are plentiful."

Mark nodded and looked around the area. "Is there anything to see here?"

"Except mosquitoes?" he asked wryly.

"Yeah," Mark answered in the same tone.

"There's an old Russian fort."

"Sounds good. Can you tell us how to get there?"

He looked at him with raised eyebrows. "You can't miss it. It's over there." He pointed behind them.

Mark and Jenny looked back at the island and saw the structure standing apart from other housing. "You're right."

"Mark, can we move?" Jenny asked, her voice strained.

"What?" he asked absently and saw the mosquitoes were bothering her. "Yes, of course." He looked at the man. "Good luck!"

"Thanks!" They waved and moved further into the island.

"Come on," he said and took Jenny by the hand. "We need to get on land. Hopefully the mosquitos lessened further into the town."

As they walked further, her nose wrinkled. "What's that smell?"

"Fish," he said. The place reeked of it.

As the mosquitoes abated, she lowered her jacket from her head and looked around. "He's right, there's no trees."

"No, it is pretty desolate," he said seeing the same thing she did.

They got closer to the fort and found that it had been turned into a mess and dining hall for the Alaska Commercial Company. "That's disappointing," Mark said as he read the signs outside.

"Let's go in anyway," she suggested.

They entered. Mark looked around. "Hey, there's still some cannons around." He walked over quickly to review them .

Jenny's mouth quirked as she followed him to his discovery. "There's not much to see," she commented and leaned on the cannon he was examining.

"But we're in Alaska," he said, trying to be positive.

"Going to write an article about this place?"

"A short one." He grinned. "I'll probably spend most of it on the size of the mosquitoes."

They walked back to the dock and didn't see their boatman. As they fought mosquitoes, Jenny said in a muffled voice through her jacket, "Just find someone to take us!"

Mark had the same thought. They inquired at the first one they saw, swatting the monster bugs.

The man answered quickly, "Sure, that will be a dollar each."

Mark pulled out the money and they climbed into the boat. Once they pulled away from the shore and the mosquitoes lessened, Mark asked, "Can you stop at some of the ships on the way to ours? I'd like to talk to a few of the passengers."

"Sure," the boatman said and started them toward the closest ships. The first one they approached, the passenger yelled down at them, "Where are you from?"

"Chicago," called Mark.

"New York," called Jenny.

"What about you?" Mark called back.

"Sweden," the tall blond man called down, "and my friend is from there also."

"Where are you headed?" Mark asked, voicing the obvious question.

"Where are we all headed?" he chided back. "Dawson! Gold!"

"You're not worried about there not being enough to go around?"

"It is gold and in the ground. We'll find it!" *They sound so sure,* thought Mark. *Will Dawson change their minds?*

They moved on to other ships and asked similar questions and got similar responses. The only difference seemed to be where everyone was from. A fair amount came from mines in California or different countries, but the balance were inexperienced farmers or businessmen looking to make their fortune.

They climbed the rope ladder at their ship and, when Mark was on the deck, he reached down and pulled Jenny up the last few rungs to join him.

"Mark!" He heard his name and looked toward the water. It was Ed! He was in a canoe with two Native guides.

"Hey!" Mark yelled back.

"I found transportation and will see you and Jenny in Dawson!" He waved enthusiastically.

"We'll see you there!" Mark called.

"Safe travels," called Jenny, waving her hand at him.

Mark looked around. The people had moved from the railing and back into the groups they'd been with since the trip started. "Do you see Helen?"

Jenny bit her bottom lip pensively and said, "You might check our room."

"I'll do that." He accompanied her there.

Once they arrived, Jenny didn't open the door. Instead, she turned to him and said, "Mark, maybe you should talk to Helen…"

At that moment, Helen's voice could be heard down the hallway. "Talk to Helen about what?" she asked. A smile was on her face, but the daggers in her eyes were for Jenny.

"I don't know, Helen. What should you mention to Mark?" Jenny taunted the other woman back.

Mark was confused at the turn of the conversation and felt he'd missed something. He walked to Helen and bent down to kiss her cheek. "I missed you this morning."

"I slept in some and then walked around the deck and you were gone," Helen said and glared at Jenny.

"We went over to see the island," continued Mark.

She feigned interest. "What was there to see?"

"Not much," he admitted. *Should I check on Mr. White? He hasn't come out of his cabin since we boarded.* A thump and scraping could be heard echoing in the long hallway. He turned and saw it was Mr. White. He was resplendent; his outfit looked like it had just been pressed. *No discomfort for him on this trip.* "Mr. White, I was on my way to check on you."

White didn't respond to that. He only asked, "When will the *Leah* be here?"

Mark answered quickly, "Sir, it could be up to two weeks in port waiting for the *Leah* to return from Dawson."

"Two weeks!" White and Helen said at the same time.

"That's what we were told," muttered Jenny, watching White and Helen closely.

White smiled suddenly and said, "Mark, introduce me to this young lady."

I guess that leaves me out, thought Jenny. She shook her head as White moved closer to Helen. She and White acted like they didn't know each other. This was going to end badly one way or another. Jenny quietly stepped into her room and left the three to talk.

"Yes, sir, this is Helen Stuart and this—" Mark said and turned to where Jenny had stood "—was Jenny Thomas." *I wonder why she didn't stay?*

"Ms. Stuart, are you headed to Dawson?" White asked.

"Yes, I'll be on the *Leah* next and then on to Dawson," she responded.

"Will you be mining for gold?" he teased.

"I'm not sure what I'll do when I get there. I have all of my money tied up in the required supplies," she answered with a frown and rubbed her fingers together in worry.

"You know, I have a cabin being built. I'll be in need of a housekeeper/cook. Think you'd be interested?" White asked her.

Her eyes lit up. "Yes, I would."

Mark's eyes went to Helen's hands and he wondered, *Can she cook?* She appeared to have had a genteel life. *It'll work out,* he told himself bracingly. And it would allow him to see her on a regular basis. Maybe his employer was a good guy after all. Though Mark reminded himself about Tait's warnings that Mr. Henry White was always only thinking of himself first.

Mark had turned toward the door again and knocked. Jenny answered right away. "Everything all right?" he asked. "You left us without saying anything."

"I was just tired," she murmured and saw that White and Helen were still behind Mark, talking in low voices to one another. *Such a farce.*

Helen came up to them and pulled Mark to her and away from Jenny. "Let's go walk on the deck," she suggested.

"That would be nice. Jenny, would you like to join us?"

Helen kept her voice light but her eyes narrowed. "I'm sure she's still too tired, am I right?"

Jenny saw the implied threat; she was tired, tired of the games. "Yes, I think I'll stay here and rest in my cabin."

CHAPTER 18

 he next two weeks dragged by. St. Michael hadn't given them hope that the future would be bright in Dawson. On that fourteenth day, a crewman called, "The *Leah* is in the harbor!" The passengers crowded on the railing to see it. The barge waited there for them.

The crewman called again, "Get organized, you'll be offboarding soon!" They felt the ship move toward the dock.

The passengers went to their rooms and pulled together their bags. They trudged en masse back to deck and watched as the ship moved into position to offload them. The mosquitoes were still there and people were swatting at everything. Several people got hit accidentally and a fight started.

The mood was that bad. Mark tried to stay away from the fray. The other passengers stood with their bags by the side, watching the many people being offloaded. The dock was already covered with people.

Mark looked behind them and noticed that many people were holding back and didn't have their bags with them. The reality was harsh and evidently turned people away before even seeing Dawson.

Final preparations were made and ships started to dock and offload passengers. The mosquitos once again swarmed as Jenny, Mark, Mr. White, and Helen disembarked. As they swatted them and covered their faces, White called to Mark, "Check on the *Leah* and make sure our supplies and Miss Stuart's are moved over."

White offered Helen his elbow and she took it. They walked further down the dock, toward the *Leah*.

Mark watched them go.

"Humpf," Jenny said, tapping her foot.

"Oh, I'm sorry, would you like me to check your supplies also?" Mark asked, turning his eyes away from Helen.

"That would be nice," she said wryly. *He still doesn't see it,* she thought, *even after two weeks of Mr. White monopolizing Helen's time. That girl's making a play for both of them. Mark for his looks and youth and Mr. White for his money.*

When Mark walked over to talk to the dock workers, she followed to see about the arrangements. They found a deckhand organizing the offloading. Once their supplies were confirmed to be moved over to the *Leah*, Mark looked at Jenny and offered her his elbow. "Still up for the adventure?"

"I am," she said determinedly.

They started walking and she looked over at him. "What about Helen? Are you still serious about her?"

"I like her, but I don't know. I guess we'll find out once we get there."

She nodded.

They reached the *Leah* and watched as the barge offloaded their current load. The crowd surged forward to see what was offloaded. *Would there be gold?* They didn't have long to wait as four men appeared, carrying a large strong box. It was so heavy that the men stumbled under its weight. Smaller boxes were carried on the other men's shoulders.

"Is that gold?" someone yelled out from the crowd. Everyone quieted, waiting for his answer.

One of the men with a bag on his shoulder called back, "It is!"

The crowd became animated with that answer. It was hard to not look at what appeared to be rich men leaving the barge.

"Do you think this will change anyone's minds, the ones who are turning back?" Jenny asked.

"Some might," Mark admitted. Seeing proof that gold existed in Dawson did make the trip seem more worthwhile.

The crowd was growing restless as they were delayed in boarding. It took a while to unload the people and then to move their supplies from the barge. There was security at the entrance; people were pressing forward toward it.

The barge was 175 feet long by 75 feet wide and was flat in front. The deck was fitted up with a section that would serve as sleeping berths and rooms. The other section was a covered area for eating, set up with a long table and chairs.

"One hundred and seventy-five," Mark said, looking at the crowd of people around them.

"What was that?" asked Jenny, still distracted by the gold.

"They're only taking 175 people."

"And how many tickets were sold?"

"I hope the same amount. I'm just not sure how we'll board. There seems to be thousands waiting."

"How will this work?" she asked, holding onto her bags and feeling the press of people on all sides.

Mark spotted the soldiers. It was the US Army. "I think they'll keep the people orderly."

He saw Mr. White and Helen try to ascend the plank into the barge. The officer could be heard telling them, "The process will be orderly and only people with tickets will be allowed to board. Please line up."

Mark looked around and Jenny asked, "Who are you looking for?"

"Jerry and Wade," he said shortly. Trouble followed those two and he hoped they wouldn't be on the barge with them.

"Whoever they stole the steamer tickets from must not have had barge tickets," she murmured, as she looked around.

"I hope you're right," muttered Mark. They made their way to the line to wait their turn.

"Let me by. I have a ticket!" Mr. White demanded.

"There's no preference given here," the soldier said loudly. "It doesn't matter who you are, you'll wait your turn! Get in line!"

The line moved and Mark and Jenny passed White and Helen. They didn't turn to look at them but continued on to give the man their tickets and boarded. *Finally, he is being treated the same as me and Jenny. Money doesn't seem to matter to these men,* thought Mark.

They boarded and made their way to the large area with sleeping berths on the deck; they each got one. They saw White and Helen had finally boarded and gotten their rooms settled. Once back on deck, Mark walked over to Helen and asked, "Is everything ok?"

"Yes, of course. I've been well taken care of." She smiled at Mr. White. Surprisingly, he was on the deck with them. He smiled back at her, then looked at Mark. "Did you get our supplies transferred over?"

"Yes, sir, I did. They're loading them now." They walked to the rail to watch the transfer.

Helen approached Jenny. "I hope our berths are by one another."

Jenny frowned at Helen. "I don't want anything to do with you."

"Whatever do you mean?" she asked with raised eyebrows.

"You know what I mean. I'm not like Mark or Mr. White. I know what you're doing."

Helen opened her mouth and closed it a few times, unsure how to respond.

Jenny left her without comment.

Boarding was complete and everyone found their place and settled in.

Mark looked around his very small room. "Simple but clean." He walked out and went to observe the barge; he also hoped to find Helen.

Instead, he found Jenny looking toward the sun. She glanced over at him. "Almost no nights since we got here."

"Yes, and the more north we go, the less we'll have."

"Then, in winter, will it be all darkness? All the time?"

"I hear there'll be a light show as the nights start to get longer."

"Light show?" she asked as she looked up in the sky. It was 9:00 in the evening and it had only just now started to darken to night.

"Yes. It is called the Aurora Borealis or Northern Dawn."

"What does it look like?" she asked curiously.

"I've only heard it described, but they say there's so many floating colors it looks like a stream in the sky."

"Like a stream," she said dreamily. "I can't wait to see that. Will I know when it's there?"

"They say the lights are visible to all."

"Oh, that will be wonderful."

He continued to look around the deck.

"She's still in her berth," Jenny commented.

"Who is?" he asked innocently.

She shook her head, then spoke firmly. "I hoped you'd see how she is around Mr. White. What do you think is going on there?"

Mark looked over at his friend, his eyes serious. "You just never liked her."

"I just don't like her type."

"She isn't…" he began. He heard a whoosh of skirts nearby and turned abruptly toward it. "Helen!"

"Hi, Mark, it's nice to see you," she said, pointedly looking at Jenny.

Jenny spared them a glance and said, "I'll just be going over there." She moved away. Helen let a small triumphant smile show.

"I hope Mr. White hasn't been too bothersome," Mark said.

"No, he's been very nice. Is he here?" she asked, looking around quickly.

Mark wondered at that reaction. He knew she planned on working for Mr. White when they got to Dawson, but she didn't have any obligation to him now.

"We'll probably only see him when there's a reason. He doesn't like to socialize."

"Yes," she murmured and turned her attention back to him. "It won't be long now? Before we get to Dawson?"

"I haven't been on this type of vessel before, so I don't know about the speed or water levels it operates in."

A nearby deckhand responded with, "This type of vessel moves with the river." He looked out on the fast moving water and said, "We'll be pulling out soon." He moved to help cast off the ropes from the dock.

The ebb and flow of the water shifted the boat as the ropes were removed. Jenny came to stand next to Mark and watched the vessel move out into the river.

It seemed to be pretty smooth sailing that first day, for the first sixty miles. People were sitting on the barge deck watching the sky when they were violently thrown to the side of the boat. Some were tripped up and others fell.

"What happened?"

"Did we crash into something?"

The deckhand called out. "We've hit a sand bank."

"Can't we just push off of it?" one of the male passengers called.

The deckhand who'd helped them earlier came to the group that had formed and said, "With the number of supplies and people we're carrying, there's no way to move off. We'll have to wait until the tides change and that will help us continue onward."

"Oh, that shouldn't be so bad," commented Jenny.

"How long will it be?" asked Mark.

"It can be up to thirty hours. Settle in."

People grumbled. They thought they'd finally reached the point in their trip where nothing could go wrong. *You have to expect anything,* thought Mark. They were at the mercy of the river. He was curious and asked, "I thought the sandbars would have been staked so the boats knew where things like that were."

"Yeah, but we're running so many barges with new crews, they aren't as experienced in the waterways as they used to be."

The crewman was right; they were stuck and, in the first hours, the water continued to hit against the ship, causing it to sway back and forth. The motion caused many passengers to lose their lunches over the side.

Mark wasn't exempt from the illness and grew green from the motion of the barge. He held his stomach with one hand and his mouth with the other.

Once the wind started, the rain arrived. It caused even more violent movement. Even those who hadn't gotten sick earlier couldn't avoid it now. The women on board moaned and screamed at their husbands for making them go on the trip. It was a miserable time. Over a day later, passengers stopped eating and moved out to the decks, hoping the air would help. Jenny and Helen were both sick, but they stayed silent in their misery.

That evening, the tide finally came in and helped shift the

barge off of the sand bank. When the water started to rise, the passengers quieted and watched the crew members use their poles to get them moving. Once they were back within the current, the trip became pleasant again. The channel widened and the barge stabilized.

"This is it!" one of the crewmen called to the passengers.

"What now?" Helen asked, her voice raised.

Mark patted her hand and watched where they were going.

"We're turning into the main part of the Yukon River!" called the crewman.

Everyone gathered on the deck and watched as they rounded the bend. At this point, the river was two-to-three miles wide. They watched the waters change.

"Look at the birds!"

"Ducks! Geese!"

"Aww, look at the baby animals."

The passengers were fascinated at the change in the environment. The desolation of St. Michael hadn't offered much hope that this would be the next thing they'd see.

Maybe Canada won't be so bad, thought Mark, as he took in the scenery.

A few days later, everything had been moving along at a good clip when they felt the barge slowing.

"What's happening? Are we stuck again?" asked Helen, gripping Mark's hand.

"No," called one of the deckhands. He and the others had their poles out and were guiding them to shore. "We're stopping for wood."

"Wood?" asked Helen.

"That's what's moving us; we burn a cord an hour."

"Can we get off and look around?" Mark asked.

"You should go quickly to your berths," they responded, pulling their jackets over their faces.

"Why?" he asked. He didn't need the answer, though; the

mosquitoes were already on them. The other passengers got the message and ran to their berths.

Later, as they pulled away and it was considered safe for everyone to come out on deck again, the decks were crowded with people. Mark stood with Jenny and Helen, talking to the deckhand.

"Why don't we have the problems with the mosquitos out on the water?" he asked.

The deckhand scratched the bites on his face and answered, "I think the marshes are their homes. That always happens when we get close to the shore."

Suddenly, loud howls could be heard from below decks.

"What's that sound?" asked Helen. The howls made her shiver.

"Dogs. I saw them on the lower deck yesterday," Jenny said. "They're being taken to the Yukon as work dogs."

"Aren't they dangerous?" Helen asked nervously.

Mark had asked about them when they were being brought on board. "From what I understand, they're fine with humans but have to be kept separated from one another."

"Why?" asked Jenny.

"They fight."

"They appeared built for the cold," commented Jenny. The dogs were a Malamute breed, 80 lbs. and up to 26 inches tall with thick fur.

"They're beautiful dogs," Mark commented.

Helen heard another howl and shivered. She'd keep her distance.

The barge slowed again, this time to allow local Natives, Inuits, to bring their boats alongside. The captain came out to pay for the salmon and the deckhands went down the ladders to retrieve the fish. It was freshly caught and would be what they ate on the majority of the trip. Another man was there also; he was the dog handler and was getting fish for himself.

Mark went over to him. "What'll you do with it?"

He grunted as he moved the fish. Mark reached over to help him lift them on his shoulder. "It's for the dogs. They'll eat it fresh or dried. You never want your dog hungry. They'll do anything for food."

CHAPTER 19

*A*s the days passed the sun was bright and burned off the foggy wet environments they'd gotten used to. As usual, Helen, Mark, and Jenny were at the rail watching the scenery go by.

"Look who's out there!" called Jenny, motioning to the canoes and boats. "Do you think it's Ed?" she asked, excited that they might see him again.

Mark watched them and said with a shake of his head, "No, it looks like they're headed toward us."

The passengers gathered at the railing alongside them and started calling down. "Did you find any gold?" After seeing the *Leah* offload gold, they'd expected the men to have bags full of the stuff with them. The questions continued to be called out.

"What's it like in Dawson?"

"What's the news?"

The men struggled against the push of the current. They called back, and not all answers were positive.

"Bad news, there isn't enough work to go around!"

"The food is horrible. Go back where you came from! It isn't worth it!"

This wasn't the news they wanted, and the messages caused a downward mood shift on the barge. There had been emotional highs and lows since they started—highs when gold was offloaded in St. Michael and lows when the men reported what Dawson was actually like.

Mark tried to cheer up those around him. "It might just be them. It's probably just their experience."

"Yes, that's true," Jenny said bracingly. Most nodded and moved back to sit on the deck, quieter than before.

Over the next few days, they passed more and more boats and the news didn't change.

"Turn back now!"

"Don't go, you'll regret it!"

As the cries continued, the others on the barge became more dissolute. Many of the men were pacing, their wives pulling and worrying handkerchiefs, watching them.

"Have we all made a horrible mistake?" the man who had notoriously fought with his tall wife fretted. For once, his wife didn't have an opinion. She watched him with wide eyes.

Ben came out from his berth. He'd been resting, figuring he'd get a little in before they reached Dawson. He observed the men pacing and women crying. "Mark, did I miss something?" he asked.

"Just more men coming by telling us to go back now."

"That explains it." He continued to watch the passengers and turned to Mark. "We've made it this far, might as well see it through."

"I agree," Mark said. He knew he wouldn't turn back. He'd waited his whole life for this adventure.

"Everyone's turning up," murmured Jenny. She nodded toward Mr. White. He'd appeared in the doorway. His suit was freshly pressed and he looked ready to attend a business function. He'd been the same hermit as on the steamship, with all of his meals being delivered to him.

Helen rushed over to him as Jenny watched with narrowed eyes. Mark saw and said defensively, "She's just checking on her future employer."

"Sure, she is," she commented.

Mark frowned and walked over to where White and Jenny stood.

"What's all the yelling about?" he demanded.

Mark answered. "People passing by are offering warnings that it's too rough and to go back home."

"Bah, they don't know what they're talking about. I'll be fine."

Yeah, I'm sure HE will, but what about these others who have taken their life savings to make this trip? Mark thought. *The man IS all for himself.* Mark tried to explain. "Everyone's worried we'll only have a few months to mine before we have to hunker down."

"Why is that? If men want to get paid, they'll work no matter what," White stated autocratically.

Mark just looked at him. *How is he so oblivious to the environment we're entering? Does his money keep him that removed from the everyday people?*

A group of men stood nearby and one of them spoke up. "We have to move forward. We can make more decisions when we reach Dawson." The other men agreed and things settled down.

White sneered at them. "Those men are weaklings, cowards. They just can't cut it in the Yukon."

And you can? Mark thought. He hoped there were more opportunities than it appeared. For the first time, he noticed that Helen was standing very close to Mr. White. He frowned and his gaze moved to Jenny. She noticed his interest and returned his look.

CHAPTER 20

*T*he ship continued to move at a slow pace and the days continued to drag on. Passengers noticed the scenery changing with grassy valleys and brilliant flowers. These changes brightened their spirits and helped convince them that they were headed in the right direction.

"What's that?" Mark called out. He pointed to the wagons and crates and rather forlorn people sitting on the shoreline. "Why are they there?"

The deckhand who was monitoring water levels spoke. "They were evidently dropped off there."

"But they're not in Dawson," Jenny protested.

"No. Not everyone's trustworthy. Whoever they hired to take them to Dawson probably took their money, then just dropped them here."

"Why do they have a wagon? I don't see any horses," Ben said, walking up to join the conversation.

"People don't understand the environment," the deckhand replied, "They aren't prepared. And if they stay there, the mosquitoes will eat them alive."

Everyone could see the people on shore were scratching.

"Is there anything we can do? Can we take them on?" Jenny asked. She was concerned for the families being left behind.

The deckhand shook his head. "No, We have to continue forward. We're overloaded as it is. You'll see situations like that all the way to Dawson. And it's worse once you get there."

Jenny wondered about Dawson. *If people have no place to stay now, what'll happen when the ice sets in?*

CHAPTER 21

*T*he trip was slow; it had been twenty-one days in total now. "Why do we keep stopping?" Helen complained. Everyone's nerves were stretched thin and there didn't seem an end in sight.

A deckhand with a large bag stepped up. "Mail. We're bringing news from home. These men haven't seen their families in more than a year."

That quieted the complaints, and even Helen looked abashed.

They pulled close to shore and put out the planks; a long line of men waited for them. Each man knew what was required and started calling their names out.

"Dan Parker!"

"Phil Smith!"

"Sam Strong!"

More and more. The deckhand crossed the plank and handed out the mail. Most took it and held it tightly to them. These were worth more to them than gold.

Mark made a note to get his articles and letters organized before the *Leah* left them in Dawson. He thought again about the men's faces, the ones who'd gotten mail and even more about the ones who didn't receive any. Are *their loved ones still thinking about them?*

That made him look around at the people on the barge with him. *Have they permanently left behind their lives?* Most of these men had wives and families back home. Mark continued to watch the men on board as they pushed off again.

CHAPTER 22

*M*ark was on the lower deck one morning writing articles about the trip. He was searching for a balance; he didn't want to encourage more stampeders, but he also didn't want to discourage dreamers.

Jenny got his attention by calling town from the upper deck. "Hey, come up! The river's changing colors!"

Mark put his notes in his book and started up. Other passengers followed as he ascended the stairs.

"Come on," she said and grabbed his hand, dragging him over to the rail. "It's so wonderful to see."

"Why is it white?" Mark asked, looking down.

Ben walked over to them. "I asked the same question. They said it's where the different tributaries join with the main rivers. As it joins, it looks like milk and the water changes colors upon entry."

This was the most beautiful part of the trip. Grassy areas and granite overhangs looked like massive awnings as they passed. The sun was warm and pleasant and rainbows appeared in front of them. The majority of the passengers stayed on deck all day. Several pulled out instruments, a mandolin and violins, and started to play. The group was enjoying themselves and wouldn't move from their location.

The hills they passed had little timber and thin grass. The granite formation provided the awe with the colors sparkling in contrast to the water and sun. This was also the part of the trip where the people were truly joyful, pulling together to dance and enjoy the wonderful weather.

CHAPTER 23

*T*hey exited the pass, and into the Yukon flats. With that, they left the joyful atmosphere behind. What was in front of them now was a grouping of wetlands, forests, and bogs. The music stopped and people grew quiet again. The changes brought mud and the boat's movement became sluggish. The crew were all on deck, using poles to push them along.

"What's that in the water?" Mark asked, pointing to the brown spots.

"Debris from tree cuttings," a deckhand called over his shoulder. They continued to watch the large amount of chips that had amassed.

"Will it block us?" asked Ben.

"We can push most of it out of the way. If we encounter bigger trees, we'll try to get around them."

"Look at the birds!" several people called. There were numerous colorful ones around them.

Helen joined them. "What's that?" she said, pointing to the cabins. "Is it Dawson?" Her words had people murmuring excitedly.

The deckhand dashed their hopes. "No, that's Circle City. It has more cabins than people. They all went to Dawson." The murmurs stopped and they watched the city go by.

They slowed again; this time people stayed silent. They'd seen the natives in their boats coming toward them and knew they were carrying fresh salmon.

"Yum. Fresh fish for dinner," Mark said.

That night, they had King Salmon. It weighed over 50 lbs. before it was cooked for their dinner. They sat communally at the large table and enjoyed the meal.

He saw Helen carrying a tray and asked, "Is that for Mr. White?"

"Yes, he refuses to eat with everyone else."

Another mark against the man. He says he wants the experience but removes himself at every opportunity.

Mark used the time to socialize with the passengers who hadn't been on the steamship with them. They were from South Africa, British Columbia, and many from the States.

The nights started at 11:00 and ended at 1am. He'd heard this would shift soon to longer and longer nights. *I hope we can get settled on a claim before the winter sets in.* He shivered, anticipating the upcoming weather.

CHAPTER 24

*D*awson, Canada

    After more than thirty days on the barge, they finally pulled into Dawson. People were massed at the docks. Mark squinted and couldn't see the end of the crowds. "How many are down there?"

Standing next to him, Ben said, "I hear about 10,000 people."

Mark whistled, listening to the cheers and chants from the crowd. "Are they here for us?"

The deckhand nearest to them balanced his pole and said, "No, they're here for mail. Nothing is more valuable here. Once winter sets in, there won't be any communication."

"Wait," Mark said. He pulled out the letters from his pocket and asked, "Can you get these back in the mail for me?"

The deckhand took them and gave him a long look. "Are you planning on staying?"

"Of course, why do you ask?"

"Because many won't leave the ship."

"We saw that in St. Michael," Mark murmured. "I'm here and I'll be staying." He looked around. The woman who'd berated her husband was now crying. Her husband held her close and looked at Dawson.

"Will you be going into town?" Mark asked.

He patted his wife's back. "No. I think not. We've had our adventure and we're heading back home." Mark knew the man had spent everything he had on supplies and the trip to Dawson. *He's just going to give up now? When they just got there?*

It wouldn't be just him, though. More than thirty people had decided they were ready to go home. Most had sold everything, broken up their families and then, on the precipice of their goal, were turning back.

Mark looked at the shore and saw what they did: tents, rudimentary cabins, no real houses. *What did they expect? A fully built town? A bustling city? Gold paved roads?*

Mark saw White and Helen. He walked over to them. "Sir, are you ready to go into Dawson?"

White didn't answer; instead, he pushed Mark aside to go onto the planks. Helen and Mark followed closely behind. They stopped abruptly at the bottom of the plank. They had a straight view into the town. "I am disappointed there are so many men in the streets. Why are they not at the mines?" White asked.

Mark didn't comment as his employer and Helen left the ship.

The trip is over but the adventure is just beginning, thought Mark.

"Hey, Mark!" called a familiar voice.

Mark grinned and turned toward it. "Ed!" He ran over to him and grabbed his hand. "You made it!"

"You too!"

"How was the boat?"

"Well, let's just say it wasn't something I want to do for a while."

Mark laughed. "Well, you beat us here. Have you got some place to stay?"

"I think, maybe."

Mark glanced at White and called, "Mr. White, do we have a place to stay?"

"I had a cabin built."

Mark turned to Ed, but was interrupted when White continued. "But you won't be staying there. It's for Helen and me."

Mark turned back quickly and stared at Helen. White saw the look. "She and I will be in separate parts of the house."

When Mark continued to stare at her, Helen walked to his side and said quietly, "He needs someone with him, in case of an emergency. I don't think he should be left alone."

Mark felt pulled in two. She shouldn't be staying with him alone. AND what about him? Where would he stay?

Ed said to Mark, "You can camp near me. You bring a tent?"

Mark decided he wasn't going to say anything else and turned to leave with Ed. Mr. White called out to him. "Be at my cabin first thing tomorrow to set up your day."

White stalked off, with Helen following closely behind. Mark looked at Ed. "How am I supposed to know where his cabin is?"

Ed grinned and said, "We'll find him. Come on."

"Hey, what about me?" called Jenny from the barge.

Ed called back to the girl. "Are you still with us?"

"I am," she said as she ran down the plank with her bags. She joined the duo, dropping her bags and hugging him quickly. "Nothing will stop me now."

"Town?" Ed ask them.

"Sure," Mark answered. "Show us around."

"This way."

And the three headed off together.

The amount of people in the town of Dawson reminded Mark of Seattle. Mr. White's observation was true. *Why are these men in town and not mining for gold?*

"How many people are here?" Jenny asked.

"Ten thousand was the number given on the barge," Mark replied.

"And most of those appear to be in the street," commented Ed as they dodged the crowds on the wharf.

"How big is the town?" Mark asked.

"About a mile long and it's all dirt roads; so, when it's wet, it's all muddy roads," Ed answered.

As they made their way into town, several passengers who had come in from the barge were behind them and Mark could hear grumbling. "Did you see the signs on the stores? Drinks are fifty cents, oranges a dollar, meals and a cot two dollars. I'm going to see if I can go back on the *Leah*. I spent most of my money to get here. I don't want to stay and lose the rest."

"I'm with you."

Mark, Ed, and Jenny turned and watched as the group of men headed back to the *Leah* to see if they could arrange passage.

"More are turning back," commented Jenny. She looked around. "Ed, where's the gambling house?"

"Right there," he commented and pointed to the large building up the street from them. It was a shell of a building with a roof. The sign on the front said THE DOMINION.

"That's my place, the plans I told you about on the steamer," she said firmly and grabbed her bags to head that way. "Thanks, Mark, Ed. Come by when you have a chance," she called over her shoulder.

"We will," Mark promised as he watched her run to her future.

Jenny stopped a man walking out the door. "Excuse me, can you direct me to Gertie?"

"She is in there," he said. "You'll know her because she has a diamond between her front teeth."

"Much obliged," she said and walked in the door. She had

been in communication with Gertie about a job and a place to live.

~

"Is there something between you two now?" Ed asked.

"No," Mark said absently. "I'm still with Helen. I think."

"And she's with Mr. White," his friend reminded him.

"She's working for him," Mark said laconically.

"Sure, sure she is." Helen had Mark fooled, but not him. Rather than make hard feelings between him and Mark, he decided to drop the topic and said instead, "Let's head over to where I've set up my tent."

"Is it nearby?"

"No, definitely not. All that's around here is typhoid and dysentery."

"Then let's get out of here!"

They headed out of town and up the hillside near a church. There were tents set up and a number of cabins nearby.

Once there, Ed said, "Go ahead and set up your tent. What all do you have on the ship?"

"The stove, food, mattress. All the other items that we were required to have."

"Great. We will need to contact the barge and have our supplies moved here."

"You don't mind?"

"Of course not. It'll be nice to have a friend around."

Supplies were organized and delivered to their site. Ed and Mark sat down for a meal of beefsteak and evaporated potatoes. While they ate, Mark asked, "Any movement on setting up your business?"

Ed laughed. "We just made it about a week ahead of you. No, I have been scouting out the competition."

The hours were slipping by, but the sun was still shining.

"Want to head into town?" Ed asked.

"Let's go."

They walked back into town and into the crowds. "What's everyone doing in town?" Mark asked.

"Well, most are here for the gambling."

Mark shook his head. "Really? All of that work and spending it that way?"

"Yeah. That's what I've seen."

"Isn't that the place Jenny went into?"

"Yeah. It's the biggest gambling location in the area."

"And the women? What do they do there?"

"They're mostly dancing girls."

"Dancing girls?" Now, Mark was worried about Jenny more than ever. "We need to get in and make sure Jenny's okay."

Ed had figured she was just fine, but Mark would need to see her. At the door, there was a pileup of people. But Mark was determined and pushed his way into the establishment. His focus was Jenny, and he spotted her on the dance floor with a man. He strode over and grabbed her by the shoulder and spun her around. "What're you doing?"

Jenny's smile evaporated when she saw Mark's face. She held up her hand to her dance partner and said, "I'm doing my job, the one I came here for. I'd appreciate it if you'd leave."

"But what are you wearing!" he sputtered out the words.

"What's wrong with what I'm wearing?" she argued back, holding out her skirt.

He pointed to her chest and then legs. "That's... that's..." Mark sputtered. "It's too low and too short!"

The man who'd been dancing with her decided to step in. "The little lady looks just fine and is dancing with me. Got a problem with that?"

"Yes, do you?" she asked Mark.

He seemed to become aware of where he was and that he

was causing a scene and could possibly cause Jenny to lose her job. He lowered his head. "No, I guess I don't," he said quietly.

Ed walked up. "Hey, come on. Let's look around." *So, he isn't with her, huh?* He shook his head. *If she's chosen this path, he'll have to move on or accept it.* He tried to distract his friend with the different gambling tables.

Mark looked around and saw large piles of gleaming yellow on the tables. "Is that... is that gold?"

"Yeah. See that man sitting in front of those large scales? He'll weigh the gold and hand out the money." Ed saw Mark was still upset about Jenny. "Mark, Jenny's doing what she has to, to make a living. It's not like she can work in the mines."

"I know. I just didn't think this was her plan."

They continued to walk around, watching people spend money. Mark noticed that the men didn't appear to be drunk or violent. "This atmosphere is odd," he commented.

Ed saw what he did. "It's the Canadian laws. They keep the people in line."

"Are they so different from back home?"

"No but the law enforcement moves fast. There's no delays in the punishment phase. It's just the process and delays aren't tolerated."

"I'll have to be careful."

"Just know the laws and you'll be fine." *And don't fight over women in The Dominion,* thought Ed.

"Who's the sheriff?"

"They call him Magistrate here, Captain Starnes. You'll know him by his uniform. He and his Mounties, that's what the police are called, patrol the area and guard the town and mines."

"Is that why everyone seems so..."

Ed filled in the word, "Sober?"

"Yes. It is odd, the mood, I mean. I expected to find this was a party town with booze and gambling and whatever else. Rather like California."

"I saw that also. Canada is different; even those from the States behave better. Wanna head back to the tents?"

"Yeah," Mark said as he looked back to where Jenny was still dancing.

"Come on," Ed said, dragging his friend outside.

The duo started walking toward the hill and saw Ben Jones outside, sitting near the bank. "Hey, Ben," Mark greeted.

He looked up. "Ed, Mark. Have you gotten settled?"

Ed answered for them. "Not yet."

"What do you have there?" Mark asked, gesturing to the paper in his hands.

"A list of claims I'm going to investigate."

"Would you mind if I go along with you? I need to find one for Mr. White."

"I'd like that. We'll need to leave tomorrow. Ed, did you want to go with us?"

"No, thanks, I have other plans."

Ben nodded and looked over at Mark. "Meet me here in the morning?"

"I'll meet you here after I confirm with Mr. White. Probably around 10:00am?"

"See you then."

Mark and Ed headed back to their tents, ready for bed.

"In the morning, we'll find Mr. White for you," said Ed, yawning broadly.

Mark nodded and moved to his tent. He felt unsure about his future here. Jenny was the last thing on his mind that night.

CHAPTER 25

*T*he next morning, Ed called to Mark. "Time to get up."

"How can you tell?" Mark muttered. Daylight was perpetual in Dawson. He exited his tent and saw Ed had made breakfast. "What's to eat?"

"What there always is: bacon, beans, and bread."

"Yum." Mark suddenly missed home, especially Mrs. Spencer's cooking. Pushing those feelings down, he took his plate and started to eat.

"It's food." Ed shrugged. "We need to be conservative with our supplies, so we eat what we have to but not much more until we're able to get work or find gold." He sat next to Mark, balancing his plate on his knees.

"I'm supposed to be working for Mr. White. You know, pay was never discussed."

"He expects you to work for free?" Ed asked in disbelief.

"Well, he did pay for my trip," he pointed out.

"I don't like it. Tell him you need a salary," Ed said, his voice firm.

They finished breakfast and cleaned up. Mark huddled in his

coat and asked, "How can it be so sunny and yet so cold at the same time?"

"Just make sure you keep your coat on and don't take it off. The cold can be dangerous."

"How do we find Mr. White?"

"There's little choice. Let's head this way." Ed indicated a group of rustic cabins. They looked around. "Any ideas?" he asked.

Mark finally pointed. "Probably that one." The ones around the cabin looked rustic, but this one was fashioned out of wood tailored specifically for the home. It was exactly what he expected; everyone else lived in squalor except Henry White.

"You think that's his? It's nice," Ed commented. He had noticed it before but had not seen anyone enter it.

"I do. The man doesn't like to be uncomfortable." Mark knew Mr. White would expect him to go to the back, but he refused. He went directly to the front door and raised his hand to knock.

"I'll leave you to it," Ed said. He didn't particularly want to have anything to do with the man.

"Will I see you later?"

Before Ed could answer, the door opened and Helen appeared in the doorway.

Ed called out a goodbye, and Mark waved absently, his attention all on her. "How are you?" he asked. *What's your relationship with Mr. White and me?*

She looked a little frazzled. "Come in," she told him. "I'm getting breakfast ready for Mr. White."

"I smell something…"

"Oh my gosh!" she said and ran toward the door that must have led to the kitchen.

Henry White came out of a side room and saw Mark. "I'm glad you're here early. We need you to find me a claim. Tell me what you plan to do first."

"I figured I need to start investigating claims, do some field work."

"Yes, that's the best move. Get with me before committing to anything."

Helen came out with White's breakfast and he looked at Mark. "You can leave now."

Mark looked over the man's shoulder at Helen. She shrugged her response.

"Yes, sir." He was outside before he realized he hadn't asked about pay. He could do so later. *Okay, now how do I find the claims?* he wondered and headed toward town to look for Ben.

Yesterday, he'd been too overwhelmed with finally making it to Dawson to really see the town. As he walked down the long dirt road, from his position, he could see the ships were still in port. This morning, unlike the day before, no one appeared idle. Everyone seemed to be working.

He passed several businesses set up in temporary tents: an auctioneer selling mining sites, and next to him a dry goods salesman with tables of bread and piles of dry goods. More men were working on the buildings, turning the tent city into a real town. The banker seemed the busiest with trunks of gold dust behind his table and men a mile long wanting to talk to him.

Mark was walking past when he noticed who was in the line. "Ed, what's going on?"

"I have a plan," his friend said in a low voice. "I just need some seed money."

Mark thought about the money he had saved. It would be better if it was working for him while he was managing Mr. White's business. "I think I can help with an investment," Mark said in a low voice. "How much are you thinking?"

Ed quickly named the figure.

The line moved ahead and Ed and Mark moved with it. "If you take the money, could you pay me interest?" Mark asked.

"I think I can do better than 10 percent monthly."

Mark grabbed his coat and pulled him out of the line.

"What're you doing?" Ed complained. "I'm going to lose my place."

"Let's find someplace quiet," Mark told him. They ducked beside one of the new buildings going up. "Now, tell me what your idea is."

Ed pointed to the docks where all the supplies sat. "The steamer captains tried to work independently and brought goods to sell. Now, they can't get rid of them, so they're offering them for a discount. The steamer captains aren't working with the regular trading companies, so I figure I can get all the 50 lb. flour sacks at five dollars each. The store is selling at eight."

Mark looked thoughtful. "That's a good margin of sale. I had a thought; people are turning back and they need money but not the goods."

Ed frowned and then grinned. "That's perfect! We buy their supplies and that'll increase our initial inventory with the added benefit of helping them get back home."

Mark was thinking. "What about storage? All of it won't fit in our tents."

"No, I wouldn't think so. I did spot an abandoned warehouse. I made some inquiries about it and it's owned by a judge. I hear his wife wants out on the *Leah* today."

"You think a deal can be made?"

Ed grinned. "For a price."

"Ed, do you have any actual money?" Mark asked.

"I do. I can get us a cabin built and pay for the warehouse if you pay for the goods."

"How much are you thinking?"

"Five hundred, plus the cost of the flour and someone to move it. We'll need horses and a wagon for about 75 to 100 a day."

"We'll need other supplies, not just flour. Can you ask about beans and rice and maybe some other goods?"

"I can."

"I need to head out to the mines. Can I trust you to move forward with our plan?"

"Yes," Ed said firmly and held out his hand. Mark took it and the agreement was in place.

Is it a mistake to hand this man I barely know money to start a business and then leave? Probably, but this is part of my personal adventure. "Let's head back to our tents," Mark said. He didn't want to be seen handing out money there in the open.

He and Ed documented their plans and the money. Each signed the agreement. Mark pulled out the money and handed it to him. "You're sure about this?"

"I can't go home and I won't work in the mines. You can count on me," he said.

"Okay then."

They stepped outside and Mark folded up his tent and placed his gear on his back. His supplies had been delivered and he had removed enough food for a month. Ed would take the rest for him. "I'll be back in a month. I hope to see some progress."

"You will," his friend assured him. "I may not be a miner, but I know how to run a mercantile."

Mark nodded, hoping Ed would still be there when he returned. Time to meet Ben.

CHAPTER 26

$\mathcal{B}$en was waiting when he moved down main street. "Ready?"

"Yes, where are we going?" Mark asked, adjusting the pack he was carrying.

"We will start in the marshes and wetlands."

They headed out and, once they were near the wetlands, they put on their hip waders. It made walking a little slow, but it was necessary. The duo followed a long line of men. They started out through the muggy water and dark moss. The groupings of moss, their foot paths through the area, appeared one-to-two feet in diameter each. He and Ben watched the men in front of them navigate the path. They went from one mossy step to another. Mark started out and, when he stepped on the dark moss the first time, he almost lost his footing. Ben reached back and caught him.

"Watch out."

"Thanks, I will." Mark studied how the men positioned their feet. They took deliberate steps to make sure they landed on solid ground. It took lots of patience. As he walked along, he happened to glance back and saw Jerry and Wade following. *Great*, he thought. *Just what we need.*

The duo were coming up behind him in a hurry, jumping from moss to moss. "That's not going to end well," he muttered. Ben looked back and nodded and turned his gaze straight ahead. Suddenly, they heard a splash and yelling as Jerry and Wade fell waist deep into the arctic mud and water. He let a smile cross his face as they moved further away from them.

The group trudged on without a backwards glance. As far as they were concerned, they weren't there as friends; they were competitors. Jerry and Wade had a few choice words to say to the other men as they pulled themselves out of the mud and water.

Once out, they studied the maps. The claims stretched along creeks that were about thirty miles in length. Ben had marked possible claims to investigate. "The ones I have in mind would be twelve-to-fifteen miles."

"It looks like some could be as far as thirty miles." *There may be fewer people to fight for claims there. Hmm*, he thought. *I may have to reconsider my plans.*

The first night, they stopped and rested at a tented camp. There were cots and food—for a cost. The cots hadn't been cleaned since the last time someone had slept on them, maybe even the time before that, but it was shelter. Ben had his map pulled out and was frowning.

Mark went over and sat next to him. "What's up?"

Ben glanced around the camp. "I need to break away from this group and get ahead. Any claims will be taken up quickly."

Mark had had the same thoughts as he watched Jerry and Wade argue with the man running the camp.

"Let's get out early tomorrow morning, before daybreak, and head to the outer areas," Ben said.

"Sure," Mark agreed. He glanced at Jerry and Wade. "Think we'll need to watch our gear tonight."

Ben grunted, turned his gaze to Jerry and Wade, and watched them. "We may not have an issue."

Mark looked over and saw what he meant. It was evident that whatever deal they were trying to make hadn't worked out and they were being taken from the camp by two large men. They took Jerry and Wade by the collars and unceremoniously hauled them away.

"Good," Mark said.

There were no disturbances during the night, and he and Ben were packed and out of camp before anyone else woke. They walked miles, the sun was already bright in the sky and stopped only for breakfast. As they were cleaning up, a few men approached.

"Where are you headed?" an older heavyset man asked.

"We're looking for claims to work," Mark replied.

"We just left one back there. You should check it out," the man with him said.

"Does it belong to anyone?" asked Ben.

"Yeah, to me," the man said. "I'm going home."

"Not enough gold?"

"I don't know. I just want out before winter sets in. You wanna see it?"

"I would," Ben said.

"Be careful," Mark whispered to him. "Newcomers can be conned and it might be an exhausted area."

Ben nodded. "I'll take a chance. Want to come along?"

Mark thought and said, "No, I think I'll continue on." He had a copy of some farther locations and wanted to get to those. He also wanted some separation between himself and the crowds.

He waved them off and headed further upstream. There were several camps he stayed at over the next few days. He stayed silent and watched the men work. Most didn't mind the young man standing near them for long hours.

Mark was particularly interested in sluice boxes. He knew

from his research that they were key to mining gold in streams. They'd been used in California and were designed to be placed in streams or creeks. The long, narrow troughs would wash away unwanted sand and gravel when it was put into the sluice, leaving only the heavier gold behind to collect.

Though he'd read about them, he needed to find out how the process worked. What he learned quickly was that there was not a set size; it depended on the stream or creek where it was placed.

The furthest camp was thirty miles from town. It would take him about three days to reach the outer camps. The days passed quickly as Mark searched for a suitable mine to purchase. The camps he passed after the twenty mile mark were busy and appeared to be prosperous. Stopping only for food and light rest, he continued on.

On that final day, he'd been walking for more than four hours since his last break, ten hours in total. Just when he was about to collapse, he reached the mine he was looking for. The edge of the camp was marked with a no trespassing sign. Mark respected the boundary and called out to one of the men working on repairing a sluice.

"Who's the owner here?"

"He's inside," the man called back.

"Can I come inside?" Mark asked.

He looked over at Mark. "Yeah, head to the cabin on the far side of the stream."

He followed the man's direction along the stream to the cabin. The door was closed, so Mark knocked and a voice called for him to come in.

As he entered, Mark saw a man counting what appeared to be gold nuggets. Mark's eyes went wide; he hadn't seen that much gold in all of his days in the field.

The man didn't seem disturbed at Mark's presence and kept

counting as he asked, "Looking to do some mining? Need a job?"

"No, sir, I'm looking for a claim for my boss."

"Well, you got here at the right time."

"How's that?"

"I haven't notified anyone as yet, but we just found this yesterday," he said, picking up a nugget from the scale.

"So, I have time to get back to Dawson and file a claim for the adjacent areas?"

The man laughed and responded with, " I see you've done your research. Yes, you have some time."

"Who owns it?"

"I do. I'm Joshua Sullivan."

"It is nice to meet you," Mark said and reached over to shake his hand. "I'm Mark Sutherland and I work for Mr. Henry White. He's a businessman from Seattle."

"Is he a good man?"

Mark hesitated and Sullivan let that go. "Are you planning to run it for him?"

"Planning to."

Sullivan sat back and looked at Mark, then pulled out some paper next to him. "Here's the claim paperwork and the price. Have your boss pay the claim office and I'll get the money from him." He reached out and handed the papers to Mark.

"Why are you doing this? For a stranger?" Mark asked curiously.

The other man sat back and stroked his beard. "I have plenty and I want to share it."

"With a stranger?" Mark asked again.

"My men are happy here with their share. There's also the fact that my brother's coming and I have a feeling he's gonna try to take everything I have."

"So, I should hurry? Can you review the claim with me?"

"Sure, let me put this away." Sullivan took the gold to the large case behind them and started toward the door.

Mark hesitated at the door to the cabin. "Sir…"

"Josh, please. We're not formal here."

"Josh, does your brother go by the name of Jerry?"

Josh stood still. "What do you know about him?"

"You're right; he's here. He has a friend with him and they're both trouble."

"How long since you've seen him?" Josh asked, frowning at this news.

"About five days, at the first camp. They were tossed out."

"Yeah, that would be Jerry all right," he said, continuing to the door.

"Josh, do you need me to stay?"

"No, I've been expecting him. I'll be on guard. Thank you for letting me know."

They closed the door and Josh locked it. He motioned to a man nearby. The man moved closer to the door. *Are the guards because of Jerry?*

They walked downstream, just south of his claim. They walked the length of the stream bed and found it undisturbed. "From what I've seen, we'll need to dig down to the gold," Mark said.

"That's our experience," Josh commented. "Do you want to observe our operations today and then head back tomorrow?"

"That would be great, thank you!"

Mark joined the team that was digging and adding to the sluice. He was able to get hands-on experience for how the process would work. They toiled well into the evening and he sat with them at dinner. That night, before turning in, Mark noticed men walking the perimeter. Josh was taking his brother seriously. He laid down on the cot to sleep, secure he wouldn't be bothered.

CHAPTER 27

$\mathcal{T}$he next morning started early with a ringing bell announcing breakfast. Josh was already there when Mark walked in. They sat together and ate. When he finished, Josh spoke up. "Now, get back to town and get that claim filed!"

"I will."

CHAPTER 28

*M*ark had everything ready to go and quickly headed back to Dawson. He took a straighter route and camped on his way back. It had been more than three weeks since he'd left and would be another two to three before he returned.

As he made his way, he found that there wasn't a lot of natural shelter. The trees were being cut down at an alarming rate for basic building supplies. He looked at the tree stumps covering the land. *What will this look like in two years?* He couldn't imagine how the landscape could recover.

Finally, he reached Dawson! He headed directly to Mr. White's cabin. He knocked quickly and waited.

White opened the door and said without an invitation, "You're back. Did you find anything?"

"I did," he said and tried to see over the other man's shoulder. "Where's Helen?"

"She's around," White said evasively, continuing to block the door. "Tell me what you found."

Mark knew that time was limited. He quickly pulled out the claim paperwork and the map to hand to Mr. White.

"Why so much money?" White asked as he read through the document.

"Because of the gold. The claim's next to a confirmed discovery. We're the only ones who know about it."

"What do we do next?"

"We need to go to the claim office and file a claim," Mark said.

"When?" White demanded.

"Now!"

White grabbed his hat and cane just off the doorway and said, "Let's go."

The duo hurried to the claim office and presented the paperwork to have it filed. "It all appears to be in order," the clerk said. "We'll take the payment for Mr. Sullivan."

White took out his bank notes and handed them to the clerk. Once the paperwork was signed off, the clerk told them, "Congratulations, you're now the owner of the claim marked on this paperwork." White took the agreement and placed it in his suit pocket. He walked to the door, motioning for Mark to leave with him.

"Just a moment. Has Ben Jones been in to file his claim?" Mark asked.

"Yes, he was in a few weeks ago. The owner of the claim was leaving on the steamship that day and wanted it finalized as soon as possible."

"Great." Mark was glad Ben was settled.

White tapped his cane on the ground to get Mark's attention. Mark hurried over to him and held the door so that he could exit. "What'll we need to start work?" White asked.

"We need experienced miners. Ones who can build a sluice and a manager for the claim."

"You can start interviewing miners today, and I'll talk to the sawmill about providing a supply of wood for the sluices and cabin."

Mark nodded. "There's a hiring hall and I expect many men will be waiting there. I'll go over and get organized."

"Report back to me with the recommendations and how much the going rate is for them."

I have to find Ed, Mark thought. *Did I make a mistake?* He was worried about giving his friend so much money and then trusting that he'd set up a business for them. *Idiot,* he thought. *You are an idiot.* He continued through the town and stopped a few people he recognized. "Hey, Bill, have you seen Ed?"

"Not lately. I have to get going," Bill said and hurried off.

A man nearby heard him and inquired, "You looking for Ed? Ed Gantz?"

"You know Ed?" Mark asked, hoping this meant Ed was still in town.

"Sure. He's the warehouse guy."

Mark ask, "Where's it located?"

The man pointed toward a location near where their tents had been.

"Thank you," Mark said and headed toward the area indicated. The old warehouse now had a sign: "Dry Goods Warehouse." *He did it! He said he would, and he did!* Mark shook his head and pushed the door open.

There was a long line inside, and it took him some time to get to the counter. Ed was there writing up receipts and calling to a young man to grab different supplies from behind them. When Mark moved to the front of the line, Ed didn't look up. "Whatta ya need?" he asked.

Mark didn't comment and Ed looked up impatiently. "Look..." he began and then realized who was standing there. "Mark!" he yelled and ran around the corner and grabbed hold of his friend's arm, shaking it vigorously. "You're back!"

"You're still here!" Mark countered.

"Did you think I wouldn't be?"

"Well..."

"Hey!" someone called from the line. "We need our supplies."

Ed looked at Mark. "Can you help out and we can talk?"

"Sure."

Mark and Ed walked behind the counter to assist the people in line. As soon as they were empty, Ed called out, "Sam! Put the lunch sign on the door."

"But it ain't lunch time!" called Sam.

"Sam! Put the sign out!" Ed said firmly.

"This actually worked," said Mark, looking around.

"Let me show you around." Ed gestured around them. "This is the main area where we keep everything on shelves in long rows."

He put his hand on the counter and asked, "You get the goods for the customers?"

"I did, now Sam does."

"How did that happen?" They hadn't talked about hiring anyone before he left.

"Well, I was all by myself and had a lot of other people's supplies to pick up."

Mark had the grace to look embarrassed. "You're right. I wish I could have stayed to help you."

"I'm sorry, that wasn't fair of me. That was the agreement; you helped with money, and I knew the rest was on me." He turned away. "Let's sit," Ed suggested.

"Bad news?" Mark asked, worried again. The warehouse looked like it was making money.

"No, it's all good," his friend assured him. "Come over to the table." They walked to the back of the warehouse and sat at a long wood table in an area that doubled as a kitchen. Ed pulled out the account books and started going over them.

"You sold all of the original inventory?" Mark asked, looking at the books. "Then what's all of this?" He waved his hand toward the merchandise.

"The captains asked if they could stock us until the ice

blocks their path. I had to decide quickly, and I gave them the profits."

"All of them?" Mark asked, feeling faint.

"No," Ed said, leaning back in his chair. "In fact, we made enough to pay back the original investment."

"You did?" Mark asked, stunned.

"*We* did," he stressed. "I have the money here."

"Not in the bank?"

"I wanted to make sure our investment was secure. A large amount of gold and cash go through the bank and, at some point, it might go bust."

"Where do you keep the money?"

"Right now, hidden," Ed said in a low voice. "It is mostly in gold nuggets and whatever cash the men carried."

"Do we have a place to live?" Mark asked. He was unsure where he'd be sleeping that night.

"Yes, and a barn for the horses and wagon."

"Horses? But why?" Mark frowned.

"How do you think we transport the product from the docks?"

"I didn't think," Mark admitted and looked through the door at the stock on the shelves. "I guess, even with a wagon, it took time and money."

"Yeah. The local barn wanted forty-five dollars a day just to rent the wagon. Horses were going to be extra. I was able to buy the horses and wagon from a family that was leaving. They took a quarter of their worth."

"Will the horses be able to stay alive through the winter?" The extreme conditions there could kill all living things, especially if they were housed outside.

"I had a place built for them here and had a fireplace put in."

Mark blinked in surprise. "Show me." They exited the warehouse, turned to the left, and Mark saw the stable. It was well built and, as promised, had a fireplace inside, which was lit. "Great idea."

"We'll need them in the spring when the ships return."

Mark worried about that. "Ed, will you make enough to get through the winter?"

"Oh, yes. We have two more deliveries coming and I've requested to double the orders for each. I should have plenty of supplies to last through the winter."

Mark let out a breath. "Okay. You mentioned a cabin?"

"I did. Back here."

They walked to the cabin and Ed stopped at the door and unlocked it.

"Locks?" Mark mentioned as Ed opened the door.

"Yeah, the man who built the cabin laughed himself silly and said locks weren't needed here. I insisted." Mark nodded as Ed turned to him. "I didn't expect you back today, so the place could use a cleaning."

They entered, and Mark saw he was right. The place had a nice big room and a kitchen. Every spare area was covered with clothes and paper. The kitchen looked to have not been cleaned since he moved in.

"Where's our rooms?" asked Mark as he looked around.

"This way." Ed guided him to the back and pushed open the only closed door. "This is it." Mark was happy to see that they had their own rooms and his mattress was in the room.

"I'll clean up the rest, I promise."

Mark smiled. "I'm just happy it isn't a tent, and I'll help you clean up."

There was a knock on their door. "Come in, Sam," Ed called.

Mark raised his eyebrows.

"Who else would it be?"

Sam stuck his head in. "We have a line outside."

Ed responded with, "I'm on my way over. Wait to open the

door until I get there." He looked at Mark. "The customers can get unruly."

"Is that why you get the supplies for the customers?"

"Yeah, the further we get into winter, the worse the desperation for supplies will get."

Mark said, "We may need to think about that."

"What?"

"Keep back some supplies, not just for us, but also a certain amount to donate. When the streams freeze over, there'll be a lot of miners hungry and possibly homeless."

"The Mounties have mentioned that," Ed said. "There's talk of using the gambling halls and having the miners sleep there if needed. But you're right. I'll let the Mounties know we can donate a certain amount. I will coordinate with Father William Judge at St. Mary's Hospital and see if he needs any donations, too."

The reference to the gambling house had Mark wondering about Jenny. "How's Jenny?"

"She seems fine. She's also profitable and happy."

"Good."

Does he really think so? thought Ed. He looked at him but he didn't say anything.

They returned to the warehouse. "I'll be back this evening," Mark said. "I need to go to the hiring hall and get some men signed up to work our new claim."

"You did it! You found something!"

"I did," said Mark.

"So, you're back to the wet, cold, and the mines?"

"As soon as we can get supplies organized."

"Who's paying for this?"

"Mr. White."

"Humph. I need to talk with you about him."

"Can it wait? I really need to get over to the hiring hall and start the interviews."

"Yeah, I guess it can," Ed said as he watched his partner leave. He wanted to tell Mark what he'd heard about Helen and White, he was worried his friend would be hurt.

Mark went into town quickly and entered the hiring hall building. The last time he had been there, it had been a tent. The town was growing quickly and there was no shortage of men looking for work. Most had used the majority of their money to get to Dawson. They had experience but no money to get their own claims. Mark walked up to the clerk and asked, "Can I set up a table for interviews?"

The man looked Mark over and scoffed, "You? You have a claim?"

"Me? No. I represent Mr. Henry White."

His eyes widened. He recognized the name; Henry White was becoming an important person in Dawson and had been getting involved in local politics lately. The clerk flipped through his book quickly and said, "You can set up a table tomorrow."

Mark next headed over to tell White the news. He also wanted to see Helen.

Mark stood waiting in the living area for Mr. White to get her. Suddenly, there was a crash that sounded from the kitchen. Mark looked toward the kitchen door. It pushed open and Helen came out, her face red. "Mark! It's good to see you." She walked over and kissed him on the cheek.

Is it? he thought. "What happened? I heard glass break."

"Yes," she said and waved her hand toward the kitchen. "Something fell."

"I was hoping you could go to dinner with me."

"I would love that," Helen said enthusiastically. "Let's go."

"Now?"

"Why not?" she asked and glanced over her shoulder. She grabbed his hand and pulled him toward the door, taking her coat.

Mark let himself be pulled away but asked, "What about Mr. White? Should you ask him?"

"Him? No," she said firmly.

"Okay," he acquiesced. He was happy that he'd finally get time alone with Helen. They started out and she was buttoning her coat and pulling her scarf over her hair.

There was really only one place to go, and that was the gambling hall. They stopped outside and saw there was a new sign in place. "Hmmm, dancing girls," she murmured.

"Is that okay?" he asked. He didn't want to make her uncomfortable.

"It's fine. After all, we have a friend here, don't we?" Helen asked with a sideways look at him.

Mark decided to answer the actual question. "Yes, Jenny's here. I've been gone a while and it would be nice to check in with her."

They entered together. The room was already full, with many people eating and gambling. On the far side of the large room was a stage.

They walked into the dining room and saw they could view the stage. Her eyes slid around the room and finally settled on Mark. She sat forward. "Mark, when are you getting back to the claim?"

"In a few days. I need to hire miners first and then people to build the sluices."

Helen nodded and asked another question. "Mark, do you love me?"

"Love?" he asked and looked around nervously. He finally reached for her hand. "I do have feelings for you and would like to spend more time with you."

"Hmm," she commented. Abruptly, she asked, "What're your plans after Dawson?"

"I'm not sure," he admitted. "I don't usually plan on the next step until the current one is up. Probably go back to Chicago for a while."

She pulled her hand from his and drummed her fingers on the table.

"Is something wrong?"

"No," she said quickly. "Everything's all right."

Music came from the back of the room, distracting him. Jenny stepped out onto the stage.

"Hey, it's Jenny," Mark said, delighted he would see her.

"Yes, it is," came a murmur from Helen. "And what a dress."

He ignored her and watched with interest. The room quieted as Jenny started across the stage. The dress she wore was deep blue and stood out as a swatch of color in the room. She stopped in the middle and began singing.

Mark listened and said over his shoulder, "Hey, she's really good!"

"Is she?"

Mark could hear Helen's fingers tapping again but refused to turn away from Jenny. The tapping stopped and he figured that Helen had finally settled back to watch the show. He couldn't take his eyes off of Jenny.

When she finished, he stood and clapped loudly, and the rest of the room joined in. Jenny spotted him and gave him a quick wave before exiting the stage. Girls came on after her and began dancing in a line.

He laughed and said, "This is fun!" He turned around to tell Helen and saw her chair was empty. He frowned, looking for her in the crowd. *Where did she go?*

He continued to look around and felt a tap on his shoulder. He turned and smiled widely at Jenny. "You were amazing! I didn't know you could sing!"

"Yes," she said softly. "We all have something we keep hidden."

He remembered Helen again and started to scan the room for her.

"Helen left," she commented, watching him.

"Left?" he asked, bewildered. "But we haven't ordered dinner yet."

"You might check outside," she said, hoping he would stay with her.

"Would you mind if I go and..."

She didn't let him finish. "Go," she said.

"I will see you soon! I want to tell you about the claim!" He started toward the door.

"Don't forget you coat!" she called after him.

He turned toward her and caught the garment she tossed his way. He ran out and pulled on his coat as he pushed open the doors to exit. People were in the way and he dodged them and kept moving. He saw Helen at a distance in front of him. She had stopped and was looking at the sky. It was still light out, even at that hour.

He slowed as he got close and asked, "Why did you leave?"

She didn't glance over to him. Instead, she continued to study the sky. "I got the answer I needed."

"Answer?" he responded, confused.

"Yes, my answer." She continued to stare and ask, "When will you be leaving for the claim?"

"Soon," he said in a distracted voice. Is *it the separation she's worried about?* "But I will be back."

She turned to him suddenly and seemed to be herself again. Her smile in place, she held out her hand and asked, "Walk with me?"

Confused, he took her hand.

She squeezed it and moved closer to him as they walked. They passed the edge of town, where they were finally alone. She pulled him to a stop. He looked over at her and took the moment to lower his head to kiss her. He expected a sweet kiss, like the ones they had shared previously. This was not that. Her mouth went open and he groaned as he felt her response. She took his hand and moved it inside her coat and ran it over her breast.

The sound of their breathing was the only thing that could be heard.

He pulled away, knowing he was fast losing control of the situation. He wanted nothing more than to take her here and now. The more he pulled away, the more she rubbed against his hands.

"No," he said and held her at arm's length. "No, I care more about you than this."

She turned away and said, "If you cared about me, you would."

He frowned and waited.

She turned back to him and saw there were tears in her eyes. "Helen," he said, and reached for her.

This time, she stepped away. "Mark, go to the mines and finish your contract with Mr. White."

"And after that?" he asked, fearing the answer. "Will you be here for me?"

"I will be here," she said noncommittally. There didn't seem to be anything else to say, and she turned from him and walked away.

Mark ran up to her and said, "I can take you home."

"No," she said, looking ahead as she continued to walk. "I will head home alone. Please respect my wishes."

He stopped and let her go on without him.

Once she was out of his sight, he turned back slowly toward town. A figure in the distance called his name, and he looked toward it. "Mark!"

It was Jenny. He hurried toward her. He let what had just happened fall from him as he got closer. "Jenny! What are you doing out here?"

"I came to find you," she said simply. "Did you catch up to Helen?"

"Yeah," he said. He refused to think about it. Instead, he asked, "Walk with me?"

She let him switch the topic and took his arm. They strolled down the street, meeting people as they got closer to the center of town.

"Jenny!" called a voice. They turned toward the running man. "I have something for you." He reached into his pocket and grabbed her hand.

"Hey!" protested Mark.

"It's okay," said Jenny, and held out her hand.

To Mark's surprise, the man put a large gold nugget into her hand.

She didn't seem surprised as she grasped it and put it into her pocket. "Thank you," she said and leaned to kiss his cheek.

"There is more to get! I will see you soon, Jenny."

"You do that!" They watched him run off.

"Who was that?" asked Mark.

Jenny laughed suddenly and said, "I have no idea."

"But… he gave you gold," he protested.

"Oh, that!"

"Yes, that!"

"They do that all the time. The men will come up to me at work or in the street and give it to me."

"Give you gold for no reason?"

"Yes, evidently it is lucky."

He thought about that as they walked. He stopped her and asked, "What do you do with it?"

"I am saving it up."

"For what?" he asked curiously.

"I am not sure."

"Will you stay here?"

"At least through the winter," she allowed.

"That is May."

"Yes, winter will be coming soon." She looked over at the man who she'd looked for every day. "Did you find a claim for Mr. White?"

"I did, and I need to hire people tomorrow."

"When will you be going to the claim?"

"Why does everyone keep asking me that?" he complained, rubbing his hand through his hair.

"Who is everyone?" asked Jenny. "Helen?"

"Yeah."

"Are you still with her?" She let the question hang.

"Yeah, maybe, I don't know. She told me to go to the claim."

She had heard the rumors about Helen but didn't think it was her place to tell him. She let the silence settle around them. She finally said, "I will miss you. Come see me when you get back."

He smiled and said, "That is what I like to hear. You will be my first stop when I get back," he promised.

Me, she thought, *and not Helen.* She smiled back. "Want to continue our walk?"

"I do." He accompanied her back to the gambling hall. He said regretfully, "I need to get going. I have a long day tomorrow."

"Yes," she said softly, wanting him, wishing he could give her a kiss goodbye.

He surprised her when he leaned over and kissed her softly.

She looked at him in surprise. He seemed surprised he had done it as well.

He stepped back and said, "Well, I…"

"Bye, Mark. See you soon." She turned and entered the gambling hall.

Suddenly, he felt cheerful again and whistled on his way home. *Tomorrow,* he thought. *I will get the men I need and head to the mines.*

He got to the cabin he now shared with Ed and tried to open the door. *I forgot it's the only house in Dawson with a lock*, he thought and laughed. He knocked and waited. Ed called, "Who is it?"

"It's me."

"Oh!" The door lock could be heard opening. The door swung open and Ed said, "Sorry, I should have given you a key."

"That would be nice," said Mark. He looked around in surprise. The place was clean. "Ed," he said, "you didn't have to do that."

"Yes, I did," he argued. "I need to live and work like the businessman I have become."

Mark looked around, impressed at the difference it made.

"I saved some dinner. Would you like some?" Ed asked.

Mark said, "Funny you should say that. I haven't eaten yet."

"I put on beans, bread, and got some ham."

"That sounds amazing." He went to the table and Ed bought over a covered plate.

Mark took the plate off the top and said sincerely, "This looks wonderful!" He ate it quickly, helped with the dishes, and went to his bed.

CHAPTER 29

$\mathcal{T}$he morning came quickly, and he made his way to the hiring hall. He had a table and a list of positions he needed in front of him. The lines were already forming. Men who thought gold would be on the ground had accepted that, if they were staying, they would need jobs.

Mark wanted experienced men—he wanted men who knew how to not only build the sluice but to stay and use it. Each man was asked many questions. Many were from California and as far away as Sweden. So, many had to be turned away. When he told them no, he watched them slink away, their disappointment apparent.

The next man sat down. "Tell me about yourself," said Mark. "Have you mined for gold before this?"

"My name is Harry Morgan and, yes, I am from this area of Canada and I lived in Dawson at the beginning of the stampede."

Mark frowned. "I'm surprised you are just now looking for a position."

"I worked several claims, but I was called home. My wife was sick." He stopped talking.

"I hope she is better?"

"No," he said and wiped his hand under his eyes. "She passed. Mr. Sutherland..."

"Mark, please."

"Mark, I need something to keep me busy."

"Tell me how to build a sluice," Mark demanded.

Harry started to explain immediately. "They are wooden boxes about fifteen feet long and are used to wash dirt that is dug up from the streams. The main thing is to have enough water to wash through; to do that, we could create a dam to build up the water. Once built, we can use rockers and move the boxes back and forth like a cradle. The goal would be to create the separation of mud and gold."

Mark laughed suddenly and said, "That sounds like what I observed on my trip to the claim. We do have another miner just up from us who said he wouldn't mind us reviewing their methods."

"That is good to know."

"What I really need," said Mark, "is a second in command, someone to help guide the men."

"Will there be extra pay?" he asked.

Mark grimaced. "Not initially, but I will see what I can do."

Harry went very still and asked suddenly, "Does that mean I have a job?"

Mark reached out his hand, and Harry took it in a firm shake. "Yes, Harry, I am looking forward to working with you."

When he started to stand, Mark asked, "Would you like to join me for the rest of the interviews?"

Harry smiled and looked relaxed for the first time since he had sat down. "I would."

"Then move to this side of the table," he said, indicating the chair next to him.

He moved over quickly. Mark explained, "We are looking for experience. Non complainers."

"Are we only looking at a few months' work?"

"No," said Mark consideringly. "I am thinking we build cabins as well as set up operations to make it through the winter."

"What are you thinking about when the ice sets in?"

"I have heard that the ground can be lit on fire and that we can keep going during even the coldest months."

He looked over at him and said, "That will allow us to hire quality men. Most wouldn't have wanted to be out of work by November."

"I think we can make it work."

The interviews started and Harry jumped in to ask questions about the details of building a sluice and mining. Their typical questions were: "Can you mine in cold temperatures?"

The first answered with, "I am from California, but I am here, so I want to stay."

Harry watched him closely and then turned to Mark and nodded.

Mark looked at him and said, "Okay, you are in."

They were on to the next man in the line. In a few hours, they had the twenty men they wanted, each with experience that would help them be successful. They asked them to stay around until the interviews were completed. After they had set their list, they called them over. Mark asked, "When can you be ready to leave?"

"Now!" several men shouted. Another said, "We need to get out of here and get the sluices built before the cold sets in."

"I need everyone to leave tomorrow. We can meet here to start."

"What about the wood and supplies"

"We will leave in the morning. Bring all the supplies you can carry with you. We can help each other out. We will send men back over the next few weeks to move the rest of the supplies."

"Where will we live?" another man asked.

"We will also be getting the wood moved up for cabins. We will take down trees as needed."

"How are you going to accomplish that?" one of the men asked.

"We work for Mr. White. He has said, for all of the extra work, there will be a bonus."

A cheer went up. Mark hoped they would be as happy in a month. It was hard work, and winter was fast approaching.

Several men from his group approached him about getting hip waders. "Go to the mercantile and tell them to put them on my account. I will settle up there as I finish here." They nodded and headed out. Harry said, "Hang on, I will go over with you!" He looked at Mark. "I will see you there."

Mark nodded and continued to sit for a long while as he organized his notes. He had received a pack from Mr. White that morning, who wasn't feeling well and didn't want anyone at the house. His note confirmed he had the wood for the sluice and shelters on the way to the site. By the time they get there, it should all be in place. He also included the first months' salary and a bonus for all of the men. Mark would keep that with him. He wouldn't mention it until payday.

He closed his notebook and started to leave when he noticed a man had walked up to him. It was one of the first men he had interviewed. He looked like he had slept outside the hall and probably had.

"I am sorry," said Mark apologetically. "We have chosen the men we need for the job."

"I need the job. I have nothing else."

Mark was truly sorry; he understood some men were suffering. Many had spent all of their money to get there and could not afford to leave. He started to stand when the man pulled out a gun. Mark sat back down hard into his chair. He held up his hands. "Wait, you don't have to do this." He kept his eyes on the man, hoping someone had run to get the Mounties.

The gun shook as he pointed it at Mark. "You... you... should have hired me! I would have worked hard for you!"

Mark stayed silent and watchful as the man continued to talk.

"I have nowhere to go, nowhere to stay. My supplies have been stolen." He started to cry.

Around them, people stayed still, watching it play out. The door burst open and two Mounties charged in and grabbed the man. The gun fell to the ground. Mark retrieved it and handed it to the authorities.

They took the destroyed man away. "What will happen to him?" asked Mark.

"He threatened you with a gun and is dangerous. We will put him in jail." Mark nodded, wishing this wasn't happening.

"You will need to come down and make a statement."

"I will do that," he promised.

There were too many unknowns when working the Yukon without men he could rely upon. Mark looked around at those still in the room. "Who ran for them?" No one answered. "Thank him for me."

He shook his head and made his way out. Store first. The store was down on the right. He entered and found three of his employees and Harry there. "Mark! Did you get hurt?" Harry asked. They had heard something was happening at the hiring hall after they departed.

"I am okay. A person thought I should have hired him."

They looked at each other. "Yeah, there are desperate people here." They knew that could have been them in another month if they hadn't gotten the job.

"Thanks for these," said Jim, and the other two men nodded.

Mark nodded and paid the cashier. "You need the right supplies. The water around here is already freezing and we don't want anyone to get sick."

The three men took their gear. Jim spoke for them and said,

"We will see you early tomorrow at the warehouse." They had decided that would be the best place to leave from.

Harry stayed behind. "Do you need anything else from me?"

"No, just be ready to leave in the morning."

"I will! Thanks for the opportunity!" He left and looked like a different man than he had seen that morning.

Once he paid, the next stop was the Mounties. He needed to give his statement. The station was at the center of town. The door opened readily and he entered. The man at the desk said, "Mr. Sutherland, thank you for coming in."

"You mentioned I need to make a statement."

"Yes, sit down." They went over the entrance of the gunman.

The Mountie shook his head and said, "I am concerned we will be seeing more of this as winter sets in."

"I was also thinking that. Are there plans for people who cannot leave?"

The man sat back and said, "We have worked on that. We will be moving them into the larger venues to keep them from freezing to death."

"And food?" asked Mark.

"Your partner Ed has volunteered some supplies."

Mark was thinking. "You might check with Mr. White."

"We have," he said. "He declined to help."

Mark had hoped that wasn't the case, but he wasn't surprised. He asked, "The gunman, will he go to court?"

"Yes, it will happen quickly."

"I am headed out tomorrow. Will I be needed?"

"No, I don't think so. We have your statement and plenty of witnesses to the events."

"Good." He started to go to the door when the Mountie's words reached him.

"I don't think he would have used the gun. It wasn't loaded."

Mark said, shocked, "It wasn't?"

"No, he just felt he needed to make his point."

"Will that make his incarceration less severe?"

"It should, but I am going to recommend he stays put here."

Mark frowned. "Why?"

"He will have somewhere warm and safe to stay. Also, we don't want others to think we go soft on something like this."

"I see." And Mark did. There were a large number of people in town who might react badly to the man being let go.

"Thank you for your help."

"That is what we are here for," he said laconically.

Mark nodded and exited the offices. The day had moved into late afternoon. He needed to pack and confirm his supplies were ready for the trip. The cabin was empty when he returned; Ed had given him a key that morning. He went directly to his room and pulled out the packs he would carry.

He started to pack and noticed a note on his bed. He picked it up and frowned as he read it. It was more instructions from Mr. White. *Why doesn't he want to see me?* The note confirmed the supplies were on their way. Mark just shook his head at the man's behavior. Setting it down, he finished his packing.

Next, he would need to write articles on the claim, environment, hiring of the men, and the big adventure. He again tempered his articles with less romanticism and added the realistic elements of mining in the Yukon. He wrote until that evening, getting things organized. He also sent a longish letter to his family and a last one to Enzo. It would be a while before he got back to town.

With the task completed, he placed them in envelopes and addressed them. He had not received any mail yet and he hoped some would get through before the ice started.

"Are you here?" Ed called and Mark heard a door slam.

"I am. I will come out." He went into the main living area. He held up his letters, "Mind dropping these off for me?"

"Just leave them, I will make sure they get off on one of the ships. Were you successful?" Ed asked, moving to the icebox and pulling out sandwich stuff.

"I was. I got a manager and twenty men."

"Any trouble?"

"Some." He described what had happened and his conversation with the constable.

"I am worried that we may have more and more trouble as the ice sets in," said Ed.

"That is what the Mounties are worried about."

"I will continue to work with them. Maybe the support will help with the desperation."

"Ed, I won't be here to help. Will you and Sam be okay?"

Ed paused in his sandwich making and said, "We will be fine. The agreement was I run this while you work for Mr. White. We will make it work." He finished compiling his sandwich and said, "Make yourself one and come relax with me."

Mark did just that and joined Ed for dinner.

Later that evening, they were sitting by the fire and a knock could be heard at the door. Ed looked at Mark. "Are you expecting anyone?"

"No." Mark watched Ed pick up a gun as he approached the door.

Mark stood quickly. "Are you expecting trouble?"

"Sam wouldn't come over this late unless there's a problem." He leaned on the door and called, "Who is it?"

"I'm Harry Morgan. I'm here to see Mark Sutherland."

Mark put a hand on Ed's arm. "He's my new manager."

Ed nodded and walked back into the room, putting the gun on the table next to him.

Mark opened the door. "Come in."

Harry walked in and said, "It's the supplies. We need a central storage location." He'd checked in with each man to see where their supplies were being managed.

"That's a good point. I should have thought about that. We

may have to delay for a few days and move the supplies somewhere safe."

Ed spoke up. "Have them bring them to the warehouse. I'll
keep them separated. That way, you can access them as you
need to."

Harry looked relieved. "I'll let the men know. Can we bring
them over tonight? The plan is to leave early tomorrow."

Ed sighed a little. He had already settled in for the night.
"Sure. Why not."

He, Mark, and Harry headed to get the wagon and horses
from the warehouse. They worked the next few hours moving
the supplies. Once everything was done, they went to their
respective homes to get as much rest as they could before they
left the next day.

CHAPTER 30

*M*ark got up early and ate a quick breakfast. He tried to be quiet and was surprised when he heard Ed's door open. His friend was pulling his suspendered pants over his long johns. Ed yawned. "Ready to go?"

"Just about. Thanks again for last night," Mark said, biting into the bread. He chewed and sat as Ed poured himself some coffee.

"We're partners. I help you and you help me." Ed frowned. Something was on his mind, but he didn't want to bring up the topic. However, Mark needed to know what he'd heard. "Mark, I didn't have a chance to mention something to you."

"What's that?"

Ed's face was set into serious lines. "Helen and Mr. White..."

"No, don't," said Mark. "That's just talk."

"Are you sure about that? They're always together and, when you aren't here, they go to dinner and shopping. I don't want to see you get hurt."

Is *he right? No! Maybe?* Mark thought. "I'm not sure how I feel, honestly. I'm confused," he confessed.

"Does Jenny add to the confusion?" asked Ed intuitively.

Mark's face turned red, but he didn't comment. Ed let it go.

Mark gathered his gear and, on his way out, without turning, he said, "Can you watch out for Jenny?"

"Jenny and not Helen?" Ed asked.

"Yes," he said and went out the door.

Ed sat back and took a long gulp of coffee, considering the changes that had occurred since Mark had returned.

CHAPTER 31

$\mathcal{M}$ ark headed to the hiring hall and, as he approached, saw that his men had gotten their supplies and looked cheerful and ready to go.

He grinned. "Everyone ready to start looking for gold?"

A cheer went up. Mark saw that each man was in their waders, same as him. The moved to the marshes, the first step to the claims.

Harry took over from there. "Men, we'll follow in a line through the marshes. You'll want to see how the man in front of you moves. We're not in a hurry; the water's cold, and we don't want to lose anybody."

The men listened and followed his directions. Harry took up the lead, and Mark brought up the rear. There were some slips initially, but thankfully no one went into the water. Their claim would take over two weeks to reach, and the group stopped at points during the trip for eating and sleeping.

Mark realized on the second day that they were near Ben's claim. "Men, I'd like to stop for the night near here. A friend has a claim, and I'd like to see how he's doing."

The men were agreeable and Mark looked at the map the

man at the office had made for him. They found it readily and saw Ben knee deep in the water. "Ben!" called Mark.

Ben looked up from his pan and, seeing who it was, grinned broadly and waved him over.

Mark turned to Harry and said, "Go ahead and get everyone settled. I want to talk to Ben."

"You made it back," Ben said. "I didn't know if you'd found a claim or gone home."

"I found a claim. I heard at the claim office that you set this one up quick."

"Yeah, it's just me, so it'll be slow going initially."

"Show me around," Mark requested.

"Not a lot to see. I have a cabin and an operating sluice."

"But you still pan?" Mark asked.

"I just can't seem to help myself," he admitted.

"Find anything yet?"

Ben leaned in. "I have. Not a lot, but enough for me to stay." He looked over at the men setting up a camp nearby. "That your crew?"

"Yeah, lots of experience there. I hope you don't mind if we spend the night here?"

"I'd love the company," Ben assured him.

Mark went to help with camp and, after dinner, they met up again.

Ben saw them off the next morning. "I'll come see you in a few weeks. See how you're getting along."

"That would be great!"

They continued on and pushed to make it to the claim by the end of the week. The men were tired but excited to be at the location they would live and work. "Let's get our tents set up and get some coffee," Mark said.

CHAPTER 32

$\mathcal{T}$he men started their first day by being separated into two groups: one to start building a cabin and the other to evaluate the area to determine the size and shape of the sluice.

The evaluations were completed and the building materials reviewed. Mr. White had gotten them enough wood for a sluice, but Harry thought they should fell trees for the cabin. Mark agreed and walked down the path the sluice would take. It would be hard work, but necessary.

They were there on a hunch that there was gold. He shook his head; they were dreaming. He finished his dinner with the men. That first night, they were all falling asleep in their dinners.

During the next few days, Harry worked on the design for the sluice box, mainly a separator. He was happy he had finished wood to work with. The men followed his directions so that the box being built would be nonmoving and would use gravity and the flow of the water to make the final separation. "What're these?" one of the men asked, looking at the drawing.

"They're layers under the box called riffles. It's like panning but on a larger scale," Harry said.

"Hmm. I have an idea on how this might work," the man responded.

Mark and another group of men were felling trees around the site where the cabin would be. They had laid a wood floor from the leftover wood as an outline and started by notching the logs so they would interlock. He gave the men plenty of breaks and tried to keep up their morale. The projects came together at the same speed. Once the walls were up, they used the leftover materials from the sluice to add a roof. Next would be getting mud to fill in cracks in the walls and roof.

Mark headed over to the sluice and heard Harry giving directions. "Place it at a shallow part of the river. Don't submerge the device; you might lose the point of separating sediments and, eventually, the gold as well." Harry had thought to bring a mesh with them and that would be good enough to capture even the smallest particles of gold. "As we go, we'll make adjustments. We're lucky that we have all the water flow we need." He looked up and down the stream. "We'll need to do the same for any claims downstream of us."

"Yes, we should be fair." Mark walked around the sluice. "What's the large rock for?" he asked. He'd seen the men moving it into place earlier that day.

"To prevent the sluice from floating off," Harry said with a grin.

"Yeah, I'd hate for all of that work to float away. How do you know you have the optimal flow of water?"

"There should be enough water flowing through the sluice to keep it clean, and the riffles shouldn't become buried under the sand. Sand is the enemy."

"When do you think we can get started?"

"Tomorrow morning, we test it."

"Then, tonight, we rest."

Mark looked around the area. He saw they'd need additional cabins but, for now, they had shelter and a way to start looking for gold.

Both crews would be on hand to make adjustments to the sluice.

CHAPTER 33

The next day, all the men were there to move the sluice into the optimal position. They diverted the water and, when the initial digging for the mud started, the men complained. "The ground's frozen! The shovels won't go through!"

"I'd expected that," Harry said. "We'll need to section off areas to burn and get the soil softer so we can dig."

The men from California began grumbling and Mark spoke up. "We have to understand this isn't the soft soil of California and we may have to take extra steps here to retrieve the gold."

They nodded and looked a bit ashamed.

Preparations were put in for the fires, and they were able to load their first mud into the sluice and have the water start the separation.

The anticipation for the first nugget was high. Most of the men jumped in to get the sluice working. Harry watched happily at the flow of water and the separation that was taking place.

A few hours later, Mark had started to send the men on shifts for lunch. He stayed and continued to watch the operation. Harry was watching closely and checking the screens. "Dam the water!" The men moved quickly and Harry reached in. He pulled out a nugget as big as his knuckle. "I think we have gold!"

"Whoo hoo!" one of the men yelled and threw his hat in the air.

Mark ran down to see and grinned. "We've found gold!"

"That we have," said Harry, tossing it in the air. The men who had broken away for lunch ran down to them.

"Where is it?" one called.

Harry held it up. The men clapped and grinned. It had been hard to get here, but now they knew they'd be staying. Harry felt the need to warn them. "We'll have good and bad days." The men nodded; this was just the beginning.

Mark took the gold and weighed it on the scale that Ed had sent with him. He opened his accounting book to document the size and ounces. He moved it to a lockbox, similar to Josh Sullivan's.

That evening, a messenger came from Josh's camp. "Please come." The request wasn't unusual. Josh had asked Mark to visit almost every night since they'd arrived.

"Tell him I'll be there." The man nodded and left.

"Josh again?" Harry asked. "What does he want?"

"I think he's lonely," Mark replied. *And probably worried about his brother's possible visit.*

CHAPTER 34

*M*ark finished dinner and walked to Josh's camp. The area was still posted and now fenced. He took his brother's upcoming visit seriously. The guard nodded at him, and he continued to the cabin. The guard at the door said, "You can go in."

"Thanks." Mark entered and saw Josh sitting by the fire darning his socks.

Josh grinned at him holding up the sock he was working on. "Mining's tough on clothes."

Mark nodded. Since he'd gotten to the Yukon, he had holes in most of his shirts.

"I'm glad to see you. I heard you found gold today."

"News travels fast."

"Gold news does. You were lucky to be able to hire experienced people."

"I was lucky," he said, "to get someone from the area to help manage the claim."

"How is Harry?" Josh had known Harry when he worked the areas.

"Better, I think. It was tough on him, losing his wife."

"Work will help him heal."

Josh saw Mark still standing. "Take a seat. I could use some company."

Mark's view since he'd entered was Josh's right side. As he got closer, he saw the left side of his face, the bruises on that cheek were now visible in the firelight. "What happened? Were you hurt?"

"Yeah, that's why I wanted to make sure you came over tonight."

Mark started to tease him that he came over most nights but saw that Josh's jaw was set. He sat, ready to head what happened.

Josh started. "I didn't tell you why I let you have that property."

"No," he acknowledged. "I wondered about that; it seemed logical that you would just increase your operations."

"Yes, that would have been logical, but I like the size of my operation here."

Mark nodded.

Josh continued. "Then you confirmed what I'd heard—that Jerry was here and on his way to me."

Mark frowned and leaned forward. "Is he the one who did that to your face?"

The other man put his hand to his cheek briefly. "Yes."

"Why would he do that?" Mark asked. Then he recalled Jerry's violent nature.

"He wants my gold."

"Did he get it?"

Josh smiled, then moaned in pain. "No, he didn't."

"What happened?"

"He showed up here with his friend, and I told my men to let me talk to him in private. When he lost patience with me, he attacked me. My men had to come pull him off of me. They took him and his friend far away with warnings to not return."

"But you think he will?"

"Oh, I have no doubt he will. Jerry hasn't changed since he was a boy in New York."

"Why come all the way here?"

"When he's desperate, he heads my way looking for money."

"And what's your normal response?"

"The last time I let him in on my business, he destroyed it and me."

"What type of business was it?"

"Property investments. I scouted the property and Jerry dealt with the investors. He used to be more personable than he is now."

"It sounds successful. What happened?"

"We were very successful," he confirmed. "Everything was going well until I found out that Jerry had sold the same property to many people. Before I could get the money back, he'd hightailed it with all of it, leaving those people without any savings." Josh went silent as he continued to work on his socks. "Mark, I want to ask you a favor."

"Sure, anything."

He grinned briefly. "You probably need to wait for me to tell you the favor first."

Mark grinned back, secure in the knowledge he'd be able to help him.

"I need to make sure that, if something happens to me, that the gold is used to pay those people back."

"Are you expecting something to happen to you?" asked Mark seriously.

Josh ignored the question and said instead, "I have a box here that's for those investors Jerry cheated." He indicated the pile of wood. "The box is hidden there. It'll close out my debt."

"You want me to take it to them?"

"Yes, I need to have this off of my conscious."

"I think I'd rather make sure you make it and give it to them yourself," said Mark firmly.

Josh shook his head. "I have everything written down." He laid his socks down on his side table and reached for his book. A piece of paper had been torn out. He handed it to Mark. "Read this."

Mark read the paper. It covered the gold to be given to the investors, but it also left the still operating mine to Mark. "You're leaving all of this to me?" he asked in disbelief. "You hardly know me."

"Yes, but I do trust you."

"I don't know what to say."

"Say yes, so I can have my mind set at ease."

Mark finally nodded and said, "I'll sign, but you aren't going anywhere."

"That's what I'm afraid of," Josh murmured.

Mark didn't know how to respond to that. "I think we need a witness."

"I've thought of that and my foreman said he'd do it for me." Josh went to the door and called out, "George!"

A lanky man ran up and took off his hat. "Yes, sir?" He looked at Mark. "It's good to see you."

"You too."

"We have that paper ready for you to sign," Josh said. Mark handed it to him.

George took it and signed quickly. He'd already been briefed by Josh on his wishes. Each man would receive an allotment and a bonus if they stayed on after Josh was gone. Mark signed next and then Josh. Mark looked at the final document and back at Josh. What had he gotten himself into?

CHAPTER 35

Gus
Gus sat in the heat and dust, watching the oil rig pump oil. It would be time to find another job soon. He lifted his canteen and took a long drink. As he lowered his arm, the paper in his jacket crinkled. He looked down at it and pulled out the article Mark had sent him. *Gold,* he thought. He'd never been motivated by money, but the adventure of the Yukon sounded intriguing.

The letter from Mark detailed the struggles of traveling to the Klondike. He studied the list that was part of the article and thought, *I can get this organized if I plan.* He reached back to the table and picked up a map of the US. *If I can get a wagon and horse here, I could move throughout the country, working and buying supplies as I go. By the time I reach Seattle I'd have everything I needed for the trip.*

He looked back at the article and saw the main issue would be the steam ticket. He'd have to see if he could get that purchased ahead of time.

Joe walked up to him and looked back at the oil field. "We did good."

Gus followed his gaze and saw many working rigs. He said, "Yeah, I believe we did." He'd stayed on after Mark left, but now felt it was time to leave.

Joe shook his head before he turned back to Gus. "You're ready to move on," he guessed.

"I am," he commented.

"You've done a great job here. We could make a place for you in management."

Gus looked down at the papers in his hands. "No, I think I have someplace to be."

"If that's the way you feel about it."

"It is."

"Then stop by and pick up your last check."

"Instead of my check, could I take a wagon and horse?"

Barney looked at him, considering. "You can have the wagon and horse as a bonus for your work with us, along with your check."

Gus smiled and said, "I knew I liked working for you."

He laughed. "I'll get them ready for you. When do you plan to leave?"

"I reckon tomorrow would be as good as any."

"Tomorrow. Okay then. If you're ever back this way, come see us." Barney stuck out his hand.

Gus shook it. "I'll do that."

Joe turned to leave, but his curiosity had him turn back and ask, "You opened the mail from Mark. Why?" He'd been surprised when Gus asked about a letter from Mark Sutherland.

"Mark was all about the next adventure and asked me to consider the Yukon next."

"The Yukon!" exclaimed Joe. "Alaska!"

"No, I think it is actually in Canada," corrected Gus.

Joe gave him a long look and finally said, "Let me know where you end up next, in case I need to get in touch with you."

"I will," Gus promised.

The next day, the horse and wagon were readied and Joe hand delivered his pay to him.

"This means a lot to me, Joe."

He watched Gus climb on the seat and pick up the reins. "Just where are you headed?"

Gus looked forward and finally said, "I'm heading north from here and stopping whenever I need the work. Eventually, I think Seattle, and then the Yukon."

Joe said, "Good luck in your travels."

"Thanks again," Gus said and clicked his tongue at the horse to get her moving. A slow steady pace kept him going across Indian Territory. The first state he would enter would be Missouri.

CHAPTER 36

M *ark*
Mark walked back to the edge of Josh's claim with George. "What do you think about this?" he asked the foreman, raising the paper they'd both signed.

"It's what he wants," George said simply. "He's a good man."

"Is he safe here?" Mark let worry color his tone.

"We'll do what we can to keep his brother from getting back into the camp." He grinned suddenly. "I think we'll have time."

"Why is that?"

"Jerry was walking funny when he left here. He'll need time to recover."

Mark nodded absently. "Be careful. He's rather stupid, but can cause lots of trouble. Let me know if you need help."

"We will."

Mark left the camp and returned to his own. He kept looking at the document as he walked. He needed to get this away from here. He needed to send it to someone he trusted. *Gus.* That would put it in safe hands and, if his friend indeed headed to the Yukon, then he'd return the document to him at that time.

When Mark got back to the camp, he called Harry over to him. "Can we send one of the men back to town to mail some letters?"

"The men would like that. Let me tell them. We can send Jason tomorrow with the mail."

Mark walked to the cabin. He told the men the plans for the following day. They immediately started writing letters to family.

Jason took the mail the next day. Mark caught him. "Remember, don't stop to talk to anyone. These have to get in the mail."

"Yes, sir. I'll avoid all to get there and return the same way."

CHAPTER 37

*G*us
Gus pulled out the list of supplies and reviewed the required items. It would take time to build the list, and he would have to work to buy the items. *And the food,* he thought. *That will have to come last.* Bad weather could ruin food-stuffs. He'd also have to wrap them well before leaving Seattle.

His trip started October 1st, and the weather grew colder as he traveled north. He stopped and layered on his shirts. He thought about that list and decided the warm clothes would be the first thing he needed. The wind started to push at them; the horse slowed, trying to get through. *We need shelter,* he thought. Lights could be seen in the distance. "Just a little more, Myrtle," he called.

The lights were a small town, and the first place he passed was a barn and blacksmith. He jumped down and walked quickly to the door. He knocked loudly and a voice called out, "Come in."

Gus stepped in and the voice barked out, "Close it behind you!"

Gus did as he was told and commented, "That storm rolled in quickly. I need a place to board my horse for the night."

The man sitting at the counter and wearing a heavy apron looked over. "I have room in my stable. That'll be a dollar a night."

"Can I stable her there now?" Gus didn't want the horse outside any longer than necessary.

"Yeah, I'll open the doors for you. Do you need feed?"

"No, I have some with me, but water would be nice."

The man nodded and stood up. "Meet me by the stable doors." Gus went out into the storm, unhooked Myrtle, and walked her to the stable door. When they got there, the door opened and the man waved them in. Once inside, Gus got Myrtle settled with water and feed.

The man once again waved for Gus to follow him back into the office. "You're new to town. I haven't seen you before."

"I'm passing through. I need to gather supplies for a long trip. I'm Gus Lopez," he said and reached out his hand.

The man shook it and said, "Martin Meed. What kind of things are you needing?"

Gus pulled out the list and showed him.

Martin whistled. "This will be expensive."

"I know. I was hoping to get work on the way to pay for the majority of them."

Martin frowned down at the list and then at Gus. "Got any experience as a blacksmith? My guy just ran off, wanted to get married or some such nonsense."

Gus looked around. "I haven't been one before, but I'm a fast learner."

He looked at Gus' stocky build and large arms. "I'll give you a chance. You can start tomorrow."

Gus thought, *My first step. It's still a long way to go, but I'll get there.*

CHAPTER 38

Mark

"Boss?" Harry inquired.

Mark continued to work on his accounting books. He said absently, "Yes?"

"Boss!" Harry said more urgently.

Mark reacted to his tone and stopped his work. He looked over at him. "What is it?"

"I have some ideas for our winter mining. Can you come outside?"

"I can." Mark stood and followed the foreman. Harry pointed up the hill from the creek. "Does the claim go into the valley gravel up there?" he asked.

Mark followed his finger and reached into his back pocket for the claim map. He traced the location. "Yeah, that's part of our claim. I thought the water was the most important for gold. What are you thinking?"

"The sluice and panning are slowing down as the cold starts setting in. I think working in that area will allow us to keep mining through the coldest of months. It's going to be shaft mining."

"I've heard something about that; another miner mentioned it to me."

"The area up there has the potential to hold more gold than the streams."

Mark and Harry walked up to the area they were talking about. Mark stomped the ground. It was already hard. "How would this work?"

"There's two steps: bringing the gravel containing gold to the surface and then separating the gold from the gravel using water and gravity separation. We'll move the men to this area and start controlled burning of the ground, then we alternatively burn and dig a shaft."

"How much will the ground thaw when burned?"

"About fourteen inches, then we dig and repeat until gold is found."

"Once it gets deep, will we need to build supports to protect the men?"

"The permafrost will make this unnecessary. However, the air might be bad, so we'll need to make sure gasses don't build up. The cool air should drop down and renew automatically."

"What then?" asked Mark, thinking.

"We'd be able to work all winter here and, when the water thaws and starts to flow again, we use the sluice to see if we find gold."

"It would be a gamble," Mark said.

"A good one, I think. We're near a successful mine and we've spotted gold in the water by panning."

Mark nodded decisively. "I think you're right. Let's continue with the sluice and do as much as we can. Once the ice starts, we move up here."

"Should we walk it out and pick a spot now?"

"No," said Mark. "I don't want anyone to know that we'll be staying. Other miners will start to leave and we'll stay behind."

"Can I let the men know?" Harry wanted them settled on the fact they were staying through the winter.

Mark thought about that. "Tell them we're firming up plans to stay through the winter. We want to keep this between us for now. I also need to confirm the plans with Mr. White and get payment for the men."

Harry nodded. "Let's get back to it."

Their day wound down. Each man had a job for dinner at night. Mark's chore was normally gathering the wood for the stoves. They had two set up, one for heat and one for cooking. Mark also made the bread—flat bread that could be eaten for days and wouldn't require time to rise. They had beans and the occasional game that got into their traps. There was also fish sold by the local Iniut, though that had slowed as well. There were no vegetables; they ran out quickly. The food was filling but not too exciting.

The men finished dinner, and everyone was settling down and talking low amongst themselves about various topics. Harry stood and Mark called over to him. "Going out?"

The foreman looked distracted when he replied, "Yeah, I'll be back soon."

Mark nodded and went back to his reading. The lamp light was bothersome, but it was the only time of day he had to read.

Harry stepped outside and pulled out his wallet. What he wanted was there. It was a letter, tattered from repeated folding and unfolding. It was the last note his wife had written to him, asking him to come home. He walked to a tree and sat down; he didn't need the light. He missed her so much. During the day, he could push the memories back but, at night, they overwhelmed him. He took deep breaths and closed his eyes.

CHAPTER 39

*G*us
Gus worked as a blacksmith apprentice for the first month. The job was something he enjoyed, and the blacksmith Martin and his wife Hannah had become friends. They knew his plan was to work across the states gathering supplies.

They were sitting together after dinner one night when Hannah asked him, "Gus, can I see your list?"

"Sure," he replied. "I have it here." He pulled it from his pocket. He referenced it several times a day.

She reviewed the list and looked over at him. "You mentioned you'd like to travel through different states gathering these materials?"

"That's the plan."

"Where did you spend most of your time before this?" she asked.

Martin sat back, tapping his tobacco into his pipe and then lit it as he listened to the conversation.

"Mostly south," Gus admitted.

Hannah listened to the wind blowing through one of their

first cool air bands coming from the north. "I think you need to stay here. Most of this can be gotten in the area."

"How do you plan on moving the supplies?" Martin asked.

"By wagon," said Gus. He listened to the wind and thought about Myrtle.

"Not in this weather," Hannah said.

"The best way would be by train," Martin said.

Gus thought about what they suggested and said, "I think that could work."

He sent his new address to Barney in case Mark sent any mail. He wanted to have it delivered to him.

And the mail did arrive.

"Gus?" Hannah called.

"Yeah," he said over his shoulder. He was moving the hot iron into water to cool the metal.

"You have mail."

"Yeah, I hoped you wouldn't mind. I wanted to see if my friend Mark had sent any letters giving me details on what to expect on the trip."

"No of course not, but could you come over to pick it up?"

He frowned and wondered why she didn't just leave it there. The work took up his attention and, when he had a break, he walked to the house. He knocked on the door and heard Hannah call him in. He entered. "You mentioned mail?"

"Over there." Hannah indicated with her knitting needles. She sat in her chair, paying attention to her knitting and the baby playing on the floor.

Gus walked to the small pile on the table. He looked and saw none were for him. "I don't see mine."

"Oh, not that one," she said. "Check that bag." He looked around for a bag and noticed it by the door.

"Is it on top?"

"No, it's the whole bag. Take a look inside."

He pulled on the drawstring and saw mail piled inside the

foot tall bag. He pulled out the first few letters and continued to dig through, seeing his name on each.

"How long since you received your mail?" Hannah asked, laying down her knitting.

"Been a few years, I guess," he admitted, looking down at his past. He could hear it yelling at him to pay attention.

"Looks like you have a lot of reading to do."

He looked a little faint at the amount of mail. "Yeah, I'll take these and look through them after work." He took the bag back into his room and went back to his job.

It was hard to get his mind off of the letters, but his job required absolute concentration. He didn't want to accidentally injure himself, as the recovery time would push back plans. At the end of the day, with work completed, he went back to his room.

Before he could delve into the bag, he heard a knock. He opened the door and saw that it was Martin with a plate of food. "Hannah wanted you to have this," he said. "She figured you wouldn't want to leave the mail once you got started."

Gus smiled slightly and took the plate. "She's right."

Martin could tell Gus wanted to be alone so he said, "Tell us if you need anything."

"Thank you." He watched Martin leave and the door closed behind him.

Gus walked back to the bag, poured it on the floor, and sorted the letters into three stacks. Ones from Mark went in one stack; what appeared to be letters from a bank went in another. The final stack was letters from Martha and Isaiah Ball. The stack from them was much taller than the other two.

Mark first, he thought. He picked up the first letter and opened it quickly. It was newsy and told him that people were disappointed that the gold wasn't just lying in the streets. When they arrived in Dawson, it was a tent city and many people refused to leave the barge. They couldn't deal with the reality of the actual place. Claims were limited and many men were working other claims and not their own. *Things are changing quickly here,* Mark wrote. *Tent buildings are now actual buildings with solid walls and roofs. The weather is changing quickly and ice will be blocking the steamer paths soon.*

March, thought Gus. *That will be when I'm able to get to Dawson. This is reality and not a fantasy.* He'd read the journals that Mark had left, and it had been clear that the work was hard and rarely did one strike it rich. A few did, but most didn't. He understood that going was an adventure, but also hard work. And he didn't plan on making it rich. He looked at the letter again, happy he'd received it.

There was one letter from Joe. He opened it and it said simply, "It's time." Gus knew what he meant; it was time for him to face his past.

Yes, it is, Gus thought.

The next stack appeared to be from a bank. He moved those to the side.

He stared at the last stack from Martha and Isaiah for a long time. He shifted through the stack and placed them in date order based on postal markings.

Letter one: *House built. Crops planted and cattle started. House and land are secure.*

Gus had sent money from each of his jobs to pay for security on the house. The man he paid kept an eye on the house when the Balls were sleeping. He couldn't have them suffer the same fate his family had.

Letter two was more good news. Martha was going to have a baby. He held the letter to his chest and cried for his wife and son and for Martha's future child. The last line said the same thing the first letter did: *Partner, any time you want to come home, we're here.*

Letter three was more newsy: crops, cattle sales, the birth of their baby. This news made Gus happy. Additional letters after this one listed two more births.

Gus read years' worth of letters, learning all he could about the Ball family: the children's names, their successes, failures, happy times and sad. The next letter, he gripped harder when he realized what it said. Martha's family had come after them again. They had tried to buy their land and when they wouldn't sell to her father or her brother, they tried to burn them out again. Though, this time, the security man spotted the invaders around the house spreading fuel. This time, the men were caught and gave up who'd hired them.

The trial went differently this time; Martha's mother and sister-in-law testified against their husbands. Martha's mother was angry that they'd tried to kill her child and her grandchildren. It was time for this to be over. The two Wilson men went to prison for thirty years. Martha's mother and sister-in-law chose to sell their property to the Balls, so instead of losing their property, they'd gained extra land around them. The two Wilson women had decided to leave and go back east where their extended family had remained.

He crushed the letter to his heart crying tears of joy. "It's finally over!" he shouted to the heavens.

Gus looked down at the letter again and read the last line. It was different from all of the letters before. *You can come home now,* it said.

He fell to his knees and cried again. He cried for his dad, his mom, his wife, and finally his small son, Benjamin. It was finally over. *Is it still home?* he wondered.

He wanted—no, he needed—to go back. The trip would take a few weeks by train to get there and back again. He started to stand and remembered the last stack from a bank. He picked them up and studied them. They looked to be from a bank in Texas. Frowning, he opened that one first. It was a bank account in his name. The first letter was when the account opened, and there was a small balance. As he opened each of the annual statements, the amount had increased or decreased over time. The final statement showed a high balance. Gus was stunned; he never meant for Isaiah and Martha to open this account for him. He wasn't sure how he felt about it. He needed to talk to them.

It's time, he thought, *time to go home.* He wanted to see where his family had been laid to rest.

He left his small house and walked to the Meed's door and knocked. Hannah opened it. "Gus! We didn't expect you." She saw his face and asked, "Are you okay? Is there something you need?"

"Can I come in?" he asked quietly.

"Of course." Hannah walked over to her chair and sat down. "Is this related to your mail?"

"Yes. I wanted to let you know that I need to head home for a few weeks."

"Home?" She looked at Martin. In the months that they had known Gus, they had never heard him talk about his home before. "I saw some of the letters were from Texas. Is that your home?" she asked tentatively.

"Yes, I need to take care of a few things. Can you do without me for a while?"

"You do what you need to. We'll be here," Martin said.

"There will always be a place for you," Hannah told him. Martin nodded his agreement.

Gus nodded, grateful he had found people that he could call friends. "I'd like to head out early tomorrow." The weather was mild and clear today and he wanted to take his horse.

"We look forward to hearing from you. Would you like me to fix you some food for your trip?"

"That would be wonderful, thank you." Gus was distracted, thinking about the trip in front of him.

"Stop by here in the morning and I'll have your food ready," directed Hannah.

Gus shook Martin's hand and nodded at Hannah.

The next day, he was at their door as the lights came on.

Hannah pushed her hair back into a bun with a pin and said, "Come in, I set everything up last night."

"Thank you."

When he didn't say anything more, she asked, "Are you nervous?"

"Yeah," he said.

She took that as the final words and finished putting his food into a bag he could take with him. She handed it to him. "We'd like you to come back to us."

"I plan to," he said as he took the bag and started to leave.

"We'll continue to work on your list!" she called to him.

He turned back and put a hand in his pocket. "Here's fifty dollars. I've been saving for it. Will you take this for me?"

"I will," she said, and took it.

He was grateful for the help. He headed out and found Martin had pulled up the carriage and hooked Myrtle up. "I'll give you a ride to the station." Even by train, the trip would last a week. "Will you be okay in third class? We can see about getting you to first or second class."

"No," Gus told him. "I'll be fine."

They headed to the station and Gus stepped down with a nod to his friend and took his bags. He boarded the train, settled in third class, and waited for it to leave. The scenery went by and Gus stared out the window, seeing nothing. Everything was a blur. All he could think of was what Isaiah and Martha had said: "Come home." Is *it home?* he thought. *I don't know.* He didn't know how he felt about returning—nervous?

The week went by faster than he expected and, when he left the train, he hesitated and thought to reboard and leave. There were too many memories here. The people disembarking pushed him down the steps, helping him make his decision.

I need a horse. He headed to the ticket office to ask about one. The clerk had been adjusting his files when Gus walked up. He looked up at him and his eyes widened. "Gus!"

"Gregory," Gus acknowledged. He'd known the man right away. They'd grown up together and had been friends. Gregory had been one of those so-called friends who had disappeared after his family was killed.

"I need a horse," Gus prompted.

Gregory waved to his left. "The smithy has some. You remember where that is?"

"I do. Thanks." Gus started to walk off.

"Have you come back to stay?" Gregory called to him.

That stopped Gus, but he didn't turn back to him. "I'm not sure," he said and then continued outside.

Once outside, Gus was shocked by what he saw. When he left, the town had a single dirt road with a few buildings. Now, as he looked all around, he saw the town had changed as much as he had in the past ten years. Businesses lined both sides of the long street. Banks, mercantile, grocers, a drugstore—everything a much bigger city would offer, all with a sidewalk connecting everything. He continued to marvel at the changes when he found the smithy. A sign declared there were horses for rent. He entered and the transaction only took a few minutes, and he was on his way to the ranch.

He rode at a steady pace, expecting to see the same things he'd left behind. He reached the entrance to the ranch and slowed the horse down to read the gate. The sign read: L&B Ranch -- Gus Lopez and Isaiah Ball proprietors. They'd included him on the name! Tears started to form, and he shook them off. He got down from the horse and opened the gate. He walked his horse through the opening and closed it behind him.

He climbed back on the horse and increased the pace to the house.

He didn't know what to expect; the picture in his mind was of his burned-out house. A shape appeared in the distance; it was a large home. It looked cheerful, white and blue, and as he got closer, he saw that there were bushes and roses surrounding it. Crops could be seen from the house and the barn still stood to the left of the house.

He slowed his horse and he heard a child's voice call out, "Ma, someone's here!"

Gus got off the horse and stayed in the shadows, waiting and not approaching the steps.

Martha walked out the door, wiping her hands, and asked the child, "Someone's here? Who is it?"

Gus stayed where he was and called over, "Martha. It's me."

Martha frowned over at him and blinked slowly. She couldn't believe her eyes. It was Gus! She took off running toward him, and he caught her in a fierce hug.

"Mommy?" a small girl of about four ran up and pulled on her mom's dress. "Who's that man?"

Martha ignored the question. "Richey," she called to an older boy of about eight. "Go and get your pa!"

"Who should I say is here?"

She hadn't taken her eyes off of Gus. "Tell him Gus, our partner, is finally home."

The boy ran to do as his mother asked. Gus watched him run to the barn. A few moments later, Isaiah and Richey ran out. The older man had a grin on his face that almost went ear to ear. He stopped abruptly in front of Gus and held out his hand. "Welcome home."

Gus felt the sting of tears and didn't wipe them this time. The two men hugged.

"Why don't we go inside," Martha said, wiping her eyes with

her long apron. "Kids, come with us. I want you to meet your Uncle Gus."

Gus' eyes spilled over and he said, "I want to know everyone's names."

They went in and Gus looked around. The floor plan was similar to his previous home. There was a large, open living room and the kitchen was on the far side. A large fireplace was the centerpoint of the room.

Isaiah and Martha planned to give him some time to get settled, but their three-year-old had other ideas. "Uncle Gus!" she called out as she ran up to him. She'd heard about him her whole life and, having him here in person, she couldn't hold it in.

Gus picked her up, laughing. "And what's your name?"

"It's Beth."

"How do you do?" Gus had read the letters over and over again and knew each of the children's names. He looked at the other kids, pointing to each and said, "You'd be Jonathan, and you'd be Anne."

Martha and Isaiah smiled; Gus had made their kids' day.

"Kiddos, why don't you run and play? We need to talk to Uncle Gus," Isaiah said.

"Ohhh, do we have to?" the kids whined.

"I'll be able to spend time with you later," Gus told them.

"Do you promise, Uncle Gus?" Beth wheedled.

"I promise."

This mollified them, and the kids went upstairs to play. An argument started as they were climbing the stairs, and Martha called up a warning.

"Gus, sit down. How long have you been on the road?" Isaiah asked.

"This time, a week by train," he said.

"We didn't know you were coming. But we hoped. We always hoped," Martha said. Isaiah nodded in agreement.

"I got your letters," Gus said, looking down at his hands.

"Which one?" she asked, knowing they'd been sending them for the last ten years.

"All of them," he admitted. "I avoided getting my mail."

"On purpose?" she asked intuitively.

"Yes, I just felt that I had to keep going to the next thing."

"We're glad you finally stopped and got the letters," said Sarah.

Gus reached into his bag and pulled out the bank statements. "I also saw these."

Martha and Isaiah looked at one another. "We're partners," Isaiah said, "and partners share in the profits."

"But cattle and crops don't bring in money like this. There's way too much money here." The first statements had made sense to him; the money in the account had risen and fallen based on weather and other factors. Ranches could make or lose money over the years. The last few years, the money had only continued to build. "Why's there so much?"

Isaiah looked at him and simply said, "Oil."

"Oil? Where?" Gus hadn't seen any derricks.

Isaiah sat back in his chair. "They're way in the back. We didn't want to hurt the cattle or contaminate the water. We've kept it limited."

"This is real then?"

"It is."

Gus sat back in his chair, shocked.

"Would you like something to eat?" Martha asked.

"Please."

She went to the kitchen to give the two men some time alone.

"You got them? The Wilsons?" Gus asked in a low voice.

"Yes."

"How did it finally happen?"

Isaiah started to explain. "The tension between us had been

building. They wanted your land, and we had it. When the oil was found, they tried to do the same thing as what they did to your family, burn us out."

"Was everyone here?" Gus asked, his expression blank.

Isaiah reached over and took Gus' hand. "No, I had prior warning that something might happen. The security guard helped us get out to a safe place before anything started."

"Thank god," Gus said, gripping his friends' hands. "Tell me all of it."

"Martha's mother and sister-in-law stepped up and testified. They decided that they couldn't be part of another family being destroyed. They met and got word to me. We got them out and set them up."

"Was there any damage?"

"No. We stopped the two Wilsons and the current sheriff took them in."

"This time, they didn't get let out?"

"No, the evidence was conclusive."

Gus lifted his eyes up and prayed to god, thanking him for this outcome. He didn't think he could lose this family in this manner. He forced himself to ask the next question. "What happened to her mother and sister-in-law?"

"They've moved back east. We gave them a fair price for the land and homes."

"You said the two Wilsons were put away for thirty years. Is that a guarantee?"

"There's no guarantee," Isaiah admitted, "but the land is ours by deed. The town has also built up, so we have more law enforcement."

Martha was listening at the door, and when there was a lull in the conversation, she pushed it open. "Gus, I have sandwiches and a beer for you."

"Thank you," he said gratefully and walked into the kitchen.

He sat at the table and quickly ate his food. When he finished, he took a long draw on his beer. "That was good."

"Have you come to stay?" she asked. "We have a room here for you."

"Or one of the houses. We can help you fix it up," Isaiah offered. He hoped his friend would come home.

Gus sat back in his chair. "I'm not sure where home is for me anymore."

Martha reached over and said, "It is always here with us."

He didn't say anything.

"We don't expect anything, but we would love for you to be a real uncle and part of all of our lives," Isaiah said.

Gus' eyes filled with tears. "I want that also."

"Then stay," they both said at the same time. They all laughed.

He took a deep breath and said, "I have one more adventure in front of me. Will you be a little more patient with me?"

"We'd wait forever if we thought you were coming home to us," Martha said. Isaiah nodded in agreement.

"Tell us about your next adventure," Isaiah said.

"The Yukon."

"Canada," Martha said, her eyes wide. "That's so far away. Why there?"

"A friend is up there and I want to go up and check it out. I met him when I was in Oklahoma."

"What were you doing there?" she asked. She was interested in where he'd been the last ten years.

"Working oil wells," he said laconically.

They heard that and laughed until they cried. "Oh, my goodness," she said, nearly out of breath. "What a coincidence."

"Yes, I have done that work off and on."

"What else have you done?" Isaiah asked

"Working with cattle movements, general handyman work, and lately working as a smithy."

"Wow," Martha murmured.

"And when those jobs ended, I just moved around until I found the next one."

"And now you want to go to the Yukon?"

"Yes."

"What does that involve?"

Gus pulled out his list and handed it to them. They looked over the list. "Why so much?"

"There's a danger of clearing supplies out of the areas that need them and a danger of starving to death."

"That makes sense. But why are you headed there? You'd only worked with Mark in Oklahoma."

"It's this," he said, pulling out one of Mark's letters. "He didn't just send me a letter; this was also included." He pulled out another piece of folded paper and opened it.

"What is it?" Martha asked.

"It appears to be a will, leaving a gold claim to Mark."

"Why would he send that to you?" asked Isaiah, moving closer to read it over Gus' shoulder.

"The letter said he needed it somewhere safe and was counting on me joining him in the Yukon."

"There must be a reason Mark thought he needed to get it to someone he trusted."

"I agree, and I'll be taking this with me." Gus folded the will back up and returned it to the envelope.

Martha whispered into her husband's ear. "Yes," he said and kissed her quickly.

"Gus, would you like to see the oil wells?" he asked.

"I would, and the other changes you've made." They stood up to leave.

Martha stopped them at the door. "Isaiah, make sure you go by both houses and see if Gus might want one of them." She looked over at Gus. "For when you move back permanently."

Gus nodded and said, "I'd like that."

They headed out to get their horses. "Oil wells first?"

"Sure."

They started and the land was so familiar to Gus that he didn't speak as they rode. The property was spread out and the oil wells were a long distance from the house. They saw them from a distance and Gus asked, "Only three?" The oil fields he'd worked at had many more.

"I don't want to ruin the land," Isaiah said. "We'll have them take what they can from these three."

Gus looked over and saw the barrels. "You have transportation issues," he commented.

"Yeah," he admitted. "We're waiting to find out if we'll send them by wagons or rail."

"They paid you for your mineral rights?"

"We're leasing it to them. So, the rest is up to them."

"I'll be here to help with this."

"I'd like someone who knows what they are doing. Would you like to go see the houses?"

"I would… but first, I'd like to see my family."

Isaiah nodded. "Martha thought you might. Come with me." They turned the horses around and headed back. He led them toward a grouping of trees overlooking the stream below.

They brought the horses to a stop and, as they stepped to the ground, Gus said, his voice low, "This is exactly where I would have chosen."

"I'm glad," Isaiah said simply.

They walked over to a small gated area. There were four stones.

"I'm so sorry that I left you to manage all of this," Gus said quietly.

"No, we wanted this for you. I think we were always meant to be partners, family." He watched Gus and asked, "Would you like some time alone?"

"No, please stay. I've been running from this, and now I see they're at peace." The graves were well tended and, even in the cooler weather, flowers were placed on them.

"Martha and the kids come up here once a week and tend them." The tears fell and Gus wiped them away. "Would you like to see the houses?"

"The east one, please. I like that land."

"Let's head over there." They crossed the land, and he pointed out the cattle and crops.

"How many hands do you have working?" Gus asked, thinking about the future.

"Five."

"Where do they stay?"

"We've turned one of the barns into a bunk house."

"Why so close?"

"For security. We converted it with some of the money you sent."

Gus nodded.

When they got to the house, Isaiah asked, "Would you like to go in?"

"No," Gus said, looking at the house. It would need paint and work on the porches. He could guess the status of the rooms. "Tear it down."

"Tear it down?"

"Yeah, I'd like to design my own home."

Isaiah looked at the house consideringly and said, "I think we can make that work. If you draw out what you want, I can have it built before you return."

"That would be amazing."

"Let's go to the house and we can map it out. "

CHAPTER 40

*G**us***

They hugged, and the kids cried.

"I'll be back, I promise."

"We're holding you to that," Martha said.

"The house will be waiting for you," Isaiah said.

Martha hugged him again.

Gus said with a thick voice, "I have to get on the train or I'll stay forever."

Martha cried and let him go. The little family watched as he boarded the train and continued to watch as it pulled out, taking Gus away again. Though, not for long.

CHAPTER 41

*M*ark
  The cold was moving in quickly, and the permafrost was thickening. There was less and less water in the creek, and the ice had to be broken up and melted for drinking. Every day, they fought the freeze and used fire to thaw the ground. They burned a shaft down to bedrock. The frozen muck was removed by pick, shovel, and windlass. The system worked best in the winter, when the temperature difference between the air in the shaft and the surface created a good draught. In warmer weather, the smoke could be dangerous. They had piles and piles to work once the weather warmed up and the water started to flow again. There had been no additional interaction with Jerry and Wade.

Mark sat by the stove one night and thought, *It's odd I haven't heard from Mr. White.*

CHAPTER 42

*G*us

Gus got back to his job and life with the Meeds as a smithy. Hannah and Martin had worked on his supply list and he found his house filled with supplies when he returned. He settled back and waited for the ice to melt.

CHAPTER 43

*M*ark   "How long will you be?" Harry asked, watching Mark pack his duffel.

"Not long. I need to update Mr. White on the gold we've found."

"Will you be warm enough?" They'd worked through the heavy winter and hadn't left the mine. Mr. White had managed to get them supplies, so they were able to keep working. The cold had reached a point where even the shaft work couldn't be done.

"I'll take my time and stop at the camps on the way."

Harry nodded. "If it gets to be too much, come back."

"I will."

Mark was excited to head back to Dawson. It was March and the ice was finally starting to melt. There were shelters along the way where he could stop. He left the men, who were talking together and waved him away.

The trip was slow, but necessary. He brought his accounting books but left the gold behind; it would have been too heavy to carry.

The last few months had been hard work, and he continued to see Josh each night; Jerry hadn't shown up since he'd been run off. Josh's face had healed and he seemed happy.

Mark thought about the will. He knew that Jerry would be back. *I wonder why we haven't seen him. Maybe he froze in the cold.* That thought made him happy as he continued to walk. The trip took more than a week, and extreme conditions caused him to take shelter whenever he could find it.

The town could be seen in the distance. He wanted to go to The Dominion and see Jenny first. He had missed her, but his duty forced him to head past the establishment to Mr. White's home. The accounting books he had with him weighed heavily in his bag.

The snow was falling again, and he could barely see as he approached Mr. White's door. He raised his hand and beat heavily on it. The wind had picked up, and he wanted to get to shelter. The door opened quickly and, surprisingly, it was White himself.

"Yes, who is it?"

Mark pulled down his scarf and said, "Sir, it's me." His eyes widened and he looked quickly over his shoulder.

"Let him in, Henry."

Henry? Mark thought.

White stepped back and allowed him in. Helen came up to him with a large towel.

"Why don't you get the snow off here and hang your coat on that peg," she said.

He did as she directed and followed them into the living room. The fire was lit and the room was warm. Mark watched as Helen went to sit down and picked up some knitting. White took up the chair next to hers. Mark frowned.

White broke the silence and asked, "How's the mining going? Has there been more gold?"

"Yes, I have the accounting books with me."

"And the gold?"

"When spring comes and the ice melts, we'll transport it to you."

"Good. Please hand me the books."

Mark reached into his bag and pulled out the four books. "I made daily entries of the findings; the weights are also listed."

"Yes, we'll need these to figure the taxes to the Canadian government."

"Of course."

"Can I keep these?"

"Yes, those are for you." Mark didn't mention it, but he had a full set back at the camp.

White stood and walked to his strong box to gather the payroll. As he handed it to Mark, he said, "I included your pay there as well. You more than made up for the trip cost."

"Thank you, sir."

"Will the men stay and start again in the spring?"

As Mark counted the money, he said, "The bonus provided here will allow me to keep them on."

They finished business and Helen spoke up. "Henry dear, I'd like to speak to Mark in private."

White looked over and saw her set face. "Yes, of course."

Mark watched him leave. *Dear?*

"Mark, sit down, please," she said.

He walked over to the chair the older man had vacated and sat.

Helen smiled suddenly and said, "I didn't recognize you."

He reached up and stroked the hair on his face. "Yeah, it's the beard. There's not a lot of shaving going on at the claim."

"It looks good on you."

"Thank you." He had so many questions. The last time he'd seen her, she'd been very upset. "How have you been?"

"Me? I'm fine."

He looked around the room and saw some of her items. A

shawl she had worn on the ship was spread on the back of the settee. Pieces of decorative glass were placed around the room.

Helen looked and saw what he did. "I married him, Mark."

He didn't say anything; he just looked forward.

"Mark?"

Finally, he turned to her and asked, "Is that the reason for…"

"My amorous attention the last time you were here?" she supplied.

"Yes."

"I was growing closer to Henry, and he offered me set plans for the future."

"And I didn't." He felt a loss but was unsure what else he felt. *Regret? Relief?*

"I didn't do this to hurt you."

He remembered what Jenny had said about Helen and that she'd spotted this back on the steamship. He could tell Helen wanted him to play a part and gracefully accept this. He decided to go the other way. "When did this start?"

He had veered off the script, and she seemed to be unable to answer. Finally, she said, "Here, of course."

"Are you sure?" he pressed. "I seem to remember your being with me and also seeing Mr. White."

"I only helped him get his meals or spent time playing cards with him," she said, admitting to the contact.

Stupid! he thought. *Jenny was right all along.* Mark shook his head and started to stand.

She stopped him with her hand on his arm. "Mark, I do have feelings for you."

He looked down at her hand. "Then I feel sorry for Mr. White." He shook off her hand, stood, and went to the door. She hadn't moved from her spot and watched as he pulled on his heavy gear.

"Mark, will you come see me in the spring?"

"For what reason?" He didn't turn around and said over his shoulder, "Tell White that I'll continue to run the claim."

"I will."

Stepping out, he pulled up his scarf and pushed against the wind. Once back on the main road, he looked left toward the warehouse and right toward the gaming room. He turned right. Jenny was who he wanted to see now.

Mark trudged the final steps to The Dominion. He remembered that they'd be offering shelter during the winter months. "Close the door!" came a yell from all corners of the building. Mark did as they asked and pulled his hat off and dusted off his beard. He stroked it; it would have to go, but for now it kept his face warm.

"Mark! Is that you?"

He turned to the familiar voice. "Jenny!"

She walked over to him and reached out a hand to stroke his beard. "What's this?" she teased.

"Face protector," he said with a smile, happy to see her. He'd been surrounded by men for the past three months and she was a welcome relief.

"Mark, did you come straight here?" she asked, watching him closely.

"I went by Mr. White's first. What's happening here?"

"We turned it into a shelter once the freeze took hold." She took his hand. "Come sit."

He allowed himself to be led to an area where mattresses were laid on the floor. They sat on one and Jenny asked, "Did you talk to Helen?"

"Yes. When did they marry?"

She kept his hand in hers. "Just after you left to go to your claim."

They could hear the wind picking up outside. She looked out and said, "You might stay here tonight... with me." She saw his frown and hastened to assure him. "We'll only share a room, nothing else."

He wasn't sure what nothing else entailed, but he could think of nowhere else he'd rather be. "I would love that," he said sincerely.

Jenny smiled and let him up to her room. No one said anything as they walked upstairs. Her room was down the long hall. They heard some of the other girls entertaining in their rooms. She opened her door and waved him in, closing it behind them. The room was cold, and he was happy to see it had a fireplace. He went directly to it and started to build a fire. While he was working on it, he heard her moving around the room.

He heard the springs on the bed as she sat. "Will you go back soon?"

"Yeah, I need to take some supplies back and pay the men."

"What are they doing in this weather?"

"Mostly inspecting the sluice and checking the area for anything out of place."

"Are you worried about something happening?" she asked.

"Do you remember Jerry and Wade?"

"From the steamer?"

"Yeah. Have you seen them around town?"

"Not in a while," she admitted. "They were thrown out of here for cheating early on, and Wade got to cut wood as his fine."

"Really?"

"Yeah, Commissioner Walsh determined the best way for him to pay for his crime was to cut wood for our shelters."

He nodded and asked, "And Jerry?"

"As usual, Wade took the blame."

"So, once again, no consequences for him."

She nodded.

"There has been more trouble from them. I'm working a claim near Jerry's brother."

"This is the one Jerry said would take him in and share his gold?" she scoffed.

"That's him. Jerry's already started trouble and was run off from there also."

"Be careful." She studied him, "You came here instead of your cabin? Why?"

"You've been on my mind since I left," he admitted.

"Me and not Helen?" she asked, looking down at her hands.

He reached over and took her hands in his. "Look at me." She lifted her eyes to his and he said, "You."

"Want to get ready for bed?"

"Yeah, it's been a long day of walking."

"You go first," she said. "I can wait."

He took out his clothes and toothbrush and headed to the bathroom down the hall. He was able to get in and out quickly. He entered, drying his wet hair, and was wrapped in a robe.

"Your turn."

Jenny nodded and grabbed her things and headed down the hallway.

Mark settled in the bed and smiled when he saw she'd rolled a blanket up and placed it down the middle.

The lights were out when she returned to the room. She laid down her dress, slipped out of her robe, and got into the bed.

She didn't say anything and lay on her back. *I'm finally where I want to be.* She turned to the rolled-up blanket. *Well, almost.* She had an overwhelming urge to throw the blanket across the room. Did she dare?

Her hand went to the barrier to grab it and, instead of wool, found Mark's hand.

"Wanna get rid of this?" he asked.

"Yes!"

He pulled the blanket out from between them and tossed it across the room.

Laughing, she rolled into him.

He kissed her long and hard. Leaning back, he asked, "Is this what you want?"

She pulled him back to her and kissed him. "More than anything."

Later, she laid with her head on his chest.

"Wow," he said.

"Yeah." She smiled.

"We could have been doing THAT all this time?"

She giggled. "I think we would have had to take breaks to work."

"Well, none of that now!" he swore and pulled her on top of him.

CHAPTER 44

"It's morning," she said softly.

"Ugh. Is it?" he asked. "How can you tell?" he murmured into her hair.

"The men downstairs."

He heard the noise. It sounded like... he didn't know what it sounded like; he just knew it was loud.

"Is it like this every day?"

"Since the jobs dried up and the river iced over, we've had a full house."

He got up, pulled his pants on, and picked up his shirt. He looked over at Jenny sitting up in the bed, with the sheet just pulled over her breasts. It was a picture he wanted to keep with him. The room was quiet as he finished getting ready. He packed his bag and turned to her as he ran his fingers through his hair.

"Are you getting up?"

"Yeah," she said. "I need to help with breakfast."

When she didn't move, he asked, "Is something wrong?"

"No." But she still didn't move.

Concerned, he walked over to her and sat on the bed. "Something is wrong."

Instead of addressing that, Jenny asked instead, "Are you going back to the claim today?" Her head was down, her fingers twisting the edge of the sheet.

"I am. I need to stop by and check on Ed and Sam, and then I need to get back." He didn't mention the payroll he carried.

She nodded and leaned back on her pillow with her eyes closed.

Mark touched her cheek.

Her eyes opened at that.

"Tell me what's troubling you," Mark said.

"When you return, will we be together again? Or was this because you were upset about Helen?"

He took her chin and turned her toward him. "This was never about Helen. This is between me and you."

"Is there a me and you?"

"Yes, I think so."

She wiped her eyes and said, "I need to get ready for the day." She turned away from him and dropped her sheet as she wrapped a robe around her.

"Are we okay?"

She looked back at him. "If it's just the two of us, then yes. We're okay."

"I have to get moving," he said. He didn't want to leave if she needed him.

"I know, be careful." She walked over, leaned into him, and kissed him on the cheek. She left the room to go to the bathroom.

Mark took his bag and headed downstairs. As he descended the stairs, he saw that the men were up and milling around. A number waved over to him as he walked toward the door.

At the door, he stopped and put down his bag. He pulled on

his heavy coat, scarf, and knit cap. Next were his gloves. Only his eyes were visible through small holes as he exited. The storm had died down and the wind was not blowing. If it weren't for the ice, the cold would've been almost manageable. Making his way carefully down the icy streets, he headed toward the warehouse.

It stood at the end of the street and, as he got closer, he saw a sign on the door. Closed until spring. *Hmm*, he thought. *I wonder if supplies are low*. He changed direction and headed to the back. The cabin was to his right and the warehouse to his left. He lifted his arm and banged on the warehouse door, then walked over to knock on the cabin door.

Both doors opened at the same time—Sam at the warehouse and Ed at the cabin.

"What do you want?" asked Ed.

Mark lifted his mask and revealed his face.

Ed called to him, "Come in! Sam, close that door!" Mark went into the cabin. "Welcome back!" he said as he helped Mark with his bags.

After Mark unwound the scarf from his face, he said, "You closed the warehouse?"

"Take off your coat and I'll explain." Mark removed his coat and set his scarf and bag to the side of the door.

"Did you travel overnight?" Ed asked.

"No, I got back last night."

Ed's eyebrows raised. "Hmm, and where did you stay?" he asked with a smile.

"I went by Mr. White's."

He shook his head. "I told you before you left that there was something there."

"I know, you and Jenny caught on before I did. You don't have to keep rubbing it in."

Ed looked at him and observed, "You don't appear to be all that upset."

"I'm not. I think I saw something last time I was in town that

266

gave me some doubt about her feelings."

Ed stood and went to pour some coffee. He held up the pot. "Want some?"

"Yes, please."

Ed came back, handed a cup to Mark, and sat down to drink his own. "So... you didn't mention where you stayed last night."

"I stayed with Jenny," he admitted.

"Oh?" Ed broke out with a wide grin.

"Yes, and don't you tell Jenny I mentioned it to you," Mark scolded his friend.

"Who, me? I'm the soul of discretion," he said, still grinning. He'd known for a while that Jenny loved Mark.

Mark looked around and asked, "Now, tell me what's happening with the warehouse. Did we run out of supplies?"

"Why don't we go over and take a look?"

Mark nodded and followed Ed over. He had a lot of money wrapped up in this investment, and he needed to know he wasn't going to lose it all.

They opened the door and ran as quickly as they could over to the warehouse. Ed banged on the door and Sam opened it. He stepped back quickly to let them in.

"Follow me."

Mark did, and they went into the main room. It was fully supplied. "What?" he asked, looking around. "Why are we closed?"

"You need to tell him," Sam commented.

"Tell me what?"

Ed sighed. "Once the ice set in and the men were laid off from the majority of the camps, they came to town and spent their money. It was getting rather desperate, and we spoke to the commissioner. That's about when The Dominion was set up as a shelter. The food distributions started to go through the Mounties directly to the shelter. We no longer had a need to stay open."

"And..." prompted Sam.

Ed sent a long glance at Sam. "And... you remember Jerry and Wade?"

"Yeah." Mark thought about what Jenny had said about their cheating at The Dominion and being tossed out.

"Well, they came here and tried to break in."

Sam took over. "They broke down the door and attacked Ed, demanding money."

"I was fine."

They broke your arm!

Mark swore under his breath. Now that he remembered, he'd noticed Ed hadn't used his arm when he served him coffee. "Is your arm okay?"

"The doctor says it'll be fine, eventually."

"How did you get away?"

Ed looked at Sam and said, "Sam got out the back and got the Mounties."

"Are Jerry and Wade in jail?"

"No, when they realized Sam had gone for the Mounties, they left."

"They just left?"

"Yeah, the Mounties have a reputation. Wade had to cut wood as punishment for the incident at The Dominion and I don't think he wanted to do it again."

Mark nodded and asked, "When was this?"

"Around Christmastime. Why?"

"Jerry's brother sold me the claim next to him. You remember what Jerry said on the *Leah*?"

"Yeah, that his brother would give him gold and share his claim with him."

"Well, it didn't work that way. Jerry beat up his brother and then his men gave him and Wade a beating and ran them off."

"Have they shown back up?"

"We posted people to watch each night, and Josh's crew

monitors the perimeter. Have you had any trouble here since then?"

"No."

Mark nodded and frowned, stroking his beard.

"What's bothering you?" Ed asked.

"Where are they? Once they left Josh, it sounds like they came back here. And now?"

"I have no idea, but they're probably up to something. Will you stay for a few days?"

"I can't," Mark said regretfully. "I have men waiting for me. I have their pay." He looked at the time. "I need to head out soon."

"Wait," Ed said, "have you eaten?"

"No, I haven't," Mark admitted.

"Come to the cabin and eat first, then you can head out."

"Sounds like a plan."

They went back to the cabin, and Ed put together a breakfast of beans, bread, and meat.

"Every time I eat this meal, I miss home more and more," Mark murmured.

Ed grinned. "What, you don't like my cooking?"

Mark said, "No I *love* it."

"Oh, shut up and eat your breakfast," Ed said, smiling at his friend.

They both finished and Ed gave him meals for a few days. "Will that be enough?"

"Yeah, I plan on stopping to see Ben Jones. I should be able to get a meal there." Mark got his coat and hat on and wrapped the scarf around his face and pulled on gloves.

"Be careful. Stop frequently to rest."

"Yes, mother."

Ed smirked. "Jackass."

"I promise to be careful," Mark said sincerely as he headed out into the cold and back toward camp.

CHAPTER 45

*M*ark walked through the frozen marshes, and the pace he set was slow but necessary. He came upon camps that had been busy and working before the ice set in. Now, they were mostly empty. Some people were still there, managing the claim until the spring thaw happened and they could return to mining.

Three days into the trip, he was close to Ben's place. He'd meant to check in with him earlier but had stayed busy with his claim. He went over the hill and saw Ben's cabin. *There should be smoke coming from the chimney.* Concerned, he headed that way.

With Jerry and Wade still around, he slowed down and studied his surroundings. If Ben was here, he'd have checked to make sure his sluice was in working condition. He went down to the stream. The sluice was in pieces. *That isn't right.* There was no sign of digging in the area.

The cabin was next. Mark walked over to it, and as there were no windows, he leaned against the door, putting his ear to it but didn't hear anything. Finally, he knocked and it opened under the pressure. "Ben?" he called. "Are you here?" The inside of the cabin was as cold as the outside. He left the door opened to allow light in. The small cabin had two rooms; in the first room, the table was turned over, the chairs on the floor, and the small kitchen had cabinets that had been torn off the walls. Mark walked through to the other room and called again, "Ben!" The second room was the bedroom, and it was in the same state of disrepair.

Where is he? Is he alive? Should I stay and try to find him?

The wind was starting to pick up again, and Mark looked around regretfully. *I have to get going. It isn't safe here and I have the payroll.* He went back out of the door and made sure it was secured. From there, he kept to himself and continued walking until he couldn't walk anymore. By the time he got back to camp days later, he hadn't slept and had only stopped when needed.

CHAPTER 46

*G*us
Gus boarded the steamship in Seattle and saw the same things Mark had: crowds of desperate people trying to board and get to Dawson. He hoped the ice was melted enough to get all the way there with his supplies. He watched the crowds recede in the distance as the ship pulled out of Seattle. *I'm on my way.*

CHAPTER 47

M *ark*

It was dawn but still very dark when Mark finally arrived at the claim. He was struggling with fatigue and forced his legs to continue moving forward to the cabin. The men were still asleep when he entered. He walked over and collapsed onto his bed. Hours later, he felt a hand on his arm, shaking him. "What?" he asked, trying to open his eyes. When he finally was able to focus, he saw George, Josh's foreman, there next to him.

"Mark! You have to wake up!"

"What's going on?" he asked in a groggy voice as he struggled to sit up.

"It's Josh, he's been attacked."

That woke Mark up. "Was it Jerry and Wade?"

"Who else would it be?"

"Where is he?" He hadn't removed his pants or shirt before he laid down and walked over to retrieve his coat, cap, and scarf.

"In his cabin. We've patched him up, but it's bad."

"Do you need us?" Harry asked.

Mark shook his head. "No. Stay here for now. We don't want those two in the camp. Have the men walk the perimeter. And take guns."

"I'll make sure."

Mark and George headed out at a fast pace and arrived at Josh's claim in a short time. The guard at the door moved away so they could get in. When Mark looked around, he didn't see Josh.

"Bed," George said.

Mark hurried to the bedroom. He found Josh there, holding his stomach and curled up on the bed. "It's a gut wound," the foreman said.

Gut wounds were a sure way to kill someone. The state Josh looked in and the blood on the clothes showed he didn't have much time.

"Josh," Mark said. "What happened?"

"It was Jerry," Josh said with a grimace, holding out his hand to Mark.

Mark walked over and took it. "Why did he do it?"

"I wouldn't tell him where the gold was. That gold has to get back to the people who were cheated."

Mark knelt down next to the bed. "It will," he assured his friend.

The held off tension drained out of Josh as he heard Mark's words. He kept a grip on Mark's hand and settled back on the bed.

"Would you like anything?" Mark asked.

"No, I don't have much time now."

"No! That's not true! We'll pack you up and take you to the doc in town," Mark said and looked over Josh's shoulder to where George stood. The foreman shook his head. Tears started to form in his eyes and he shook them off.

Josh started talking about how much he enjoyed his life in the Yukon, the people he'd met, the work—rambling in his delirium. A few hours later, Mark and George pulled the sheet up over his head.

"What do we do now?" Mark asked.

"You do as he asked. You get that gold out of here and to those people."

"Jerry and Wade are probably watching for that."

"Probably."

Mark went to the wood pile where Josh stored the gold for the investors and took it out. "There has to be a way," he muttered.

George nodded. They both looked at the box. "I have an idea," Mark said.

Once the plans were formed and the gold packed up, Mark took his heavy bag and walked to the door. "I'll be back and we can work out how we want operations to run."

"That'll be good." George knew Mark was in charge now.

"For now, contact Harry if you need anything."

"I will."

"Thank you," Mark said sincerely.

"Thank you," George replied.

Mark nodded and left the room. He was accompanied by the men from Josh's camp.

Harry met him at the perimeter. "How is he?"

"Dead."

"Oh no! What happened?"

"Jerry and Wade. What else?"

"I kinda figured as much." Harry saw that the bag Mark carried was bulky and appeared to be very heavy. "Do you need help with your bag?"

"No," Mark said. "I have it."

"What now?"

"I'm headed back to town. We'll need the Mounties. Jerry and Wade are still around and I think they're going to cause more trouble."

Mark walked inside, washed up, and got a filling breakfast. The payroll was distributed to the men. Cheers went around at the size of the bonus.

The gold at their camp was locked in a box and under the floorboards of the cabin, so he knew Jerry and Wade wouldn't find it easily. Now, he just needed to get Josh's gold to a safe place.

CHAPTER 48

*M*ark started out and, an hour into the trip, he heard a branch breaking behind him. He stopped, pretending to drink from his canteen. As he expected, the sound stopped. There was someone following him. He wanted to stay ahead of whoever it was. The further he went into his trip, the worse the weather was becoming. The winds tore at him, but he persevered. He needed to get back to town. Josh deserved justice.

Whoever was behind him was increasing their speed. He held tightly to his bag and started to run blindly. There was a ravine nearby; he slowed and found it, staying close to the edge. The snow continued and he could feel the ground dissolve under him; he tumbled down into the ravine. As he fell, jagged limbs tore at his clothes. By the time he stopped, he'd lost his scarf and his jacket had been torn open. As he lay in the brush, the rain felt like frozen drops on his face.

He heard voices from above.

"Do you see him?"

"No!"

After a few minutes, the voices slowly rescinded. Mark lay

his head down in the brush, then slowly pulled himself up. Everything ached but nothing seemed broken.

Up or down? The men following him may expect him to go back up, so the only way he could go was down. Hours later, the snow had started to melt, but there were now mounds of ice. It still covered everything. Oddly, he felt he was getting hot. *I need to take off my coat*, he thought. *That'll make me feel better.* He pulled himself into a sitting position near a large rock, his arms didn't cooperate as he tried to remove his coat. He still as voices got closer to him.

"Did you find him?" one of the men yelled over the howling wind.

"He has to be around here!" came another voice.

"If he is, he's either dead or half frozen. Let's go back to camp. He can't go anywhere. We'll take the gold from him, even if we have to pry it out of his cold, dead hands."

He heard them leave, feeling safe and warm, he settled in. *Just for a moment.*

CHAPTER 49

*T*he heat was too much, and he pushed back at the pressure on his chest.

"You must keep the covers on," a soft voice said. He let that voice settle him down.

"Will he live?" a gruff voice said.

"I believe he will, the fever appears to be breaking."

"I hope so, we do not want to be found with a dead white man."

The conversation drifted away.

Mark pushed at the cover. *Covers? Where am I?* He opened his eyes and looked around. He wasn't outside any longer. The structure was all wood and animal skins with a heater in the center with a long vent to the roof.

He continued to look around and saw a heavily pregnant woman who was Inuit. She was making bread and a man sat nearby talking in a low voice. *Her husband?* Mark was surprised they were still here; so many had been moved to the reservations. It wasn't fair that they had to abandon their land. Were they hiding here?

"Hello," he croaked out.

They looked over at him. The woman walked over and placed a hand on his head. "You have been sick, a fever."

"How did I get here?"

The man answered from where he was sitting. "I was hunting and found you. I brought you back with me."

Mark did remember that he had been so tired and warm. He realized that he'd been freezing to death. He'd ignored the warnings. "Thank you for taking me in and saving my life."

The man nodded his acknowledgement.

Mark tried to sit up. "My bag?"

"It is here," the man said. "It is safe."

Mark settled back down into his blankets.

They were a silent people, only speaking when necessary. When dinner was brought to him, it was fish.

"Has the ice broken up?" Mark asked. Ships would be coming through and people would flood the area again. *I wonder if Gus will come.*

"It has started."

For them, it would be good to sell fish but would be bad when the new arrivals took their land.

Mark stayed with them for a week, as he needed his strength back to get back to town. He still had at least three days of travel ahead depending on the weather.

As he was set to leave these silent people, he knew they didn't trade in gold, so he told them, "If you ever need help, I own the claim toward the mountain."

"Do not mention us to any white man, that is the help we need," the man said.

"Do come with fish, we will buy all you have," promised Mark.

The man nodded solemnly at him.

CHAPTER 50

*M*ark thanked them for their care and continued his trip, no one followed him this time. He was conscious of his very heavy bag and wanted it somewhere safe. As he entered town, he looked toward The Dominion; he would prefer to see Jenny, but he needed this taken care of first. He turned toward the warehouse. He'd like a long sleep after the very long walk.

As he got closer, he saw a squad of Mounties were around the front doors. *Has there been trouble again?* He forced himself to walk faster. When the Mounties saw him, Mark saw one nod toward him. Before he knew what was happening, they surrounded him. "What? What's happening?"

Ed ran around the corner, "Mark!"

"What's happening?" he asked again as a Mountie placed cuffs on his wrists.

A sergeant spoke up. "Mark Sutherland, you're being arrested for theft and murder of two people."

"Who am I supposed to have killed?"

"Josh Sullivan and George Landry."

"George is dead?" Mark said faintly.

"It was reported a few days ago. Both bodies were brought to town. At what point did you kill the men?"

Mark was completely confused. "I killed them...?"

"Yes, when did you kill them?"

Mark gave the sergeant a questioning look. "I killed them?" He was dumbfounded by this and looked to Ed for support.

The Mounties started to take him away and Mark yelled out, "Whoa! Waitaminnit! Ed! I didn't kill anyone."

"Mister Sutherland, we have an eyewitness report that says you killed these men," the sergeant said.

"Who are the eyewitnesses?"

The sergeant pulled out a notebook and read through a few pages. "Ah, here we are. The report was made by Jerry Sullivan and Wade Pettyford."

"Jerry and Wade?" Mark asked. "*Jerry and Wade!* You'd believe those two over me?"

"Mark, calm down," Ed told him. "I know you didn't do it. Go with them and we'll get this sorted out."

Mark looked at his friend and stopped struggling. The Mounties walked him to the station.

CHAPTER 51

Once in the station, they took Mark into a room with his belongings and opened the bag. "No gold," Sergeant Riley said and dumped the rocks out on the floor. "Why are you carrying heavy rocks?"

Mark didn't comment and just stared straight forward.

"Have you anything to say for yourself?" Commissioner Walsh asked as he walked into the room.

"I didn't kill anyone. It was Jerry and Wade."

Walsh and Riley looked at one another. "That's who reported the murders," Walsh said.

"Josh was stabbed by Jerry and, when I left the camp, George was alive. "

"Mr. Sullivan says that you tried to steal the claim from his brother and, when he wouldn't give it to you, you killed him and Mr. Landry."

"The claim is now mine," Mark confirmed. "Josh—Mr. Sullivan—deeded the claim to me, if anything happened to him."

"As I understand," Walsh began, "you had just met Mr. Sullivan a few months ago. Why would he leave his claim to you and not to his brother?"

"They didn't have a good relationship. What about the other men at the camp? They can tell you we were friends."

Riley shook his head. "They aren't talking and they only say that you were there almost every night."

"I was there. Josh liked to talk after dinner and he invited me."

They both looked at him and Walsh said, "We'll need to put you in a cell until we get more information."

As they took him toward the cells, Jenny and Ed rushed in. "Mark!"

Mark turned toward them. "Jenny," he said.

"Ma'am, stand back. He won't be allowed visitors until we've processed him. Come back in an hour."

When Jenny started to protest, Mark said, "Jenny, come back later. Please?" He didn't want her mixed up in this.

"Okay, but I'll be back in an hour," she promised and left the station with Ed in tow.

"What'll happen now?" Mark asked.

"Evidence will be presented to the local judge and then we'll see if you stay in jail," Walsh replied.

"What evidence?" Mark asked, confused.

"Right now, we have two men dead and you were the last seen in their company. We have witnesses who say you killed the two men. You disappeared for a time after that, and now you say you own the claim."

"I do own it."

"No will was found," Riley said. "Therefore, it belongs to Mr. Sullivan's brother."

"There's a will," he insisted.

Walsh raised his eyebrows and asked "And where's this will?"

"I sent it away to keep it safe." *Gus*, he thought, *are you on the way?* "Have the ships started to arrive?" he asked.

"The first one is on the way now that the ice has broken," Riley confirmed.

"Who witnessed the will?" Walsh asked. "We could use that person to support your statement."

"George Landry," Mark admitted.

"Really?" the commissioner asked. Mark could hear the doubt clearly in his voice.

"Yes, really."

"That's convenient," Riley said sarcastically.

"Mr. Sutherland, it sounds like you have a problem," Walsh told him.

"No, Jerry and Wade are the bad guys. They've cheated at the gambling hall and they broke my partner Ed's arm."

"That isn't murder."

Sergeant Riley took Mark to his cell. He walked in and collapsed on the cot and waited.

CHAPTER 52

*A*n hour later, Jenny and Ed arrived and were escorted back to him. The door opened to the hallway where the cells were located. Jenny ran in first, toward Mark's cell. He grabbed her hands when she placed them through the bars.

"What's happening? People have been murdered?" she asked breathlessly.

"When I was at the camp, Jerry and Wade went to talk to Josh to get him to give them some of his gold. Josh refused. He and Jerry got into a fight and Jerry stabbed Josh. By the time I got there, Josh was almost gone. I stayed until he died and I made my way back to town to report the death. And when I got here, I was told that not only had Josh died, but also Josh's foreman, George Landry."

"What's this about a will?" Ed asked. "They say you're trying to steal the claim from the rightful owner?"

"Josh was afraid Jerry would kill him and steal the gold. He wrote out a will deeding me the claim and George was the witness. Josh wanted to use the gold for a certain purpose."

Jenny leaned forward and whispered in Mark's ear. "I have it."

"Thank you," Mark said to her, not revealing that he knew that the it was Josh's gold.

Ed was left out of that conversation, but didn't comment on it. "So, what're we going to do now? We don't have a lawyer here."

"I don't know," Mark admitted. "Everyone who knew of my relationship with Josh is dead."

"Where's the will?" asked Ed.

"I sent it to a friend to keep it safe."

"How will that work if it isn't here? Can we contact him?"

"I'm hoping he's on one of the ships that's making their way here."

"How soon do you think until they start arriving?" asked Jenny.

"Any day now," Ed replied. He was waiting on supplies for their warehouse.

"Then we wait," she said.

CHAPTER 53

The evidence against Mark was evaluated and determined by Commissioner Walsh to be adequate enough for a trial. Mark's future was in jeopardy. All of his hopes hinged on Gus' arrival; hopefully he had the will with him.

Mark's cell had a window, and voices could be heard through it. "Ships! Ships are here!" Mark prayed that Gus was one of the passengers.

Jenny and Ed headed down to the docks. "Any idea what this Gus looks like?" he asked.

"Shorter, dark hair, dark tan skin. That's all I know."

They watched people disembark, looking for men who might fit the description. None did until a dark-haired man with a dark beard walked down the gangplank.

Jenny took a chance and called, "Gus?"

The man looked around. Jenny waved frantically toward him. He waved back and made his way down with the crowds. He walked up to them.

"Are you Gus?" Jenny asked hopefully.

"I'm Gus. Were you sent by Mark?" He would've been the only person he knew there.

Jenny started with, "I'm Jenny Taylor and this is Ed Gantz. We're friends of Mark."

"Nice to meet you. Where's Mark?" he asked, looking around.

"That's why we're here. Come with us," said Ed. They led him to The Dominion.

"Is this a gambling establishment?" Gus asked, confused.

"It's where I work," Jenny explained.

They entered and sat at a table and Jenny ordered lunch for them. With spring's arrival, the businesses had opened again. Men had started moving back to their claims, and the atmosphere had started to return to normal.

"What's going on? Is Mark at his claim?" Gus was getting more confused by the minute.

Ed said, "Mark's been arrested."

Gus was shocked. "Arrested? What's the charge?"

Jenny answered in a low voice, "Murder of Josh Sullivan and his foreman George."

Gus knew those names; they were on the will he carried. "Why do they think Mark killed them?"

"The Mounties had two witnesses who said they saw Mark do it," Jenny replied.

"Who said that he did it?"

"Josh's brother Jerry and his friend, Wade."

Again, Gus knew those names. The will had stated that no one other than Mark could have access to the claim and gold. It had deliberately excluded Jerry. "I need to see Mark," he said and started to stand.

Jenny reached over and took his hand. "Eat first. We'll also take Mark his meal."

Gus acquiesced and sat back down.

The food arrived and they ate in silence, each worried for Mark.

The takeaway arrived for Mark, and they headed to the Mounties' station.

They entered and Jenny went to Sergeant Riley to give him Mark's lunch to examine. After it was checked, he gave it back to her. She and Ed were allowed through. They stopped Gus before he could enter. "Who are you?" Riley asked.

"I'm Gus Lopez, Mark's lawyer."

"You are? Where did you get your degree?"

"Chicago-Kent College of Law in Chicago."

"We'll need to confirm that."

"Of course, can I see him now?"

"Yes, of course."

Mark, Ed, and Jenny had heard the conversation and looked at Gus as he entered. Mark called out to his friend. "Man, you arrived! I just had a feeling you would."

"Yes, I made it here."

As Gus approached, Mark leaned forward to say in a low voice, "Be careful about the lawyer bit. They'll find out you're lying."

"I'm not lying. I practiced for a few years until the incident. Then I didn't," he said simply.

Mark opened and closed his mouth and finally got the words out. "Do you have the will with you?"

"I do, but I think we'll hold it back for now."

Jenny and Ed stood listening in. Gus looked over at them and asked, "Can we talk alone?"

"Yes, of course," said Jenny. "We both need to get back to work."

"I'll need some information from both of you later." They nodded and headed out. Gus pulled up a chair and sat while Mark ate.

"Tell me about your interactions with Josh Sullivan, Jerry, and the others."

Mark went into details on his relationship with Josh and what he'd asked of him.

"One of the charges is that you stole a large gold stash," Gus said. Mark went silent on this topic and Gus went on. "I'll need to review all the evidence and see where we go from here." He stood up to leave.

"Wait." Mark said. "You can stay in my room at the cabin. Just head down to the warehouse. Ed's there and he'll let you in."

"Thanks, I appreciate that."

"Gus, is everything okay at home?"

"You know... it is," he said with a smile.

Mark smiled back; jail cell or not, his friend had come when he needed him. "Hey, Gus. It's really good to see you."

"It's good to see you, too, Mark." Gus turned and left the station.

CHAPTER 54

a s Gus walked through town, he thought about what Mark had told him. Evidently, Mark had taken the gold, but he had his reasons. Gus also knew his friend didn't kill those two people, and the will proved that. What was in question seemed to be the brother and his character. He had thanked the Mounties upon leaving and promised he'd follow up with them. On the way to the warehouse, he ran into Jenny and Ed on the sidewalk.

"Hey, sorry!" Gus said as he stepped back.

"No, we were waiting for you," Jenny said.

Gus looked at Ed. "Mark said I could use his room at the cabin."

Ed said, "Of course, would you like to go there now?"

"I would. Can you both come with me? I have questions about Jerry and Wade."

"Yes, I'll go with you," said Jenny.

They started walking. "You had a run-in with Jerry and Wade at The Dominion?" Gus asked her.

"Not personally. Jerry cheated at one of our tables and the floor manager had them tossed out."

"He reported it?"

"Yeah, but Wade said he did it and he took the punishment."

Gus looked over at Ed. "What about you? I understand they broke your arm. You didn't report it."

Ed rubbed the arm. "I didn't press charges. I should have."

"Will you make a statement now?"

"I will and so will my assistant, Sam. He saw what happened."

"Good."

Ed said, "You know, they were on the ship with us on the way out here. I always wondered where they got the tickets. They didn't have any on the train here and were trying to intimidate people there."

"That may be hard to prove, especially if no report was filed." He glanced at Ed.

Ed looked shamefaced. "Yeah, that's true."

"We also need someone to go to neighboring camps and find anyone who'll speak about Mark's relationship with Josh."

Jenny looked over at Ed. "Do you think Sam would go?" she asked.

"We can ask him. He might like that," said Ed.

"We need to move quickly. I'd like to get this tossed out before the trial starts," Gus said.

They knew what they had to do.

CHAPTER 55

Sam immediately agreed and got a list of questions from Gus. He'd return with the right person.

"Where are Jerry and Wade?" Gus asked.

"While the claim is up in the air, they're staying in town. The trial should hand the rights to Jerry," Ed replied.

"We need to find them," said Gus.

"It is unlikely they're staying out of trouble," said Jenny.

"Then we also look into that."

Ed said, "I can ask around."

"We'll regroup here this evening."

Ed was worried. "Sam will be about a couple of weeks. It takes that long to get to the claim and back."

"Then we'll have to get as much done as we can in the meantime."

Each went on their way—Jenny to The Dominion and Ed to the hotels.

Ed kept his hat pulled down over his eyes. The manager had confirmed Jerry and Wade were staying there. They were there on credit, as they had no money.

"Why are you letting them stay?" Ed asked him.

"They're thoroughly nasty individuals and I have no way to get rid of them."

"Have they threatened you badly?"

The manager dropped his chin to his chest. "Yes," he murmured. "I didn't want more trouble."

"Yeah, none of us did. If only one of us had reported it, we might have saved lives."

"What can I do to help you?"

"Keep an eye on them and let me know if something happens."

"I will," the manager promised.

"And we'll need a statement from you for Mark's lawyer."

He nodded. It was the right thing to do.

"Be at my cabin tonight." Ed pulled his hat down again and made his way out. He ran into Jerry.

"Hey, watch where you're going, ya idgit!" Jerry said, shoving Ed away.

"I will," Ed mumbled. "Sorry."

Jerry started toward him but stopped and said, "Ah, you ain't worth my time." He continued on into the lobby.

Gus prepared his dinner as he was waiting for the promised witnesses. The door opened and Ed entered.

"Is that dinner?" he asked. "Got enough for two?"

"Make that three," stated Jenny, coming in behind him.

"Better make it four," said the owner of The Dominion, walking in with her. He was there to make a sworn statement that it had been Jerry, not Wade, who cheated.

"Is this everyone?" Gus asked, looking around.

"One more," said the hotel manager, coming in at the end of the small parade.

"I believe this is it," answered Jenny.

"Then I'll need help with the food."

Everyone pitched in and sat at the table. After they ate, Gus took each statement down.

"Is it enough?" asked Jenny.

"It doesn't exonerate Mark," said Gus.

"What would?" asked Ed.

"A confession from Jerry and Wade."

Ed squinted his eyes and asked, "And or OR?"

"And. It's time to meet with Mark," said Gus.

CHAPTER 56

*L*ater, Gus reviewed all of the data with his friend.

"I have an idea," said Mark.

"Tell me."

"Mr. White owes me a favor. What if he pretends to take Jerry seriously as a businessman and leaves Wade out?"

"Pitting the two against each other?"

"Yeah. Given their temperaments, I imagine they'll turn on each other in a minute."

CHAPTER 57

"Why do I have to do this?" Mr. White muttered to Helen.

"You should help. Plus, this will make you a hero, helping prove a man is a murderer."

"But why do I have to do it?" There was a slight whine in his voice.

"We did Mark a bad turn, and he's been an excellent manager for you," she reminded him.

"That's true."

"And, you're smarter than them. You need to pretend to be wanting a partner, someone who's as smart as you. Butter him up."

He nodded. He could do that.

CHAPTER 58

"Why are you invited and I'm not?" Wade asked.

"Because Mr. Henry White," said Jerry, "has heard of my vast business experience and, when my inheritance comes in, he'd like to partner in some businesses."

"And you're just going to leave me behind?" Wade whined. "We are together in everything, you said we would be together always. That I just had to do as you told me."

"That was before the money. It is *mine*," he stressed and pulled his coat on. "*Not yours*." With that, he sauntered out to go to his appointment.

Wade sat and glared at the door wishing he had somewhere to go. *The Dominion! It was Jerry who got thrown out of there, not me.* He grabbed his coat and headed over to the gambling hall. Ed and Gus stood outside and watched him from the shadows. He passed them with an angry scowl on his face.

"It's begun," Gus said.

Ed grinned. "It's up to Jenny now."

Jenny watched the door, and when Wade entered the hall, she waved the security off. They had been instructed to let him in. He sauntered to the first gambling table, grabbing another customer's beer on his way. *Okay, here we go,* she thought.

Jenny went over to him and said casually, "Hey, Wade, how are you doing? Where's Jerry?"

He swung toward her with an angry frown and smiled slowly. "Well, hello little lady. What's your name?"

"Wade, it's me Jenny. Where's your buddy?" She needed to remind him why he'd been so agitated. Jenny waved a server over and gave him another beer.

He slammed it back, glad he finally had a friendly ear to vent to. "Jerry thinks he is soooo smart."

"Why don't we move to a more secluded table?" she asked with a slow smile and waved for another beer.

The beer was delivered. She carried it to the table for him and said, "Come this way." He followed. She sat them strategically with Gus, Ed, and Sergeant Riley in street clothes at the next table.

"So, tell me how much smarter you are than Jerry."

"Yeah, why does Mr. *Henry* White want to talk to just him and not me?"

"Everyone knows you're the better person. And I bet you know something that he doesn't want you to share," she said and touched his arm.

Emboldened, he leaned forward and said in a low voice, "I know that Mark didn't kill those men. Jerry did. I wuz there." Wade giggled, picked up his beer, and took a drink. Riley started to stand. As Wade continued talking, Jenny hastily waved to stop him.

"There wuz also that other man; we put him in the river." He giggled again. "What wuz his name?" He snapped his fingers as the name came to him. "Ben!" he said triumphantly. "That proves I'm smarter, right?"

Riley took him by the collar. "Yep, you're smarter. Why don't we head down to the station and document all of your smartness."

Wade grinned stupidly and said, "Jerry won't get his inheritance now, right? And he'll be with me?"

"He will definitely be with you, in jail. And no I don't think he will get the inheritance." Riley looked over at Gus. "Can you come with us?"

"I can. I also have a document to show you that will probably close this issue out."

Jenny and Ed hugged and followed. They went to the station, and Wade happily gave over a full confession.

"Where's Jerry Sullivan?" Commissioner Walsh asked.

"He's with Mr. Henry White. They're having a business meeting. Without me," Wade said belligerently.

"Yes, well, he isn't being invited to your business meeting here."

Wade sat straighter and raised his chin. "Well, he'll see, won't he? I'm the smarter one."

"Take some men and go get Jerry Sullivan," Walsh said to Riley. "He's at Henry White's house."

"Yes, sir." Riley and two officers headed out and returned in a short time with an infuriated Jerry. "I don't care what Wade said, I had nothing to do with it. It was that Mark Sutherland fella. He killed my brother and everything should go to me."

Gus took that moment to pull out the will. "I think this will clear a few things up."

Walsh read the document, then looked at Jerry. "No, Mark Sutherland is the owner of the claim and all of the gold from such claim."

Jerry lunged at him. Riley took the initiative and hit him on the head. Jerry slumped to the floor.

"Get him into a cell," Walsh declared.

Gus asked, "Could we also get Mark out?"

"We can."

In a few moments, Wade and Jerry changed places with Mark.

"You! What did you do!" Wade yelled at Jerry.

Jerry sobered up with each word that spewed from Wade's mouth. Once again saying that everything was Jerry's fault. He was a looser that he should have discarded years ago. Jerry watched Wade continue to rail at him. The words finally penetrated the hazy cloud that always buffered him. *Why have I followed this man for so long? I have to be more than this.*

Mark stood in the office and looked around at his friends. Jenny ran over and he pulled her close.

"I don't know what I would do without you," he said. The group laughed. *Emma was right,* he thought. *You need people that you care about around you.*

"How about coming to The Dominion for some drinks and celebration?" suggested Jenny.

"That sounds amazing," he said and all four left the station.

He whispered in Jenny's ear, "Where is it?"

"We buried it behind the cabin."

"In the church graveyard?" he exclaimed.

"On the edge of it," she said defensively.

He laughed. "Thank you for doing that for me." Mark had had two of his men move the gold while he led Jerry and Wade on a chase. Even if they caught him, they wouldn't have found the gold. He wanted to honor Josh's final request and get that gold back to the people Jerry had cheated. The list of names and locations was included with the gold.

Next steps, he thought. He now had a claim to manage, a wonderful girl, and the best of friends. *Where do I go next?*

Ed stopped abruptly. "Wade mentioned that he'd helped kill Ben Jones and put his body under the ice."

"Oh no!" Jenny exclaimed. "We forgot that piece of the puzzle."

"I'd wondered," said Mark. "We need to help them look for him. Let me run back."

He went in and saw the commissioner at his desk. "Sir, when you go look for Ben Jones, can I come with you?"

"Do you have an idea where he might be?"

"I know his claim. They might have put him in the river near there."

"We'll head out tomorrow morning."

"I'll be here."

He went back out for that drink; it was a quieter night because of the news about Ben. The next morning, Ed, Gus, and Mark joined the Mounties and Wade in the search.

They stood at Ben's cabin and the commissioner stated, "Wade, this is where you're the leader. We want you to show us what happened here."

Wade stood straighter and pointed to his left, away from the cabin. "We camped over there." They walked to where he indicated. The trees had been roughly cut back, forging a path. "I cut the path."

"Why?"

"So Jerry could see the cabin clearly. We watched Ben and saw him move the gold back to his cabin."

"What happened then?"

"Christmas Day had come around and Jerry figured we could go knock on his door. You know, as a friendly gesture."

"At this time, what did you think was happening?"

"I thought we'd steal the gold, maybe rough him up some."

"What did happen?"

"Well, at first he was welcoming, it being Christmas and all, and I think he was a little lonely." They listened, not interrupting. "We sat and had us a drink. Ben kept studying Jerry. He finally asked if he knew us from somewhere. We looked a little different because of the beards," he explained, touching his. He went on. "We told him no, but then he said, 'Jerry and Wade' and asked us to leave."

"How did Jerry take that?"

"He didn't take it well at all. Jerry pulled his gun and demanded the gold."

"And Ben?"

"He said he'd worked too hard all on his own and he wouldn't give it away for nothin. Jerry don't like to be told no," Wade said, rubbing his head. "Jerry, he didn't even warn him. Just pulled the trigger and BOOM, shot him in the head."

Mark felt his chest tighten and his eyes fill with tears. Ben was a good man, and he'd desperately wanted to find him alive. That was not to be.

"What did you do with the body?"

"We took off his clothes and burned them in the cabin's oven."

"We should check there for any debris," Mark said.

Walsh looked at two of his men. "Go check the cabin." They headed toward it.

"You," Walsh said to Wade, "where did you put him?"

Wade hung his head, and he raised his arms toward the Yukon River. "Yonder. We cut the ice and shoved him in. Jerry figgered the water would carry him far far away."

"Show us the exact spot," Walsh demanded.

Wade walked toward the river. The ice was starting to break up and flow. "There," he said weakly.

Mark walked over to Wade and shook him. "Where is he?"

"Man, I don't know! I really don't. Maybe Jerry wuz right and he washed downstream."

"Let him go, Mark. It won't change anything," Ed told him.

Mark let the man go and then pushed him away. Wade tripped and fell. "Hey!"

"Sir!" an officer assigned to the cabin called as he ran up. "We found something."

"What is it?"

The officer held out his hand. In it were some buttons, charred clothing, and sock garters. "I recognize those," Mark said, picking up the garters. "Ben always wore these. He complained his socks never stayed up."

"Put that into an evidence bag," Walsh said. "I'll send men downstream; since the ice is breaking up, the body may still surface."

They headed back to town, sure they had their man.

Mark asked Wade, "Will you be able to hold your own against Jerry and testify about his murderous activities at the trial?"

Wade looked up suddenly. "Yes, I've been an idiot and I'll finally have my own say. I'll also take responsibility for my role in all this."

"Thank you, Wade." They escorted him back into the station.

A few days went by and word came back that a body had surfaced six miles down the river. It appeared that he'd gotten stuck on a submerged tree.

The funeral was arranged and paid for by Mark. After Mark spoke, Father Randal said a few words over him. The small group walked back together. Mark ran up to where Mr. White and Helen stood. "Mr. White, thank you for your help."

"You never killed anyone," White muttered and looked away.

"Don't let him fool you. He wanted to help," Helen said and took her husband's hand.

"Helen said it was the right thing to do," White commented and laid his head on his wife's.

And you listened to her, Mark thought. He gave them another look. *Did they fall in love?* White smiled more and Helen looked happy.

Jenny walked up to him as Helen and Mr. White walked away. "Maybe it wasn't the money," he said.

Jenny knew what he was talking about and commented, "I

think it was initially, and then it wasn't." She looked at him and asked, "What now?"

"Yeah," Gus asked. "What now?"

Mark looked around at his three friends—Jenny, Ed, Gus. "I'm not sure. I have to go to my claim and work out what happens next."

"I'd like to go with you," Jenny said.

"Me too," said Gus. He had yet to see the gold mining that had drawn him there.

Mark nodded. "We can head out tomorrow. Are you and Sam okay at the warehouse?" he asked Ed. Sam had returned with several men ready to testify on Mark's behalf. It had turned out they weren't needed, but Mark was happy to have the support. The men had taken a well-deserved break in town before heading back.

Ed responded. "We're good, stocked up, and the next orders placed."

"Great!"

"What about Mr. White's claim?" asked Gus.

"I talked to him about replacing me with Harry and giving him a raise. I think it's time for that relationship to end." The group laughed.

"Will you be coming with me tonight?" Jenny murmured in his ear.

"Just try to stop me," he said.

CHAPTER 59

enny and Gus met Mark early at the cabin the next morning. The duo weren't dressed appropriately at all. Mark laughed. "Okay, let's get organized. It's still cold out there and, with the ice breaking up, we won't need ice shoes, but now the hazard of falling in the water is back. You'll need to wear hip waders."

He made sure they were packed and dressed before they started out. He was the expert and leader this time. It was funny how times had changed. They walked closer to the camps and stayed at some on their way. Gus was fascinated by the tools and the methods used to find gold.

Mark noticed and asked, "Do you plan on staying for a while?"

Gus thought about the house being built for him and the family waiting. "I think I'll stay for this adventure, but not long enough for ice to set in again."

Mark thought about that as they continued on.

They reached Mr. White's claim first. Harry ran up and had lots of questions. "Let's go inside the cabin and I'll let you know what happened," Mark said. He noticed the men were outside near the dirt piles.

"We're starting to move the material we dug out through the sluice."

"Finding anything?"

Harry grinned. "Yes, that's where the real gold is."

Gus asked, "Would you mind if I go down to observe?"

"Go! Feel free to lend a hand if you'd like," suggested Harry.

Gus grinned and said, "I believe I will!"

"Harry, do you know Jenny?" Mark asked the foreman.

"I've seen you at The Dominion. It's nice to meet you. I know the men will love seeing a pretty face." Jenny smiled and followed them to the cabin.

"And the man running to help is my friend Gus Lopez," Mark said.

They took off their coats and Harry stoked the fire.

"I heard about Ben, and I know you wanted to check on him. I stopped you," Harry started.

"No, you reminded me that I had responsibilities here. And I don't think I could have saved him."

"It was Jerry and Wade?"

"It was mainly Jerry, but Wade was his helper."

"That sounds like Wade," he said dryly.

"Wade is actually testifying against Jerry and providing key evidence."

"Wade found his backbone?"

"Yeah, but he'll probably be in prison for the rest of his life. Not Jerry. He's in line for a swift hanging."

Harry stood and got them coffee. "So, you're here to tell me you're not my boss anymore."

Mark looked surprised. "How did you know?"

"You inherited Josh's claim. Why should you work this one?"

"Well, now, you're the new general manager. I have your bonus with me and a confirmation of a raise from Mr. White."

"Will I be allowed to replace my position?"

"Yeah. Mr. White would like you to return to town and bring the gold with you. He'd like to secure it. And while you're there, you can add the man you'll be down."

"I'll get the men organized, though it'll take two men to move it."

They stayed the rest of the day and spent the night. The three made their way to Josh's claim the next morning.

The area guard waved at Mark to allow his group in. "Jerry and Wade have been taken care of," Mark commented.

The man lowered his gun. "They got the two of them?"

"They're in jail awaiting trial."

He nodded and said, "Good. Josh would have been happy about that. Bill's acting as the foreman; he's in the cabin."

Mark nodded and they headed over. "Is it a successful operation?" asked Gus.

"Very, though they've been mining for over two years. I wonder if there's a limit to it?"

They went into the cabin. It was a shock for Mark; he knew Josh was dead, but he still expected to see him in his large chair. Instead, it was Bill, one of the workers. "Mark," he said, standing quickly and walking over with his hand outstretched.

Mark took it and shook. "I hate that it's under these circumstances."

"Me too. Sit down."

"Thank you. This is Gus and Jenny."

"Nice to meet you."

"You too," said Jenny and Gus nodded.

They sat and Mark asked, "Can I see the accounting books?"

"Yes, of course." Bill stood and got them from the cabinet behind the desk. He handed them to Mark.

The group sat quietly while Mark examined them. "They seem all in order."

"I tried to record every finding and get the weights in the books."

"Thank you. Would you like to stay on and have a promotion to foreman?"

Bill let out a breath. "I would," he replied.

"We'll also need a new manager," Mark commented.

"Won't that be you?" Bill asked in surprise.

"No," he said, looking over at the wood pile where the gold had sat. "I have to fulfill a promise."

Bill nodded. "Then who'll be here with us?"

Gus spoke up. "I will."

Mark looked at him in surprise. "You want the job?"

"For a while, but not through another freeze. I can learn the operation and find a stable manager for you."

"Thank you," Bill said.

Mark stood up. "We'll head back to town and get organized."

"Will you take the box with you?"

"I already have it."

"No, you don't have the second box. That one is yours," Bill said, his voice firm.

Mark frowned. He didn't know about a second box. Bill got up and walked to the wood pile and pulled another lockbox out and opened it. It was full of gold. "The first box is for his debts and this one is for you. George told me to make sure you understood that."

Mark sat back. "Should I share it with you and the other men?"

"We got our share before. This is Josh's and he wanted you to have it."

"Then I have a lot of thinking to do."

Gus and Mark walked outside. Jenny was lying down inside; the cold was bothering her.

Mark said, "Gus, if you stay, I'll make you a full partner in everything that's found, after paying the miners."

"I already said I'd stay; that isn't necessary."

"I think it is. I'll also give you a large bonus before I leave."

"I'll keep you informed of the accounts."

"What I could see from the accounts, it's that the profits seem to be slowing. Which tells me the mine is drying up."

"I'll stay and continue to monitor it. If it becomes nonprofitable, we shut down operations?"

"Yes. You can offer it to one of the men if they want to stay."

They walked back and rested.

CHAPTER 60

*T*he next morning, they and two men with the heavy boxes headed back to town. They joined the team that was taking a heavy box to Mr. White. Once they arrived, they split at the edge of town, with Harry going to Mr. White's home and the other men accompanying Mark to his cabin.

He escorted Jenny back to The Dominion. "I'll see you tonight. Right now, I need to go get my steamer tickets."

Jenny watched him go, the grief welling up in her. She had listened to the conversations and realized, *He said me, not we. What part do I play in his future? Am I just a woman he knew on his adventures in the Yukon? Just another person within his personal narrative?*

CHAPTER 61

$\mathcal{M}$ ark entered The Dominion that night. "Mark!" called Gus. "Over here!" He was staying in town until Mark departed. Mark grinned and headed toward him.

Jenny saw him enter and her eyes followed him around the room. Her chest tightened. If he didn't want to be with her, she didn't want to be with him. He could take his gold and just go away!

Gus hugged him and asked, "When do you leave?"

"Soon! I just wanted to do one more thing," he said, looking around.

"What's that?"

Mark continued to search the room. *There!* He saw Jenny standing by the piano, sending him a side eyed glare. She turned away, pretending not to see him.

Mark suddenly jumped up on a large table and yelled, "Jenny! Jenny Taylor! I have a question for you!"

The room quieted as they waited for her to respond. Her face was blank as she turned to him and called back, "And what would that be?"

"Will you come on an adventure with me?"

She put her hands on her hips and called back, "Is *THAT* the question you wanted to ask?"

"No, it isn't!"

"Well," she asked. "What's your question?" Her heart pounded, thinking what it might be.

"Will you marry me?"

She ran toward him and the crowd lifted her up to the table where Mark stood. "Well?" he teased. "What's your answer?"

"Yes!" she shouted joyfully and jumped in his arms. He caught her and held tight as the room cheered.

Gertie walked over and said, "Now that we have that settled, can you get off my table?"

"Yes, ma'am," said Mark. He climbed down and helped Jenny descend.

"Outside?" he asked in her ear.

Grinning, she said yes. He had his arm over her shoulder and was walking down the dark sidewalk.

Ed and Gus ran up and threw their arms over Jenny and Mark's shoulders.

Mark looked at his friends happily. "What matter wounds to the body of knight-errants? For each time he falls, he shall rise again and woe to the wicked!"

Ed asked, "So, now are we tilting at windmills?"

"Weren't we always?"

HISTORICAL NOTES FOR 1897

Aurora, Texas

Was there an alien landing? I can't be sure but when I found out about the event, I couldn't wait to read it. So, Mark was right about people being curious about the subject.

The young girl, Mary that Mark interviewed was a real person and her story about her parent going to the site is part of the historical record. Mary also mention Charlie Stephens who also was a witness to the event that occurred in Aurora. Many times, over the years request were made and declined to dig in the cemetery. Evidence was once again to be found inconclusive (1973).

In 2008 Tim Oates, grandson of Brawley Oates gave permission for the land under the well to be dug up. Nothing was found, except the water tested for large amounts of aluminum present. There was no other items found. At the cemetery, ground penetrating radar was tried and approved because it did not disturb the graves. The radar could not prove conclusively what types of remains were there.

Bartlesville, OK

The oil drilling historical information was provided by my son. He works at the Houston Natural Science Museum on the 4th floor. The Weiss hall has all of the details I needed to put together how drilling operations were run at that time. They have actually operating equipment that I was able to review.

Yukon

The difficult trip to the Yukon changed a lot of peoples minds about staying once they reached Dawson. It took a special breed of people to not only make the trip, but stay and work for the gold.

Ben's murder was based on an actual event. The man was murdered, his clothes burned and placed in the river, under the ice. He was also found downstream because the ice block any further movement.

Notebook Mysteries

Books
1 - 2 - 3

KIMBERLY
MULLINS

ABOUT THE AUTHOR

Kimberly Mullins is the author of series of books titled "Notebook Mysteries" and a book called "Divided Lives", under the pen name-K.R. Mullins. Her stories are based on historical events occurring in the 1880s to 1912. She holds a BS in Biology and a MBA in Business. She lives in Texas with her husband and son. When she is not writing she is working as a Process Safety Engineer at a large chemical company. You can connect with her on her website www.kimberly mullinsauthor.com.

Photo Credit: Blessings of Faith Photography

 twitter.com/kremullins_kim

Milton Keynes UK
Ingram Content Group UK Ltd.
UKHW020747231123
433129UK00017B/1144